PRAISE FOR S

D1111442

Hunt Them Down

"In *Hunt Them Down*, Gervais has crafted an intelligent and thoughtful thriller that mixes family dynamics with explosive action . . . The possibilities are endless in this new series, and this will easily find an enthusiastic audience craving Hunt's next adventures."

—Associated Press

"[An] action-packed series launch from Gervais . . ."

—*Publishers Weekly*

"Nonstop action meets relentless suspense . . . The blood flows knee deep in this one as Gervais uses his background as a drug investigator for the Royal Canadian Mounted Police to bring a gritty authenticity to his latest thriller."

—*The Real Book Spy*

"Gervais dishes out lavish suspense to keep a reader glued . . ."

—Authorlink

"Superbly crafted and deceptively complex . . . This is thriller writing at its level best by a new voice not afraid to push the envelope beyond traditional storytelling norms."

—*Providence Journal*

"Another simply riveting read from author Simon Gervais, *Hunt Them Down* showcases his mastery of narrative-driven storytelling and his flair for embedding his novels with more twists and turns than a Coney Island roller coaster."

—Midwest Book Review

"From the first page, *Hunt Them Down* is a stick of dynamite that Simon Gervais hands you, masterfully lights, and then dares you to put down before it explodes. Don't. It's worth a few fingers to read to the end."

—Matthew Fitzsimmons, bestselling author of *The Short Drop*

"Your hunt for the next great adventure novel is over. If Jack Reacher started writing thrillers, he'd be Simon Gervais."

—Lee Goldberg, #1 *New York Times* bestselling author of *True Fiction*

Time to Hunt

"An action-packed thrill ride with plot twists around nearly every curve."

—*Kirkus Reviews*

"Gervais consistently entertains."

—*Publishers Weekly*

THE LAST PROTECTOR

THE LAST PROTECTOR

SIMON GERVAIS

THOMAS & MERCER

Text copyright © 2021 by Simon Gervais
All rights reserved.

Published by Thomas & Mercer, Seattle

www.apub.com

Amazon, the Amazon logo, and Thomas & Mercer are trademarks of Amazon.com, Inc., or its affiliates.

ISBN-13: 9781542022941
ISBN-10: 1542022940

Cover design by Kirk DouPonce, DogEared Design

Printed in the United States of America

To Lisane, Florence, and Gabriel.
The sun lightens the day.
The moon illuminates the night.
And you brighten my life.

PART ONE
SIX YEARS AGO

CHAPTER ONE

Bagram Air Base
Afghanistan

Brigadier General Maxwell White pushed his burner phone away and buried his face in his hands. What had started as a minor headache had transformed into a migraine of gigantic proportions. The top of his skull felt as if it had been lodged in a nutcracker and split open. Suddenly nauseous, he pushed himself upright in his chair and leaned back, closing his eyes. He didn't open them until he was sure the room had stopped spinning.

He reached for the bottle of water beside him and drank half its contents before turning his attention back to the burner phone. He stared at it for a few seconds, fighting the temptation to smash it beneath his combat boots.

Sighing heavily, he grabbed the phone and looked at the screen. His face grew paler as he read one last time the draft email he knew would end his career. Never in a million years had he thought it would come to this, or that he'd find himself on the wrong side of the law. What he was about to do went against everything he stood for. True, it could be argued that he didn't always play things by the book, but never before had he committed what amounted to treason.

Treason. The word reverberated within him. It made his flesh crawl. It made him feel dirty, unworthy of his rank. Just a week ago, the thought of leaking classified military intelligence to five prolific investigative journalists would have been unconscionable. He had always seen himself as a patriot and a firm believer in the military chain of command. He wasn't known as a shoot-from-the hip maverick who chucked the rule book in favor of expediency.

But this? This was different. If he had known CONQUEST would have led to such bloodshed, he would have never agreed to go along with it.

History would have plenty to say about the men who'd been complicit in those atrocities. He'd already been silent longer than he should. But if he stood up now, maybe history would treat him more kindly as a whistleblower, even if in the short term it ruined his career and the deepest bonds he'd formed in his military career. It would be so much easier to simply turn a blind eye and keep quiet, but when it came to his country and the American people he had sworn to protect, Maxwell White had never chosen the easy path.

And he wouldn't start now.

The stakes were too high. This was bigger than him and his career. Not saying anything would mean surrendering the moral high ground of the United States and its people.

He was about to press send when his thoughts switched to his son, Clayton. His whole body stiffened as a new wave of self-doubt burst to the surface. A combat rescue officer with the 57th Rescue Squadron, Clayton was presently deployed in Iraq. There was no doubt in the general's mind that his son would suffer too. Within days, hours maybe, Captain Clayton White would be pulled from his unit and placed in detention. They would of course release him once they realized he didn't know anything, but his son's promising career would be ruined.

It broke Maxwell's heart to know that his actions would negatively impact his family. His wife, Carolyn, who had remained loyal to him for more than thirty-five years despite his endless deployments, didn't deserve what was coming. He wished there was another way, an alternative that would see him remain anonymous. But there wasn't. To be taken seriously, he needed to come out of the shadows. And he couldn't wait any longer. He had sworn an oath, and if Maxwell White was anything, he was a man of honor. He had to see this through.

"Sorry, Clay," he said out loud, his finger tapping the send button.

CHAPTER TWO

Fayetteville, North Carolina

Lieutenant General Alexander Hammond wasn't fast enough. Still suffused with sleep and reluctant to remove himself from a lingering dream that found him cycling the majestic mountains of Andorra with his wife and daughter, he was unable to silence his phone before it woke up his wife. Heather stirred uneasily beside him, a groan escaping her lips. Hammond pulled back the duvet and reached for the damnable instrument. He accepted the call but didn't speak until he'd left the bedroom and closed the door behind him.

"Hammond," he said into the receiver.

"We need to talk, Alex. Is this line secured at your end?"

Hammond recognized the voice and became instantly alert. "It's not. I'll call you right back," he said before ending the call.

He went downstairs and stopped by the kitchen on his way to his study. He turned on the coffee maker. He had a feeling he wasn't going back to bed anytime soon and would need the caffeine jolt. In his office, he switched on the desk light and put on his glasses. He then went to his personal safe, which was hidden behind a framed painting of his daughter. He entered an eight-digit code on the keypad. The safe contained stacks of bills in various denominations and currencies, a 9 mm pistol with three spare magazines, and an encrypted phone.

Hammond powered up the device and punched in a number he hadn't dialed in more than six months.

"Thanks for calling me back so rapidly," the man said by way of greeting, a faint British accent coloring his voice.

"I'm secure on my end. What's up?" Hammond asked, his heartbeat faster than usual, knowing nothing good could possibly come from this middle-of-the-night phone call. Especially with this man.

"You were right, I'm afraid."

"I usually am. What's this about?" Hammond paced back and forth on the thick Persian carpet his wife had insisted on buying during a two-week cruise a decade earlier.

"Maxwell White," the man replied. "He's turning out to be a problem."

Hammond stopped midstride. A shiver shot up his spine. Among all the potential issues he knew could come his way, this was the one he wished he'd never have to deal with.

"You can't be serious," he said. "Maxwell would never turn on us. Besides, there's no way he could find the evidence," he said. "I buried it too deep."

"He's an intelligence officer," the man shot back. "And a good one at that."

"What are you saying?" Hammond asked, light headed.

"He knows about the purge. And about the fact you lied to him about the resolution of CONQUEST."

"Goddamn it!" Hammond exploded. "This was never supposed to come to that."

Hammond exhaled loudly, feeling the beginning of a massive headache. "How big a problem do we have on our hands?"

"The kind that requires immediate attention."

Hammond swallowed hard and squeezed the phone until his arm shook. Unless he intervened on his friend's behalf, Maxwell White would be dead before sunrise. Hammond was unsure what to say or do. Not a common occurrence for him.

"Is there another way to approach—"

"The decision's already been made," the man said, interrupting him. His voice was firm and unwavering. "He tried to send an email containing critical material about CONQUEST to five investigative journalists. All of it very damaging to you. And to me."

Hammond winced. It was as if he had been gut punched.

"He tried?" he asked. "You intercepted it in time?"

"It never really left his burner phone. As I said, you were right to suggest we keep an eye on him."

Goddamn you, Maxwell, Hammond thought, shaking his head.

He sighed. "Am I the last one to hear about this?"

"Yes. He's a friend of yours, Alex," the man said. "We all know that. We needed to be certain you weren't aware of his endeavors."

"I know you wouldn't have called if you weren't absolutely sure I wasn't in on it," he said, resigned. It felt as if the weight of the world was on his shoulders. Maybe it was.

"We felt we needed to let you know. As a courtesy, of course," the man said.

"Of course," replied Hammond. He heard the gruffness in his voice, as if he had just gargled with nails.

"Krantz is already on his way. He'll handle everything. You don't need to worry about a thing. Just do as he says."

Hammond despised being ordered around, exceptionally so by Krantz. He was about to push back when the man said, "And, Alex, don't even think about not cooperating with Krantz. Because I won't hesitate to bring you down too. Not for a second."

The call disconnected, leaving Hammond gaping at his phone, weighed down by the heaviness in his chest.

What the hell were you thinking, Maxwell?

8

Hammond had damned himself the moment he'd agreed to participate in CONQUEST. The American lives saved could be counted in hundreds. But now that his former associate had resurfaced, Hammond wasn't so sure it had all been worth it.

And why didn't you come to me first?

The phone rang. Hammond stared at it, wondering if he should answer it. There would be no turning back. Whatever he decided to do in the next minute would impact the rest of his life. Hammond sat down behind his desk, afraid his rubbery legs would give out under him.

He answered on the sixth ring.

"I was wondering if you were going to pick up, General. I'm glad you did."

Hammond instantly recognized the voice. It was as if Abelard Krantz was missing the fundamental frequency of a human's voice. The normal melody of speech was completely absent.

"Our mutual friend told me you'd be calling."

There was a weird-sounding chuckle at the other end of the line. "I'm glad you two are still friends. He was actually wondering if you'd be willing to sacrifice Maxwell to save yourself. Good call, General."

Bastards, Hammond thought.

"What do you need from me?" he asked, doing his best to keep his anger out of his voice.

"His flight plan for tomorrow."

The muscles in Hammond's neck tensed. "No way," he said, thinking about the helicopter's crew. "You're not taking down a chopper to get to him. You'll have to find another approach."

"There's no time, General," Krantz replied. "Give me Maxwell's flight plan. We both know our mutual friend holds all the cards. Do you really think he'll leave your precious Heather and Veronica alone if you betray him?"

At the mention of his wife's and daughter's names, Hammond felt his body grow rigid. He was about to tell Krantz to go to hell when his eyes settled on the framed family photo that sat at the corner of his desk. His heart faltered.

"One moment," he replied as he powered on his secure laptop. While his laptop contained its own interface, his access to the information-sharing network would be recorded. That was something he could not afford. It took him a moment to connect to the special communications adapter that had been provided to him by a friend at the NSA. Once plugged in, the adapter ran a self-diagnostic protocol and initiated several software routines aimed at masking his presence. A few keystrokes later, he had Maxwell's flight plan details on his screen.

He closed his eyes and forced back the bile rising in his throat.

Once he was sure he wasn't about to throw up, Hammond gave Krantz the intel he needed to kill Maxwell White.

CHAPTER THREE

Northern Iraq

Captain Clayton White grabbed his harness as the HH-60G Pave Hawk
search-and-rescue helicopter darted straight up, then banked steeply to
the right while the pilot did his best to evade another burst of machine-
gun fire coming from below.

"Damn it!" yelled an air force staff sergeant, one of the two pararescuemen seated across from White. "I hate it when they do that."

White wasn't a big fan of being shot at either. But it came with the
job. White and his team of eight pararescuemen—or PJs—supported
by two Pave Hawks and their crewmen, were the only rescue team
positioned to cover the battlefield of northern Iraq and Syria, which
encompassed over 150,000 square miles. And today, White's team was
the best hope of survival for two Marine pilots who had been forced to
crash-land their SuperCobra attack helicopter in ISIS-controlled territory after sustaining significant battle damage. The closest Marine
TRAP—Tactical Recovery of Aircraft and Personnel—team, usually
tasked to cover the southern part of Iraq, was too far away to give
the two stranded Marine aviators a realistic chance. The TRAP team's
MV-22 tilt-rotor aircraft had the range, but by the time they could get
to the pilots' location, it would be too late. ISR—intelligence, surveillance, and reconnaissance—provided by a Reaper drone had confirmed
that three ISIS technicals were racing toward the downed American

chopper. Typically open-backed civilian pickup trucks or four-wheel drive vehicles, technicals had mounted weapons systems like machine guns, light antiaircraft guns, or even antitank weapons. And troops. Fast and maneuverable, technicals had become ISIS's de facto cavalry.

White willed the Pave Hawk to go faster. They all knew what awaited the downed airmen if they were captured by ISIS.

"I have comms with Major Steck, sir," the copilot said to White. "Call signs Bandit-One and Two."

"Okay," White replied. "Patch me through."

A moment later, the copilot gave White a thumbs-up.

"Bandit, this is CSAR-One, how copy, over," White said.

"CSAR-One, this is Bandit-Two. You're loud and clear. How far are you?"

The copilot, who was still listening to the frequency, showed four fingers to White.

"We're southeast of your position, four minutes out."

"Good copy, CSAR-One. Please note Bandit-One is in bad shape. His legs are pinned under the flight instrument panel."

"Is Bandit-One conscious?" White asked, his mind racing ahead toward a multitude of possible scenarios.

"He's been in and out of consciousness since the crash," Bandit-Two replied. "But when he's awake, he just mutters some incoherent shit."

"CSAR-One copies," White said, keeping his voice smooth and steady despite the constriction in his chest. "ETA is now three minutes. CSAR-One out."

Damn. The three incoming ISIS technicals were going to be a problem. With Bandit-One's injuries, White's team wasn't going to be able to pull off a quick in-and-out rescue prior to their arrival. It was going to take some time to extricate the Marine from the SuperCobra's cockpit. The last thing White wanted was to get jammed into a firefight across open ground with an unknown number of ISIS combatants. The .50-caliber machine guns likely mounted in the backs of their vehicles could lay down an incredible amount of firepower and would shred him, his men, and the two Marine pilots to pieces. With no QRF— quick reaction force—in the vicinity, it was on him to find a way to secure the crash site.

"You guys all set?" White asked the two PJs.

One of the PJs had a tablet on his lap that was linked directly to the Reaper drone's feed. He had a worried look on his face, which was never a good sign. In White's true-to-God opinion, United States Air Force pararescue jumpers were not only the best-trained technical rescue medical personnel in the world but also fearless warriors. Only the most resilient and focused airmen became PJs or combat rescue officers. The pipeline to enter this elite group was one of the most grueling in the military. It lasted two to three years and boasted an 80 percent attrition rate. Trained and efficient in everything from mountain climbing to free-fall parachute operations, PJs and combat rescue officers were also skilled deep-sea divers and capable of entering and clearing an enemy compound. So, if one of White's men was worried, there was indeed a source of legitimate concern that needed to be addressed.

"Talk to me," he said to the PJ holding the tablet.

"It's not good, sir," the PJ replied, handing over the tablet. "The technicals are only ten clicks away."

White looked at the screen. His man was right. The ISIS vehicles were making good progress. The Pave Hawk would reach the crash site before the technicals, but White's team would only have a couple of minutes to complete the rescue. It wouldn't be enough time.

"Two minutes out," the copilot said, craning his neck toward White. "What do you want us to do?"

White had to come up with some sort of a plan. And fast. The fate of the two Marine aviators rested in his hands.

CHAPTER FOUR

Northern Iraq

Clayton White wasn't a fan of hastily formed plans, but life, especially in his line of work, was full of surprises. Any plan was better than no plan at all. White's strategy was simple but dangerous. His men had argued against it, and the Pave Hawk pilot and copilot hadn't seemed convinced, either, but White had politely but firmly terminated the discussion. He had made up his mind.

"Thirty seconds to crash site," the pilot said.

White glanced around the helicopter. The intent faces of the two PJs told him they were ready to go. The crew chief was moving around, preparing the Pave Hawk for the insertion of the two PJs. Five hundred feet from the SuperCobra, the Pave Hawk slowed, its nose flaring slightly as it dropped low enough to allow the two PJs to jump out. From where he was seated, White saw Bandit-Two on the ground near the tail section of the gray SuperCobra, a fire extinguisher next to him. The Marine aviator was clutching his rib cage, and even from a distance, White could see the man was in pain. The SuperCobra lay on its side, its fuselage twisted and blackened, smoke still gushing from its turbines. The landing skids had been ripped apart.

Half a moment later, the Pave Hawk's turboshaft engines revved, and the heavy rotor picked up speed, spitting skeins of small rocks and sand erratically across the landing zone as the helicopter gained altitude. White trusted the PJs to do their job. There wasn't much these guys couldn't accomplish. But with the ISIS technicals fast approaching, it was up to White to give his men the time they needed to extricate Bandit-One from the wreckage. White took another look at the tablet to confirm how far away the technicals were, then turned his attention to the copilot.

"See the bend in the road and these elevation lines on both sides?" White asked, his finger tapping a spot on the digital map. "Drop me there."

"You got it," the copilot replied.

White went down his mental checklist, visualizing how everything would go once he hit the ground. He then checked his M240B machine gun and accepted an AT4 rocket launcher from the crew chief.

"You sure about this?" the crew chief asked. "The door gunner thinks he can—"

"I've got this," White interrupted him, slapping the crew chief on the shoulder.

"Sixty seconds," the copilot said.

White felt the nose of the Pave Hawk dip as the chopper dropped to a mere thirty feet from the ground as it worked its way down a small valley, the scenery outside whipping by too fast for him to make out any details. Suddenly, the helicopter lost speed, and the pilot brought it down to within four feet of the ground. White unbuckled his safety harness and jumped out of the chopper, landing hard on the semipaved road below, his knees and ankles protesting the impact. He crouched down to reduce his size as a target and waved at the crew chief.

The Pave Hawk gained altitude, and the pilot turned the chopper 180 degrees on a dime. The noise was so loud it briefly numbed White's senses and thoughts. The moment it was safe to do so, he sprinted toward the steep rocky hill on the west side of the road as the helicopter disappeared behind the hill on the opposite side.

White moved as fast as he could, but the extra ammunition he carried and the high-angle climb slowed him down considerably. Out of breath, his legs burning, White took cover behind a large rock a third of the way up the hill. He brought the M240B to bear and scanned the area for threats.

Relieved he wasn't in immediate danger, he was about to continue his climb when his radio came to life with a flash of static. "SCAR-One, this is Victor-Two. Radio check, over."

"You're five by five, Victor-Two," White replied, recognizing the voice of the copilot. "Are you in position?"

"We're standing by, SCAR-One. Just let us know when. Victor-Two out."

One hundred meters down, the road wound its way through the rocky-sided valley until a seventy-degree bend in the road forced any sane drivers to slow down in order to keep their tires on the road. White hadn't seen any vehicles yet, but that sharp bend was why he had decided this was the best place to ambush the ISIS vehicles.

The bend was the perfect kill zone. Still, one hundred meters was too close for comfort. He needed to go higher. He probed the surrounding area and noticed an outcrop of palmlike trees nestled among boulders halfway between his position and the top of the hill.

Perfect.

———

White advised the copilot of his exact grid location, then flipped out the bipod of the M240B. He settled into his firing position, his chin resting on the buttstock of the machine gun. He could hear the Pave Hawk hovering on the other side of the valley, but he was confident that the sound of the ISIS vehicles would keep their occupants from hearing the chopper.

There was nobody else around, only a languid breeze, and, like everything in or near Mosul in August, it was boiling hot. White's already sweat-drenched uniform clung to his body like an unavoidable second skin. He felt a drop of sweat trickle into his eye and wiped his forehead with his sleeve before taking a drink from his canteen.

The distance from his concealed firing position to the bend in the road was about 175 meters. The elevation would give him an additional advantage against the ISIS fighters. The plan was for him to ambush the lead vehicle. He had thought about using the AT4 first, but he'd be in trouble if he missed. The most crucial part of the plan was to stop the convoy long enough for the Pave Hawk's door gunner to engage the technicals with the minigun. At a firing rate of four thousand rounds per minute, the minigun could chew through the technicals easily, but since the helicopter was their only way out of the danger zone, White wanted to minimize its exposure to ISIS fire as much as possible.

White hadn't been in position for more than three minutes when he spotted dust and grit whirling in the distance. He pulled his binoculars to his face and fixed his sight on the dust trails. What he saw made his jaw tighten.

The three technicals he'd expected were indeed coming his way. What surprised White wasn't the fact that one of them was mounting a .30-caliber machine gun; what made him cringe was that the two other technicals were equipped with DShk heavy machine guns. Sometimes called Dushka—which meant "sweetie"—the DShk was capable of firing 12.7 x 108 mm rounds at an effective range of two thousand meters. The DShk had a stellar reputation for blowing coalition helicopters out of the sky. To make matters worse, White counted at least five men per vehicle, discounting the drivers. He was about to face a lot of firepower. Surprise and accuracy were going to play a major role in the upcoming engagement.

"Victor-Two, this is SCAR-One, over."

"Go ahead for Victor-Two."

"Three technicals approaching my position from the north. Traveling speed is approximately fifty miles per hour. The lead vehicle is equipped with what seems to be a .30-caliber machine gun. Vehicles two and three have DShk heavy machine guns mounted on tripods. How copy?"

"Victor-Two copies. Standing by."

White double-checked that he had easy access to the AT4 rocket launcher, the hand grenades, and the extra ammunition he had carried for the M240B. He then settled in behind his weapon with a deadly coolness born of years spent in combat zones. He knew what was about to happen. He had experienced it before. Many times. Too many times. He would kill his enemies, and he would do so without even the thinnest bit of regret for the combatants in his sights. No longer human, the ISIS fighters were simply brutes to be slain.

Tracking the technicals with his M240B, White saw them slow down considerably about two hundred meters before the bend. The thrill and anxiety of impending combat gave White the adrenaline rush he had come to expect. He focused on breathing normally, keeping his breaths even in and out, so that he could hold the front sight of the M240B just a little higher and to the left of where he wanted the first round to hit.

"Victor-Two, this is SCAR-One, engaging in three, two . . ."

White wasn't thinking anymore. He was in his bubble, his mind clear of any doubt. He applied the necessary pressure to the trigger, and the M240B started to chew through the belt of ammunition. The machine gun's bark bounced over the countryside as the steel-jacketed rounds found their targets. The bullets hit the side of the lead technical, punching through the door panel and killing the driver and two of the combatants seated in the bed of the pickup truck. By the time the gunner standing behind the .30-caliber machine gun realized what was happening, White had worked the muzzle back toward him and unleashed a two-second burst. White watched his tracers disappear into his target. The lead vehicle, now without its driver, came to a stop. The driver of the second vehicle stomped on the brakes just as the Pave Hawk appeared over the hill across from White's position. The door gunner opened up with the minigun, casting the side of the helicopter in bright orange, rounds and tracers lashing out relentlessly at the ISIS convoy. White smoothly transitioned to the AT4, bringing the rocket launcher up to his shoulder. He took careful aim at the third and last vehicle. Its driver, who was in the process of backing up, was doing his best to create as much distance as possible between his vehicle and the Pave Hawk. White observed the ISIS gunner manning the DShk jerk the heavy machine gun's barrel upward to meet the chopper. Since the AT4 was a recoilless, preloaded weapon system, White had only one shot. He had to make it count.

White and the ISIS gunner fired at the same time. White knew for sure that at least one of the ISIS combatants aboard the third vehicle had seen the plume of smoke behind the rocket, but it didn't matter. The 84 mm rocket traveled the distance in the blink of an eye and slammed into the side of the technical, transforming the vehicle and all its occupants into a rolling fireball. White let go of the rocket launcher and turned his attention to the Pave Hawk. To his horror, the chopper had been hit. White wasn't sure if it was from small arms fire or the DShk, but the Pave Hawk had started turning erratically, black smoke trailing behind it.

White swore, the enormity of the moment taking hold. His plan was quickly falling apart. Rounds suddenly chewed into the boulder to his right, sending him back to his M240B. Even though the Pave Hawk door gunner had pulverized the first and second technicals and had cut down many ISIS fighters with effective fire, White still counted half a dozen combatants armed with rifles and rocket-propelled grenades. And by the look of it, they were quickly getting organized into two groups of three men. That wasn't something White could allow to happen. At a ratio of six to one, they'd flank him in no time.

The first ISIS group sprinted north alongside the road. White drew a bead on them and fired three short but accurate bursts. Two men fell. The third man dropped to his belly and rolled to his right until he was out of sight behind a medium-size rock a few feet away.

While White was engaging the first group of ISIS fighters, the second had taken the opportunity to retreat behind the cover of the lead technical. Two men from the second group opened fire, their rounds slapping the air above White's head. He was about to return fire when he spotted one man hoisting himself into the bed of the technical. White swung the M240B in his direction and pulled the trigger just as the man reached for the .30 caliber. White's rounds punched the would-be gunner in the chest and neck, knocking him back. Before White could take aim at the two remaining ISIS fighters, a fiery streak of light coming from his right grabbed his attention.

RPG!

The grenade exploded behind him less than forty feet away. Then, as if working in concert, tracer rounds fired by the second group began to whistle to his left and right. The two ISIS fighters behind the technical had zeroed in on his position and were pinning him down. To his right, the man who had fired the RPG was reloading. White didn't take time to aim, he just unleashed a long burst of his machine gun and continued to keep pressure on the trigger until he saw the RPG gunner stagger backward. The man fell on his ass, accidentally triggering his freshly reloaded launcher. The RPG exploded at his feet. Only his boots, with the man's feet still in them, remained. Before White could engage his next target, a new barrage of 7.62 rounds peppered the earth and rocks around him. White turned his head toward the lead technical just in time to see the intense red glow of yet another RPG.

The RPG hit a small boulder less than twenty feet below his firing position and exploded. White was shoved backward while being showered with bits of sharp rocks. He hit the ground hard as rounds continued to skip close by. He tried to breathe, but the explosion had sucked the air out of his lungs. His jaw hurt like hell, and he had a strong metallic taste in his mouth. Disoriented, he raised his head, looking for his M240B. The machine gun lay to his right, well past the semiprotective enclave the boulders offered. White dragged himself back to his firing position and glanced at the lead technical, the last known position of the two ISIS fighters, and saw that the two men were leapfrogging their way toward him, covering each other in sequence. There was no way he was going to get to the M240B before being cut down.

Damn. That left him with his pistol and the three fragmentation grenades he carried in the grenade pouch of his plate carrier. White drew his pistol from its holster and took a moment to strategize his next move. What about the Pave Hawk? Had it crashed? With all his energy spent on staying alive, he had momentarily forgotten about the helicopter. White glanced at his watch. Less than sixty seconds had elapsed since he had first engaged the lead technical.

"Victor-Two, this is SCAR-One, over," White called out over the radio.

No answer. He was about to try again when he spotted one of the ISIS fighters only fifty or sixty feet away. The man was slowly climbing toward him. Maybe he thought White was dead, killed by the last RPG he had fired?

The man was thin, with sharp facial features. Like the other ISIS fighters, he wore a black headscarf and tan-colored body armor. He had a six-inch-long, disheveled black-and-gray beard. His eyes were small and filled with anger, hate, and fear. White slowly angled his pistol toward the man, afraid any brisk movement would catch his eye. He assumed the second fighter was trailing the first one.

He was wrong.

A strong voice coming from behind startled him. White's Arabic was rudimentary at best, but he had no difficulty understanding what he'd been asked to do.

How in hell did he get here so damn fast? White wondered, weighing his options. None of them were good. He slowly got up and raised his hands to his side, still holding his pistol. The second ISIS fighter yelled at him again to drop his pistol.

If he was to make a move, it was now or never, before the first man arrived. It would become exponentially harder to take down two men aiming rifles at him. It was a fact of life that action was always faster than reaction. Even though White's initial move would require precise timing and a bit of luck, it was imperative he made himself a harder target to hit. He had to make the ISIS shooter react to *his* action, not the other way around. With that in mind, and with lightning speed, White pivoted forward 180 degrees on his right foot and then leaped to his left, bringing his pistol up and aiming for center mass. He had time to fire two rounds before the ISIS fighter pulled the trigger. A bullet grazed White's right arm at about the same time he crashed into a small pile of rocks. The ISIS fighter, hit by White's bullets, staggered back, his face ashen from shock. White fired again. The man's head snapped back, and his rifle fell from his lifeless hands.

Pain shot through White's right arm. With a gasp, he pulled himself upright. He touched his arm and clenched his teeth. The bullet had carved a path through the meat of his arm. The wound didn't look good and it hurt like hell, but he had to move. Or he'd be dead in seconds. His right arm became numb, and he transferred his pistol into his left hand. There was no point grabbing the ISIS fighter's AK-47; he wouldn't be able to operate it.

A grenade landed with a thud ten feet away. White sprang into action and ran in the only direction he could—up the hill. The grenade exploded and White fell forward.

Fuck.

Hot, searing pain shot up through the entire length of his left leg. Deep red blood soaked his combat trousers where a piece of shrapnel had embedded itself. Below him, less than seventy feet away, two ISIS fighters were taking aim at him.

How's this possible? he asked himself, realizing too late he had missed one ISIS man. *That explains why the third one surprised me.*

As he raised his pistol, and through the thickening of his mind, White wondered what would happen to the downed Marine aviators. He hoped his actions had bought his men the time they needed.

Then, from behind the hill, the distinctive sound of long blades chopping the air emerged, loud enough to draw the fighters' attention. By the time they pointed the barrels of their rifles toward the Pave Hawk, it was too late. The door gunner fired a long burst from the minigun, killing both men instantly.

White tried to get to his knees but failed. The sand around him had turned red. With a last surge of lucid energy, he determined that the shrapnel must have nicked an artery. Desperately holding on to consciousness, he saw the Pave Hawk pilot skillfully bring the helicopter to a hover above his position.

Too late, he thought as he felt himself free fall into darkness.

CHAPTER FIVE

Landstuhl Regional Medical Center
Landstuhl, Germany

Captain Clayton White sat up in bed and looked at his right arm. The nurse had removed the large bandage and swapped it with smaller white strips covering the twenty-four stitches he'd received.

That's gonna leave a nasty scar, he thought.

In the last seventy-two hours, White had received three surgeries to remove the two—not one as he had originally thought—pieces of shrapnel embedded deep in his left leg. The Pave Hawk's crew had saved his life. As he had feared, shrapnel had indeed scored a hit on an artery. But luckily for White, by the time they reached the SuperCobra's crash site, the crew chief had already stopped the bleeding. The two Marine aviators had been rescued, and despite being hit numerous times by small arms fire during the initial engagement and losing its communication systems, the Pave Hawk had carried them all home.

White couldn't be prouder of his team. They had once again proven their courage and ability to take care of business amid the worst of conditions.

These Things We Do, That Others May Live.

White's only regret was that he wouldn't be returning to his men in Iraq for at least a month. His doctor had been unyielding about this. With a sigh, White stared moodily at the view outside his window.

There wasn't much to see. The only thing he could make out from his bed was another tan-colored wing of the hospital. At least the window was open wide enough to let in fresh air. White's thoughts moved to his father, Maxwell, a brigadier general currently serving with JSOC in Afghanistan. No doubt his dad had heard what had happened to him. White wondered if his dad even cared.

Of course he does, he thought, chastising himself for even thinking it. His relationship with his mostly absent father was too formal to allow any intimacy between them. His mother, Carolyn, was the glue that kept the family together. That remained true to this day. Yet, for a boy who had grown up with an absentee father, White had inherited his father's strong characteristics, values, and beliefs. White had always been a tad afraid of his dad, but he had never felt the weight of his hand. As he looked back on his boyhood as an army brat, or even his early manhood, when he'd made some bad choices, he couldn't remember an angry or a hasty word spoken by his father that wasn't deserved. His dad had rarely praised him, but he'd never unduly criticized him either. And deep down, White knew his father was proud of him. He'd seen a glimpse of that pride in his old man's eyes when he had graduated from the Air Force Academy as a second lieutenant, despite the fact he had done so with a history major and a minor in French studies.

But the thing that meant more to him than anything his father had ever said to him had come the day he'd earned the maroon beret of a combat rescue officer after twenty-four months of grueling training. General Maxwell White hadn't said a word as he'd shaken his son's hand. But his nod had been filled with pride and fatherly love.

A confident knock on the hospital room's door redirected White's gaze away from the window. Expecting a nurse or a doctor, he was surprised to see Lieutenant General Alexander Hammond march into his room. General Hammond was wearing his dress blues, and his shoes were polished to a perfect shine. At six foot four inches, he was an impressive figure. Even more so with the breast of his tunic heavy with ribbons showing his military qualifications and awards, including a Combat Infantry Badge, parachutist's wing, and a Silver Star. There was also a Purple Heart with an oak leaf cluster, which denoted a subsequent award of the same medal. The three gleaming silver stars on Hammond's epaulets were the ultimate proof of his long and distinguished military career.

White attempted to sit straighter, but Hammond stopped him with a hand.

"Please, Clayton, at ease," the general said, closing the door behind him.

To say that White was shocked to see Hammond was an understatement. As commanding officer of Joint Special Operations Command, Hammond was one of the busiest men in the United States. One of the most powerful too. JSOC's main task was to execute special-operations missions worldwide. The fact that Hammond wasn't in Washington, DC, or Fayetteville, North Carolina, was surprising enough, but Germany? Hammond couldn't really be in Landstuhl just to see him, could he?

"It's nice to see you," Hammond said. "Glad you got out of this one with only a couple scratches."

White smiled. He had known Hammond since he was a boy. His father had served under Hammond twice, excluding Maxwell's current assignment at JSOC. Hammond's daughter, Veronica, had been White's best friend until he entered the Air Force Academy. At first, they had kept in touch almost every week, but after a few years their lives had taken them in different directions, and the time between phone calls had gotten longer and longer. They still talked occasionally, and he knew she was now a PhD candidate at Yale University. The last time they had spoken, a week prior to his deployment to Iraq, she'd been on her way to an archaeological site in Greece.

"But seriously, Clay, how are you feeling?" Hammond asked, standing next to White's bed.

"I feel fine, sir," White replied truthfully. "The doctors said I'll be able to return to my unit in a month or so."

"Good to hear it," Hammond said. "What you and that crew of yours did out there to rescue those two Marine aviators was outstanding."

For the first time, White noticed that Hammond's eyes were bloodshot and sunken, as if he hadn't slept for days.

"Thank you, sir. So that others may live, right?"

"Right," Hammond replied, looking a little uneasy. "So that others may live."

Then there was an awkward moment of silence. White spoke first.

"How's Veronica, General?" he asked. "I haven't heard from her since she left for Greece."

At the mention of his daughter, a faint smile came upon Hammond's face. Veronica was her father's pride and joy. Hammond cleared his throat and said, "She's doing fine. I told her you were injured. She's on her way to see you."

White was confused. There was no reason for Hammond to have done so. It wasn't as if he and Veronica were in a romantic relationship. They were friends. That was it. "Sir, you shouldn't have—"

Hammond interrupted him. "There's something else I need to tell you, Clay," he said, an unfamiliar gruffness in his voice.

White felt an involuntary tightening of his chest and shoulders. *There it is,* he thought. *Here's the real reason he's here.*

"It's about your dad," Hammond said, his face suddenly ashy white. "His helicopter was shot down south of Bagram by the Taliban two days ago. There were no survivors."

White felt all the blood drain from his face.

"I'm so sorry," Hammond said.

White met the general's eyes for a moment, then nodded. He had so many questions, but his first thoughts were for his mother. "Does my mom know?"

"I spoke with her a few hours after Maxwell's helicopter went down. Heather is with her now."

White's mother was one tough lady, and famously spare with her emotions. Still, the loss of her husband was going to create a huge void in her life. She'd been married to Maxwell for almost thirty-five years. This was almost one hundred times longer than White's longest relationship. He was glad Hammond's wife would be by her side to provide emotional support if needed.

"Your father was quite a hero, Clay," Hammond said. "He spoke often of you."

White didn't know if it was true or not, but it was nice of Hammond to say.

"Thank you, sir," he said. "I appreciate you coming all this way. You didn't have to."

"Your dad was a good friend," Hammond said, almost to himself. "I had to."

Somehow, that didn't make White feel any better. In fact, he felt sick to his stomach.

So many missed opportunities, he thought. His mother had tried her very best to bring the two of them closer, but their respective careers and deployments hadn't made it easy. Still, White should have made an extra effort to be more present, to call more often. But he hadn't. And now he regretted it.

"I can't believe he's dead," he said after a moment. His eyes were sad but dry.

"If there's anything I can do, Clay, you let me know," Hammond said.

"I appreciate that, sir," White replied. "Means a lot."

Hammond placed his hand on White's shoulder. "Maybe it won't be today or tomorrow. Maybe not even next year. It doesn't matter. I'll be there when you need me. In the meantime, I've got your six."

White nodded. "Thank you. What about the Taliban fighters? Were they ever found?"

For the briefest of moments, Hammond looked puzzled; then he quickly said, "Two Apache helicopters were dispatched minutes after the crash. Our choppers easily caught up with them. We got them all."

There was a reason White was a great poker player, why he'd finished in second place a few years back during a World Series of Poker event in the Bahamas. He was good at spotting microexpressions, the subtle subconscious clues someone gave out when he was lying or being dishonest—just as Hammond had a moment ago.

For whatever reason, General Hammond had chosen to lie to him. And White had no idea why.

PART TWO
PRESENT DAY

CHAPTER SIX

The Ritz-Carlton
San Francisco, California

Clayton White raced up the elegant spiral staircase that led to the second floor. The balcony, which encircled the majestic ballroom of the Ritz-Carlton San Francisco, was the perfect vantage point from which to oversee what was happening among the four dozen round tables set for tonight's event. Located near Union Square, the hotel's nine-story 1909 landmark building was a stunning tribute to beauty. The cable car stop just outside the modern yet timeless lobby made the Ritz-Carlton the perfect place from which to explore the city. The hotel's location was one of the main reasons the Society of American Archaeology had picked it for its annual awards gala.

White spotted Special Agent Marcus Thompson the moment he reached the balcony level. Marcus, a bald dark-skinned man dressed in a tuxedo who towered well over White's own six-foot frame, was standing behind the cast-iron railings at the edge of the balcony, looking down toward the ballroom, his powerful arms crossed over his chest.

"How are things, Marcus?" White asked, approaching the man from behind.

"Nothing unusual to report," Marcus answered without looking back.

White leaned against the railings next to Marcus and took in the elite crowd gathered in the ballroom. He felt like a king overseeing his subjects. The floor was varnished wood, and magnificent crystal chandeliers lit the space with a fairy-tale glow. White scanned the tables, each adorned with a spotless white-linen tablecloth, each with eight to ten people sitting around its edges, all beaming at each other. These people were the best and brightest in their field. They were the true superstars of the archaeology world, but only a minuscule percentage of the American public would ever recognize their names or appreciate their accomplishments. Their faces, with the exception of that of White's protectee, would never be seen on the covers of gossip magazines, but their names were celebrated in certain scientific circles.

Despite the seemingly jovial ambiance, White wished he had more Secret Service special agents at his disposal. As the special agent in charge of Veronica Hammond's protective detail, White had the power to order more agents to San Francisco. But Veronica had been adamant. She wanted to keep a low profile. He had, of course, insisted, enumerating the reasons having more than six agents on the trip wasn't a luxury, but she had threatened to refuse Secret Service protection entirely if he pushed any further. Veronica, the only daughter of Vice President-Elect Alexander Hammond, had that privilege. And, as White had learned a long time ago, Veronica didn't bluff. So he'd backed down. It was better to have a six-man team than no team at all.

"I'll go see if she's ready," White said to Marcus. "I'll send someone to relieve you so you can grab a quick bite before this thing starts."

"You think she'll win?" Marcus asked, looking at White for the first time.

"I don't know, but she certainly deserves to," he said before heading back to the staircase and starting down.

Four months ago, Veronica, an archaeologist specializing in aerial archaeology, whose work concentrated on observing some of the earliest traces of human activity from the air, had released a beta version of

Drain, a mobile application she had developed in collaboration with SkyCU Technology, a Silicon Valley start-up. Drain enabled the public to check high-resolution satellite imagery for signs of looting or previously undiscovered archaeological remains—the satellites could even see through one hundred feet of water. Hence the app's name: long-hidden sites became as visible as if the area had been drained of water.

Since its launch, more than seventy-five thousand users from twenty-one countries had flagged some five hundred new sites, including two underwater Aboriginal sites off the Australian coast. Those two sites, the first confirmed underwater archaeological sites found on the Australian continental shelf, had raised so much enthusiasm among the archaeological community that Veronica had decided to lead the expedition herself. Thanks to her hard work and her immense popularity on social media, she'd had no trouble securing the necessary funds. A news crew from a specialty TV channel had even embedded itself in Veronica's team to cover her first dive in Australian waters. They hadn't been disappointed. Within hours, the first of more than two hundred artifacts had been discovered, some of them dating back seven thousand years.

Invigorated by the initial results, Veronica had recently announced on social media that she and SkyCU Technology were working on an important update that would permit Drain users to see through water ten times deeper. Not only would that have a profound impact on ocean observation, but the application could potentially help inform the response to climate change. Veronica was now considering all her options, including partnering with one of the giant tech companies who had approached her and SkyCU about acquiring the app. She had a meeting with the eight employees of SkyCU tomorrow afternoon in Palo Alto to discuss Drain's exciting future.

At tonight's gala, the Society of American Archaeology would announce the winner of the Award for Excellence in Archaeological Analysis. Veronica was one of the nominees, and, if White was to believe all the gossip, she was the top contender. He wasn't surprised. Thanks to the millennials who represented over three-quarters of Veronica's followers and who never did anything without their smartphones, suddenly archaeology was cool again. The nomination was a way to acknowledge Veronica for her unique contribution to the field.

And White couldn't be prouder.

He and Veronica had been friends since their teenage years. When the helicopter his father was traveling in was shot down by enemy fire six years prior, Veronica had flown to Landstuhl, Germany, where White was recuperating from injuries sustained during a rescue operation. He'd asked for and received emergency leave from his unit and, with Veronica, had traveled back to the United States to help his mother plan the funeral. Veronica's assistance had been godsent, and, even though nothing remotely romantic had happened between them, those precious weeks spent with her were when White had started seeing her as more than just a friend. Three months later, after completing his tour of duty in Iraq and leaving the military, he'd moved into an apartment a few minutes' walk from her residence in the heart of Westville, a lovely neighborhood in New Haven, Connecticut. From that point on, the dynamic of their relationship had quickly shifted from "just friends" to something much deeper—if still not official.

"XJD-31, this is Vigil-One, over," White said into the microphone in his sleeve.

A steady voice came through his earbud. "Go ahead for XJD-31."

"This is Vigil-One, I'm going up to pick up Flower," White said, using Veronica's designated code name. As he crossed the marble lobby, White nodded at another agent who was standing close to the main entry. The agent gave him a thumbs-up, letting White know he had heard his last communication with XJD-31, the mobile telecommunications unit parked not far away.

White pressed the elevator call button. The shiny silver doors opened, and he stepped inside. White disliked elevators—small sealed boxes that could become traps in the blink of an eye. And there was no way to know what might be lurking on the other side when the door reopened. Not something you wanted when your job was to protect the daughter of the vice president-elect.

Veronica's suite was on the fifth floor, with a connecting door linking her room to White's. It wasn't an unusual arrangement for a Secret Service detail, but White's meteoric rise within the United States Secret Service would come to a sudden halt if his boss knew he had shared more than a door with Veronica. Even Alexander Hammond's direct intervention wouldn't help him. By becoming romantically involved with Veronica, White was playing a dangerous game. There was no denying that their relationship couldn't continue in its present form. But for now, being reprimanded or reassigned were risks he was more than willing to take. Never in his life had he remotely felt this close to another person.

The elevator reached the floor, and the doors slid aside. White got off, scanned the hallway, and turned right. Apart from the Secret Service agent standing at the end of the hallway, he didn't see anyone else. The thick carpet smelled like an odd combination of expensive perfume and cleaner. The walls, painted a dove gray, were decorated with canvases by local artists White didn't know.

"All good?" he asked the agent guarding Veronica's room.

"The cleaning lady came, but I told her to come back," the agent replied.

"All right," White said. "Get down to the balcony level to relieve Marcus. I've got this."

White fist-bumped his subordinate and watched him walk toward the elevators.

As White raised his hand to knock on Veronica's door, he noted the time. Six o'clock. The cocktail hour had officially started, but the dinner and speeches wouldn't begin for another sixty minutes. White knocked on the door. Veronica snatched it open as if she'd been standing there waiting for him. Upon seeing her, White's heart almost stopped. The sexy tilt of her mouth, combined with the charming glint in her green eyes and the faint but enchanting smell of her perfume, sweet and floral, made him weak in the knees—and the hounding risk of being found out all worth it.

"Come in, Clay," Veronica said, stepping out of the way to let him in. "If it's okay, I'd like to discuss tomorrow's schedule."

"There's no need to pretend," White replied with a smile, closing the door behind him. "I've sent the other agent downstairs to relieve Marcus."

Veronica was dressed casually in a pair of blue jeans, dark ankle boots, and a cream-colored sweater that showed off her curves. With her brown hair pulled back into a messy bun and her face devoid of cosmetics, she looked a decade younger than her thirty-six years. She grabbed him by the tie and pulled him close as she stood on tiptoe. Her lips, so giving and so soft, found his. Her hands brushed his face. A shiver rolled down his spine as his fingers curled around the back of her neck.

"How much time do we have?" she asked, her voice a soft growl.

"Depends if you want to skip the cocktails or not," he replied, kissing her bottom lip.

"I'd skip the whole damned thing if it meant we could be alone for two hours," she said under her breath.

White smiled and placed a silencing finger on her lips.

"XJD-31, this is Vigil-One," White said.

"Go ahead, Vigil-One."

"I'll be off comms for a few minutes," White said. "Call me on my cell if you need anything."

"Ten-four, Vigil-One."

Veronica grabbed at his belt, and in two fast, aggressive flicks she had the buckle undone. Her hands continued to move together as she undid the button at the waistband of his trousers. With nothing left to support them, the weight of White's portable radio, his pistol, and the two extra magazines took over, and his pants fell to his ankles, bunching around his feet. Veronica removed his suit jacket and began to roughly pull his tie apart. Soon, all her clothes along with his tie, shirt, and soft body armor lay in a heap on the floor next to the bed.

Veronica ran her fingers over his bare chest and down his flat stomach. He kicked off his shoes and let her push him onto the bed, unaware of the danger swiftly closing in.

CHAPTER SEVEN

Oxley Vineyards
Kommetjie, South Africa

Roy Oxley knew it was going to be a long, stressful, and probably sleepless night. It wasn't every day one ordered the assassination of the vice president-elect's daughter. Oxley didn't mind the lack of sleep. He was used to it, and he expected the staff on his payroll to deal with pressure the same way he did. So, he felt no shame in having Pierre Sarazin, the newly hired general manager of Oxley Vineyards, stand almost at attention in front of his desk at five minutes to midnight, long after the man's normal working hours.

Oxley's hands were locked behind his head and his ankles crossed atop the large mahogany desk behind which he sat as he considered the two wine bottles presented to him by Pierre. The first one was a sauvignon blanc, while the second was a pinotage, South Africa's signature variety.

"You've tasted them?" Oxley asked.

"I did."

"And?"

"I'd prefer if you'd form your own opinion, sir," Pierre replied, his French accent coming through. "I wouldn't want to influence—"

Oxley shut him up with a wave. "You're new here, Pierre," he said, "so let's make something crystal clear, shall we?"

Pierre remained silent but nodded.

"Good." Oxley swung his feet off the desk and stood. He straightened his sport coat and walked over to Pierre, entering his personal space. "There's nothing, absolutely nothing, you can say that will influence how I think. Do you understand what I'm telling you?" he asked.

Pierre blinked several times and took a small step back. "I—I'm not sure I do," he said tentatively.

Oxley eyed him for a long time. He didn't like what he saw. There was a *je ne sais quoi* about Pierre he wasn't fond of. The Frenchman was in his midforties, small, blond, and impeccably dressed, but he exuded an arrogance and superiority he shouldn't have. Not yet, at least. In Oxley's humble opinion, Pierre hadn't done or accomplished anything since he joined the winery a few months ago that warranted such pride. He didn't care about Pierre's embellished résumé, or his past achievements.

"You came highly recommended by your previous employers," Oxley continued. "Do you believe yourself to be good at what you do?"

"I was once the best sommelier in Europe," Pierre said, straightening his shoulders, a trace of a smile adorning his lips. "And I must mention that the winery I managed in California, after working at two Michelin-star restaurants, just won second place at this year's World's Best Vineyards. So yes, I believe I'm good at my job. Sir."

"Why did you apply to work for me if everything was so dandy in California?" Oxley asked, relieving Pierre of the bottle of sauvignon blanc he was still holding.

"Money, of course," Pierre said, as if the answer should have been obvious. "Nobody was able or willing to match the compensation you offered."

Oxley turned around and walked to one of the large windows facing the Atlantic Ocean. Even though it was impossible to see the water at night, powerful spotlights mounted on the rooftop and aimed toward the sea illuminated the surrounding vineyards. The house, which sat on a four-hectare lot fifteen miles south of Cape Town, had cost him a hair above US$2 million, a fraction of what it was worth. He would have paid twenty times that in Southern California for a place similar to this one.

The compound included a simply designed but elegant 6,500-square-foot two-story home for him, his wife, and his five children; two much smaller guest houses for his staff and security detail; and another midsize structure that housed a shooting range, a training facility, and a helipad. The two actual winery buildings, plus the newly renovated tasting room, were a bit farther away on each side of a small lane that crossed the vineyard to the ocean.

If all went according to plan, Oxley Vineyards' wine would be available for the public to purchase in twelve months. Not that he expected to make much profit from the sales. Breaking even within the next couple of years would be a great start. Of course, making a profit had never been the ultimate objective.

Oxley Vineyards was simply his method of worming his way into South African high society in order to make the necessary contacts he would need to run for office. It was the only way he could really change things.

Roy Oxley had accomplished much in his life. Born in Los Angeles, he was the result of a one-night stand between a British Airways pilot and a cute American waitress. It wasn't until his mother was killed in a botched robbery attempt at the small corner restaurant where she worked that Oxley had contacted his father for the first time. Surprisingly enough, his father had accepted him with open arms and hadn't even asked for a paternity test, which told Oxley that the man must have known he had a child in the United States. For years Oxley wondered if his old man had fathered more kids around the world. If he had, he'd never told Oxley about them.

Oxley became a British citizen and joined the military when he turned eighteen. He eked out three years in the Parachute Regiment followed by five years with the elite tier-one unit of the British Army, the SAS—Special Air Service. That was where he met Abelard Krantz, one of the most driven people he'd ever encountered.

After eight years of military life, Oxley had decided he'd had enough. There was only so much one could do to win the war, and he was tired of being a pawn. He wanted to be a knight instead. The United Kingdom's Secret Intelligence Service, commonly known as MI6, was ecstatic when he submitted his application. It wasn't every day—or even every year—that a decorated, combat-hardened SAS trooper was interested in joining the spy business. The fact was, most SAS operators didn't hold MI6 in high esteem. SAS troopers were door kickers, while MI6 officers were . . . well, nobody really knew what they were. And that was exactly the way MI6 wanted to keep it.

Oxley had been with MI6 for almost ten years, recruiting and running agents and helping in the execution of over half a dozen assassinations and paramilitary operations in Afghanistan and Iraq, when he was unexpectedly called back to London. It was true that things had gotten a bit out of control in Afghanistan. A few complaints had been filed against him for prisoner abuse by members of his staff, but they had all been investigated and dismissed. Roy Oxley's work was too important, and his effectiveness couldn't be denied. It wasn't an exaggeration to say that his efforts in the Middle East, as controversial and scandalous as they might have been, had helped save the lives of hundreds of British troops.

But back at Vauxhall Cross, his meeting with the head of the counterterrorism division hadn't gone well. Someone in Afghanistan had leaked information about a prisoner's death, and the situation had turned messy. Reporters had started asking difficult questions, and the chief himself had decided—for the good of the service, Oxley was told—to cut ties. But before Oxley could explode in righteous anger, his boss at the counterterrorism branch had pushed a smartphone across the table.

"Don't go too far, Roy. You're out of the service, but your services are still needed."

The next day, after completing all the necessary paperwork, Oxley had quietly retired. A week later, the phone his former boss had given him rang.

"How would you like to become the CEO of Oxley International Shipping Lines?" the foreign secretary had asked him. "Given your . . . singular expertise in certain matters, we think you'd be perfect for the job."

And this was when things had started to become interesting. And lucrative. But Oxley needed help, someone he could trust. It didn't take much to convince Krantz to team up with him. A decade and a half of fighting in one of the most elite units in the world had taken its toll on Krantz's body, and it seemed that his knees, shoulders, and back weren't what they used to be. When Oxley offered to quadruple his salary, Krantz had signed on.

Ninety days after what would be his first and only call with the British foreign secretary, Oxley was overseeing a fleet of four container ships, all financed by the good people of Great Britain through a special projects fund at the Ministry of Defence, though Oxley knew the Americans were chipping in a substantial amount too. Although three of the four ships were indeed carrying regular goods, and sometimes sensitive military equipment, to regions where the British and American governments preferred to keep their activities under the radar, one of them had been transformed into a floating prison for enemy combatants believed to be in possession of information too valuable or time sensitive for the standard prisoner-processing protocols.

The name given to the operation was CONQUEST, and the decisions about which terrorists were designated for the ship were made by a select few at the very top of the British and American special operations commands, including the American generals Alexander Hammond and Maxwell White. Due to the outpouring of support for the Abu Ghraib prisoners and the widespread condemnation of the treatment they had endured, it had been critical to keep CONQUEST far from prying eyes. Even at the height of the program, there had been fewer than one hundred people who knew about it. Even the tier-one operators who'd bagged the terrorists had no idea where their detainees usually ended up. Not that they would have cared.

The intelligence acquired from the prisoners was vital to the war effort—or at least that's what Oxley had been told by General Hammond and his British counterpart—but since it had been obtained using methods most people would have found reprehensible, Oxley had been left with a significant problem on his hands: What to do with the prisoners once they had no further value? Both the American and British governments had flatly refused to take them in. Truth was, they were in a difficult position, especially since CONQUEST had been funded through black funds.

So, seven years ago, when he got word that the program wouldn't be renewed, he was unofficially told to keep the four vessels. Neither government cared what he did with them, though someone suggested at least one of the vessels should be sunk. Oxley took care of the problem. All the problems. In a very definitive manner. And no one had asked any questions.

That was, until six years ago. General Maxwell White, whose involvement in the operation had been fairly limited, had caught wind of how Oxley had disposed of the prisoners. The man and his conscience had become a problem, though Oxley, through Abelard Krantz, had taken care of that one too.

During the following years, through an aggressive growth strategy of mergers and acquisitions, Oxley International Shipping Lines had grown into a fleet of fifty-one vessels and owned approximately half a percent of the worldwide market share of container shipping. Its rapid growth had attracted the attention of the two largest container-shipping companies in the world. Both had made offers of purchase, and Oxley had decided to accept the most lavish one. Three billion dollars. Le Groupe Avanti was days away from finalizing its financial due diligence, and until two weeks ago, Oxley had been confident that once all his debt had been paid off, there would be a cool billion left in his pocket.

That money, in combination with his status as a winery owner, would open a lot of doors for him. By the time he was done, everybody that mattered in South Africa would know his name.

And then the snag had hit. Veronica Hammond and her damn mobile application, Drain. With the upgraded capabilities planned for Drain, how long would it take for users to identify the underwater cemetery? And hadn't she mentioned repeatedly on social media that the coast of the Arabian Peninsula was one of the areas she wanted Drain users to focus on?

Bloody hell. He should have sunk the bodies in the middle of the Indian Ocean.

The irony of Alexander Hammond's daughter threatening to expose CONQUEST wasn't lost on him. It had become obvious to Oxley that Hammond wasn't going to do anything to rein in his daughter. Perhaps the man believed that he was off the hook. Oxley had wondered at times if Hammond had manipulated the covert files so that if the deaths of the prisoners ever came to light, Oxley would take the fall. Never mind that Hammond had given the instructions. Oxley had seen exactly what a short distance Hammond's loyalty extended. After all, he'd given up Maxwell White.

Oxley had way too much to lose to simply stand back and hope this was going to go away by itself. It wasn't only a question of his having to answer for his crimes—it had everything to do with the promise he had made to his wife.

Three decades after the end of the apartheid, there were still South African children falling into pit latrines due to the lack of ablution facilities. There were still so many who didn't have access to land, health care, and water. His wife, Adaliya, had been born in South Africa, and her parents, who had immigrated to the United Kingdom to escape the systemic racism of apartheid, had told him about the hard life they'd had to endure in their home country. Adaliya had sworn to him that one day she'd go back and do her part to change things. Seeing how much it meant to her, Oxley had promised her they would do it together.

How could he help Adaliya make South Africa a better place if he was behind bars? There was no one else but him who had the willingness, the guts, the money, and, soon, the contacts to enact the universal changes needed to give all South Africans access to the same opportunities and essential public services. This would be his legacy for his and Adaliya's five children.

And maybe, just maybe, it would be redemption for the role he had played in CONQUEST.

All he needed was time. Time to clean up his mess off the Arabian Peninsula. In his mind, Oxley swore again. Why the hell had Hammond allowed his daughter to pursue this?

He turned his attention back to Pierre. There was something about the man that made him mistrustful. Was it possible he was an intelligence officer? Certainly not Russian, but maybe French? Swiss? Or, worst, South African? Shipping activities often provoked national security concerns, and perhaps someone was probing around the pending merger.

Then again, it was entirely possible that circumstances had made him paranoid and that Pierre was exactly who he claimed to be.

"And what tells me you won't walk away from me if one of my competitors offers you more?" Oxley asked.

Pierre cleared his throat. "Mr. Krantz made it abundantly clear it would be a bad idea to do so," he said.

Oxley smiled. "Did he, now?"

Abelard Krantz. Oxley's go-to for everything requiring a violent touch.

"Did Mr. Krantz also explain to you what I expect from my employees and associates?" Oxley asked, inserting a corkscrew into the cork of the sauvignon blanc.

Pierre swallowed hard. Tiny beads of perspiration had formed below his hairline and on his upper lip. "Loyalty," he answered.

Oxley stopped what he was doing and set his eyes on Pierre.

"That's right, Pierre," Oxley said, dropping his voice to a menacing softness. "Total and absolute loyalty. Now, let's see if you're capable of it."

CHAPTER EIGHT

The Ritz-Carlton
San Francisco, California

Willem Van Heerden exhaled a stream of gray smoke and watched it dissipate into the evening air. Strategically positioned so he could cover both the hotel's entrance and the side street, he scanned the area, taking in the faces of the people coming and going in all directions. Except for the white Sprinter van parked in front of an antiques store one block farther east, in which Van Heerden knew the Secret Service had set up its mobile communications unit, nothing unusual had caught his eye during his long walk around the neighborhood. His target's black SUV was parked under the hotel's archway on Stockton Street, and the security vehicle, another black SUV, was idling next to the secondary exit on California Street.

Van Heerden glanced at his watch. It was time to go back in. He took one last drag on his cigarette and tossed the butt into a rain puddle. He hurried across the street, avoiding the slow-moving traffic, and entered the hotel lobby, heading directly toward the elevators. To his left, standing ramrod straight only a few steps away from the main doors, a man Van Heerden easily identified as a Secret Service agent was keeping a watchful eye on the comings and goings within the lobby.

It was a different man than the one who had been standing in the same place when Van Heerden had left the hotel one hour ago, but Van

Heerden was convinced he was one of the six agents assigned to his target's protection detail. The coiled earpiece and the American flag pin on his lapel gave him away. Nonetheless, he committed the man's face to memory. Just to be absolutely sure an additional agent hadn't joined the initial group, Van Heerden would compare it to the six mug shots his employer had provided him in his mission brief.

Van Heerden took the elevator to the second floor and walked up to the fourth floor, where his room was located. He didn't believe he was under surveillance or that the American Secret Service had taken notice of him, but old habits died hard. He didn't want anyone watching the floor location indicator on the ground level to know on which floor he exited.

Coming out of the staircase, he turned to the right, toward his room halfway down the corridor. Van Heerden removed a key card from his pocket, inserted it into the lock, and turned the door handle. He opened the door slowly, looking down at the carpet inside his hotel room. The thin sheet of see-through plastic he had left there hadn't moved. Satisfied, Van Heerden removed the **DO NOT DISTURB** sign and locked the door behind him. Next, he checked his carry-on. The four hard-to-see filaments he had fixed on the suitcase were intact. No one had searched his suitcase. Not that anyone would have found anything incriminating or of great value inside, but if the plastic at the door or the filaments had been disturbed, Van Heerden would have postponed or even called off the operation.

He pulled his phone from his pocket and unlocked it. He opened a browser, entered the username and password his employer had given him, and waited for the system to log him in. A single email popped into his in-box. The message contained an encrypted attachment. He tapped the attachment with his finger and examined the six mug shots and the three vehicles that appeared on his screen. The agent he had spotted in the lobby was indeed part of his mark's protection detail, and, as he had thought, the Sprinter van belonged to the Secret Service. The two other vehicles were the black SUVs he had seen outside the hotel.

Good. Van Heerden wasn't a big fan of last-minute surprises.

He reached under his sport jacket and drew the SIG Sauer P226 pistol from his shoulder holster. The pistol, with three fully loaded magazines and a black suppressor, had been left for him inside the rental car arranged for him by his employer. A summary inspection had shown the pistol to be in proper working order, but Van Heerden wouldn't be completely satisfied until he took it apart and cleaned it himself. Aiming at the floor, he released the magazine and racked the slide, ejecting the chambered round. He slid out the rounds from the three magazines one at a time with his thumb. He examined the magazines and checked the springs. He then fieldstripped the pistol and laid out each piece neatly on top of the writing desk, inspecting every piece carefully. From his suitcase he removed a small gun-cleaning kit, from which he pulled out an old toothbrush, a cleaning rod, a barrel brush, and a bunch of Q-tips. Dirty weapons misfired. Clean ones didn't.

Once his pistol was cleaned, he lightly oiled the moving parts, making sure to wipe any excess, and reassembled it piece by piece. He then reloaded the three magazines and inserted one of them into the SIG. He racked the slide and holstered his pistol. His actions during the course of the next hour would define how he would live the rest of his life. Success meant a nice villa by the Mediterranean; failure would send him to prison—or to his death.

Van Heerden ran an impatient hand through his silver hair. Only a few more minutes to wait. As he reached for one of the complimentary bottles of water provided by the hotel, he noticed that his hands, usually steady as a surgeon's, had a slight tremor. The tremor, as faint and feeble as it was, worried him. He had fought in numerous wars, skied on the steep faces of so-called unskiable mountains, and even survived a bear encounter. Still, he couldn't remember the last time he had shown any signs of anxiety. Was it fatigue?

Or maybe that's just what happens when you get old, he thought, drinking from the plastic bottle. His fiftieth birthday was less than two weeks away. Images of his wife—his third—and his four adult sons popped into his head.

Damn. Now wasn't the time to get distracted. Wasn't he exactly where he wanted to be, doing what he loved? Some folks pushed through their nine-to-five jobs so they could go home and live their lives. For Van Heerden, it was the opposite. The field was his home.

Well, he thought, *if that's true, why do I keep thinking about retiring to a Mediterranean villa?* Van Heerden tightened his jaw and forced the villa and his family out of his mind.

For tonight's operation, he had selected five of his best men. Like him, they were experienced operators who had all successfully completed several missions in the United States—albeit none more difficult or dicey than tonight's. As mercenaries, it wasn't the first time they would risk it all for a chance at a nice big paycheck. Each of them had different travel arrangements. None had crossed into the United States via the same route or even on the same day. After tonight's operation, they would all leave the same way they had come in—just tourists going back home after a short but pleasant stay in San Francisco.

Van Heerden retrieved a wireless earbud from the inside pocket of his sport coat. He switched on the Bluetooth connection and inserted it in his right ear. His first order of business was to reestablish communications with his men. A call sign matching one of the first six letters of the alphabet had been assigned to each of them. Since his departure from Johannesburg ten days ago, he had only heard from each man once. A quick text to confirm a safe entry into the United States.

"Barry, this is Albert. Radio check, over," Van Heerden said, pressing down on the transmit button of his handheld radio. Smoking two packs a day for years had made his voice hard and raspy.

"In position and ready to proceed," came the reply.

Van Heerden repeated the process with each man. Satisfied the comms were good and that all his men were ready, Van Heerden gave the order to execute. In his mind's eye, he saw his men move into position, each taking down their assigned target.

As for his man assigned to the Secret Service special agent positioned in the lobby, Van Heerden had instructed him to only neutralize the agent if it became absolutely necessary, due to the high volume of people gathered there. The man assigned to keep an eye on the agent was to contact Van Heerden directly if he noticed any changes in the agent's demeanor.

Although they had practiced the entire operation numerous times at their training compound in Johannesburg, Van Heerden was anxious. The American Secret Service was good at what they did. It was one thing to drill two holes in a paper target's forehead in a controlled environment; it was an entirely different ball game to pull off a covert operation deep in enemy territory. But Van Heerden had a powerful ally in his camp. Surprise.

CHAPTER NINE

The Ritz-Carlton
San Francisco, California

Clayton White, still slightly out of breath, ran his hand through Veronica's hair, relishing the silken sensation against his palm. Not for the first time, he realized he just couldn't get enough of her. Veronica Hammond made him smile. She made him happy. She made him whole. And by the way she looked at him when they made love, he bet she felt the same way he did. He'd know soon enough if it was indeed the case.

"We're playing with fire," Veronica said, her voice barely rising above a whisper.

White searched for her face, but it was buried in his side, her lashes tingling his rib cage. "What do you mean?" he asked.

"Your career. Aren't you worried about it? At least a little?"

It would be a lie to say he wasn't a tiny bit concerned about the situation. He loved his job. But if forced to make a choice between the Secret Service and Veronica, the decision would be easy. Men with skill sets like his were in high demand. Finding another position with a federal law enforcement agency wouldn't be much of a challenge, and even if that failed, he had a feeling that the private sector would welcome him with open arms.

"What about you?" White asked. "Where do you see this going?"

"In the shower," she said, laughing. "Care to join me?"

"I'm serious," White insisted.

"So am I," Veronica replied, rolling out of bed. "Your loss."

White sighed as he watched her walk naked to the bathroom. She glanced back at him, her green eyes sparkling, daring him to make the next move. It took all his willpower not to follow her into the shower. Instead of doing the easy thing and joining Veronica, White arched his spine and stretched his arm toward the bedside table where he had left his cell phone. There was no voicemail.

White had an important decision to make. He checked his phone again. Thirty minutes left before Veronica had to go down to the awards ceremony.

Plenty of time, he thought. He eased out of bed, grabbed one of the plush hotel bathrobes, and wrapped it around himself. He quietly opened the connecting doors linking his suite to hers and slipped into his identical hotel room. He headed toward the closet where, tucked away at the bottom, the room's safe was hidden. He turned on a table lamp near the closet and entered his six-digit code into the keypad.

There followed the whirl of the locking mechanism, and the safe opened. There were only three items inside: an ankle holster, a snub-nose revolver, and a small blue satin box.

———

Veronica turned off the shower and grabbed one of the white fluffy towels from the nearby heating rack. She really thought Clay would have joined her in the shower. Maybe they could reconnect after the awards banquet? The possibility made her smile. She dried herself quickly and then wrapped the towel around her head turban-style. Her skin tingled as her mind played back the last hour. Their friendship had turned into a secret love affair. That wasn't something she had seen coming, or necessarily wanted. Or needed. But damn if it didn't feel good.

Her brain, though, didn't necessarily agree with her heart. She had her career. He had his. But here they were, both taking risks as if they were love-starved fools. Admittedly, he had much more to lose than she did. If word of their relationship got out, he would not only be in trouble; it would also give a black eye to the entire Secret Service. And it wouldn't reflect well on her dad either. So why risk it all?

Deep down she knew. She bit her lip. *He loves me.*

She used a hand towel to wipe the foggy mirror, but it left too many streaks and smudges to be helpful. She closed her eyes and inhaled deeply.

As good as this is, as fun as it feels, this thing, this relationship . . . it can't continue like this, she thought, shaking her head. *And he knows it too. He has to.* She had important work to do. The revamped Drain app was almost ready. They were days away from the beta release, and she just couldn't wait to get back out there and follow the tips, wherever they might lead.

Of course, there would be quirks to fix and adjustments to make, but she was confident the app would be a success—despite her dad's constant obstruction. For a man who had always been so supportive of her, his tenacious bitching about how Drain was a waste of her talents was getting irritating. She was frustrated at the amount of energy her father seemed to spend on finding reasons why she shouldn't launch the new version. As the vice president-elect of the United States, didn't he have more vital issues to deal with?

She had fantasized about excavating previously undiscovered sites since she was a little girl and saw a documentary about the Nazca Lines in Peru and how some thought they'd been drawn by aliens. She'd quickly found that the evidence disproved that theory, but she'd been left with an enduring fascination with humankind's efforts to alter the very face of the earth. It was her realization of how much the numerous satellites that constantly orbited the planet could reveal about the past, coupled with her memory of how fascinated the public was by archaeological mysteries, that led her to conceptualize Drain.

There was no way she was going to let her father ruin her dream. His claim that it was too dangerous for her to travel through parts of the world less friendly to Americans didn't hold water. Weren't the Secret Service agents the best in the world anyway?

One way or the other, the next two years were going to be busy. She guessed that was why every moment she spent with Clay was so precious. Truth was, she couldn't picture herself without him. Was this love?

My God, am I in love? Veronica felt her cheeks blush. *Oh shit. Am I really?* Deep down, she knew the answer to that. And she'd known for a while now. She'd had other lovers, but she had never dared think of any man as hers before. Not until Clayton White.

I have no time for this, she thought, her stomach in knots. *No time at all.*

Maybe they could continue to see each other from time to time, once her father was fully sworn in, once Clay was assigned other duties? The inauguration was only six weeks away. She was planning on being there, of course. It would be nice if Clayton could be her plus-one at the ceremony. Not as one of her close-protection agents, but as the man in her life. She had a feeling her dad would approve of her relationship. Alexander Hammond didn't give his blessing easily, but it wasn't much of a leap of faith to say he was fond of Clay.

Especially since Maxwell's death in Afghanistan, she thought, remembering how devastated her dad had been about Clay's dad's passing.

Sometimes she wondered if her dad already knew about them. He was a very, very difficult man to read. If he did, he hadn't confronted her about it or mentioned anything to her mother. Veronica's mom wouldn't be able to keep that kind of secret for long.

She sighed. Heaven help her—she needed Clay in her life.

She used the hair dryer to defog the mirror and spent the next ten minutes getting ready for *her* big night.

———

While Veronica was getting dressed, White changed into his tuxedo, which wasn't super comfortable with the soft body armor underneath his shirt, and returned to her room. He replaced his earbud in his ear and performed a radio check with XJD-31 to ensure proper communications. He then confirmed that all of his five agents were in position and that the site was green, free of imminent danger. Nobody had anything to report. They were ready to go.

When Veronica came out of the bathroom, he took an involuntary step back. She was beautiful. She wore a long, fitted red dress with a pair of black Louboutin stilettos. Her unruly brown hair was now loose and cascading in soft waves over her shoulders. Her green eyes were sparkling, just like the simple but elegant diamond necklace she wore.

"You clean up nicely, Mr. Bond," Veronica said before White could utter a single word. "You look dashing in that tux."

He opened his mouth to say something witty but decided otherwise. "And you look marvelous, darling," he said in his best British accent. "Absolutely marvelous."

She gave him a flirtatious smile. "Shall we?"

He hesitated. His heart was beating so fast he thought it was going to come right through his chest. Suddenly, the only thing he could think about was the blue box in his pocket. Veronica seemed to sense his hesitation.

She frowned. "What's wrong, Clay? You all right?"

White took a deep breath, smiled, and got down on one knee in front of her. From the breast pocket of his tuxedo jacket, he pulled out the small blue box. He cracked it open, revealing a two-carat diamond engagement ring.

Veronica jumped, covering her mouth with her hands. Her eyes lit up in surprise.

"Veronica Hammond, I'm no saint, and I'm no hero. I'm just a man who loves you. But every moment I spend with you, you inspire me to become a better person. Your passion to make a difference in this world is contagious. I want in. I want to be part of your future, and you part of mine," he said, pausing before his voice cracked.

Veronica's eyes shone wet. Her bottom lip trembled.

White continued, "Most people don't believe in soul mates. I do. I swear I'll stand by your side through the good days, but also through the worst of days. Veronica Hammond, will you—"

And that's when White heard the first gunshot.

CHAPTER TEN

The Ritz-Carlton
San Francisco, California

Van Heerden knew he wasn't out of the woods yet, but the operation had started smoothly. Two of his men had already reported back to him. The Secret Service drivers were dead, and Van Heerden's men had taken possession of the two government SUVs. They had performed well, and, most importantly, silently. As far as Van Heerden could tell, no alarm had been activated. The Secret Service mobile communications unit van was next. He didn't expect the two well-trained mercenaries he had assigned to the van to encounter any serious resistance. Once the mobile communications unit was down, the two men would move out of the danger zone and go to a staging area a couple of neighborhoods away to await further instructions.

Van Heerden inserted a magazine into his pistol and racked the slide. He then released the magazine and pressed another round into it, assuring a full load. He reinserted the magazine into the pistol's grip and dropped the black suppressor into his coat pocket for later use.

"Albert, this is Chuck," crackled a voice in his ear.

"Go for Albert."

"I'm with Daniel, and our target isn't where he's supposed to be. We walked the whole floor twice. Do you want us to breach the room?"

Chuck and Daniel were Van Heerden's best men. The three of them had served together in the Recces, and they had all transitioned out of the South African military around the same time. Chuck and Daniel were highly capable warriors, hence the reason Van Heerden had tasked them with the most important assignment. Their job was to neutralize the bodyguard standing outside Veronica Hammond's door and secure the vice president-elect's daughter.

"Stand by, Chuck," Van Heerden replied. "To all call signs, this is Albert. Does anyone have eyes on Flower?"

None of them did. Was it possible that Hammond had left the hotel? If so, to go where? Barry, who was in the lobby, would have let Van Heerden know if he had seen her. Chances were that she was still in her room and that the bodyguard had simply gone to his own room to use the washroom and would be back at his post in a minute or two. Still, Van Heerden didn't want Chuck and Daniel to breach Hammond's room only to be caught seconds later by the Secret Service agent. So far his operation had remained under the radar. He wanted to keep it that way.

Chuck, just like Van Heerden, was in possession of a key card that would unlock Hammond's room, courtesy of their employer.

"Chuck, this is Albert. Wait for me. I'm on my way."

"Copy that, Albert."

Van Heerden holstered his pistol and then slipped out of his hotel room and walked down to the elevators. While he was waiting for the elevator to arrive, he scanned the length of the hallway and observed a young man exiting a room not far from the elevators. Van Heerden hoped the elevator would arrive before the man did. He had no such luck.

The man was in his midtwenties, tall and fit with light skin and longish black hair. He was dressed in a pair of expensive jeans and a designer T-shirt. He nodded at Van Heerden and stood next to him.

"Oh," the young man said. "You're going up?"

"Yeah," Van Heerden replied.

The young man pressed the down button and looked at Van Heerden. "Hey, man, do you know a good steakhouse around here? It's my first time in San Francisco."

Van Heerden had no intention of making small talk. "I don't. I'm not from here either."

"Where are you from? Is that an Aussie accent I hear?"

Where the hell's that elevator? Van Heerden thought, resisting the urge to choke the man out. *Maybe I could hide his body behind the ice machine?*

"Small world. My girlfriend is from Australia," the man continued. "Whereabouts are you from? She's from Brisbane."

There was a ding, and Van Heerden looked up. The elevator had arrived, and it was going up. Without another word, Van Heerden, distracted by the incessant chatting of the younger man, stepped into the elevator the moment the doors opened.

A mistake.

He did his best to mask his surprise, but one of the special agents assigned to Hammond was already in the elevator. The man—Black, tall, and built like a bulldozer—stood with his back to the rear wall. There was no hiding the muscular frame under the man's unbuttoned tuxedo jacket, or the Secret Service badge clipped to his belt. The special agent occupied so much space that Van Heerden couldn't stand next to him against the rear wall. Instead, he leaned against the side wall and rested his hands in front of him. Both men eyed each other. Neither was smiling. To Van Heerden's horror, the young man with the Aussie girlfriend stepped into the elevator just as the doors were closing.

"Sorry, I changed my mind," he said, looking at Van Heerden. "I think I'll go check out the lounge before heading out."

What the hell? Had he misread the young man? Was he part of a countersurveillance team? Van Heerden didn't like this one bit. If the two men were working together and they knew who he was, or why he was there, and they made the first move, he was done.

The Secret Service agent's eyes didn't stray from Van Heerden. Moreover, the agent had pushed his tuxedo jacket to the side, and his hand had moved closer to the holster on his right hip. This was tactically sound for the agent, but not so much for Van Heerden since the weapon was out of his reach and could be protected by the agent's left arm. He could feel the suspicion in the big man's eyes, and he was confident that the agent knew something was wrong but that he hadn't yet come to terms with what it was exactly. He would. Soon.

And that's why Van Heerden struck first.

Van Heerden went for the young man, the closest and easiest target. With his left hand, he drew a small combat knife from the sheath inside his waistband and stepped forward, plunging the knife hard and deep into the rear of the young man's neck, mortally wounding him. He let go of the embedded knife and turned his attention to the Secret Service agent, knowing he had the advantage of surprise.

The agent's eyes went wide in astonishment. He jerked his gun from his holster, but Van Heerden chopped down at his rising wrist with the edge of his right hand. The agent yelled in pain as his pistol clattered to the tile floor of the elevator. Then, stepping in even closer, Van Heerden whipped out his left hand in an uppercut that packed all the strength he could muster. The punch was fast and perfectly timed and would have knocked out most men. But not this one. The uppercut didn't even faze him.

The Secret Service agent drove his left fist forward into Van Heerden's face. The blow sent him backward, but the agent didn't let him fall. Instead, he kept Van Heerden close by holding him by the collar of his coat. The agent drew back his left fist and punched him again, this time right on the chin. Van Heerden's knees buckled, and he tripped over the dead body of the young man he had killed less than five seconds ago.

Van Heerden hit the floor just as the elevator stopped. The doors opened. The agent hesitated, his eyes darting between his service pistol and Van Heerden.

Van Heerden didn't make the same mistake. He reached into his jacket and pulled his SIG Sauer from its shoulder holster. At such close range, there was no need to aim. He shot the agent in the head. The man crumpled without a sound.

Van Heerden's head was spinning, but he forced himself to get up. He grabbed the agent's badge from his belt and exited the elevator, holding his pistol in his right hand. He needed his left to hold on to the wall in order to keep his balance.

Despite the ringing in his ears, Van Heerden heard Chuck's voice in his earbud.

"Albert from Chuck, we heard a gunshot. I think it's on our floor."

"Chuck from Albert, it was me. Breach the door!" ordered Van Heerden as he made his way toward Hammond's room at the end of the hallway.

"Albert, are you okay?" Chuck asked.

"I'm fine and on my way to you. Breach now!" Van Heerden repeated.

A clutch of curious hotel guests had opened their doors and were peeking outside, trying to see what was going on. Van Heerden held the Secret Service badge in the air, quietly asking the nosey guests to return to their rooms. As he spoke, pain flooded the lower part of his face. He ran his tongue along the inside of his gums and tasted blood. But, by some miracle, there were no loose teeth. He tried to remember if he had seen or heard the agent he had killed in the elevator communicating with any of the surviving Secret Service agents. He didn't think so, but he had to assume the man had.

What if he reached the mobile communications unit? he wondered, remembering he was yet to receive the all clear from the team tasked with seizing the van. *Shit.* He had to call them off.

"Erik, this is Albert," he said.

"Go for Erik."

"Are you with Frank?"

"Yes. We're about to execute. We're on foot, about two hundred feet from the target vehicle."

Van Heerden briefly considered letting them continue but decided otherwise.

"Abort. I say again. Abort," Van Heerden said. "Move to the staging area now. How copy?"

"Erik copies."

"Frank copies."

Van Heerden swore under his breath as he attached his silencer to the pistol. This wasn't how he had envisioned the operation going down. His employer would be pissed, and Van Heerden's reputation would take a hit. But now wasn't the time to worry about that. He had to stay focused. He yearned for Veronica Hammond to be inside her room, because he was running out of time. He estimated that he and his men had a maximum of three minutes to complete the mission. The hotel would soon be swarming with police officers, and once they realized who had been the target, they would cordon off the entire area and request backup from a multitude of local, state, and federal agencies.

Van Heerden was still forty or so meters away from Hammond's room when Chuck and Daniel breached it. And he was still thirty meters away when he heard two distinct double taps followed by a single shot.

One, two. One, two.

One.

Those five shots could have meant mission success, but there was only one problem. His men had suppressors. And these shots hadn't come from a silenced pistol.

CHAPTER ELEVEN

The Ritz-Carlton
San Francisco, California

The ostentatiously loud noise had broken the spell. White let the blue box fall to the carpeted floor and got up, angling his body between the door and Veronica. He drew his pistol, aiming it at the door. Veronica had heard the shot too. She was clutching his arm, her fingers digging in. All White's senses were alert.

Something wasn't right. The little voice in the back of his mind, the same one that had saved his life numerous times in Iraq and Afghanistan, was trying to tell him something. To Veronica's credit, she didn't panic. She remained calm and in control. With his left hand, White pressed the little red button on his radio that would send an alarm signal to XJD-31 and keep his microphone open for the next sixty seconds.

"This is Vigil-One. Possible gunshot on Flower's floor," he said. "We're hunkered down in her hotel room. Send additional agents to my location and prepare the stash car for possible evacuation."

"XJD-31 copy. I'll link with local law enforcement and try to get more information about this possible gunshot."

Keeping his eyes on the door and his voice low, White said to Veronica, "Go to the bathroom, lock the door, and grab the GLG Bishop knife from my toiletry bag. I left it next to your sink."

"Got it," she replied, making her way toward the bathroom.

Made of G-10, a high-pressure fiberglass laminate, the Bishop knife could inflict a lot of damage at close range. White had personally pierced a one-quart paint can with it, and he had done so without damaging the tip or the blade. Looking around the room, he realized that the connecting door between his room and Veronica's was still open. Two access points made them more vulnerable. He chastised himself for being so unprepared.

What the fuck were you thinking, Clay? His eyes briefly stopped on the blue box and the diamond engagement ring on the carpet. *Stop thinking with your dick and start acting like a goddamn Secret Service special agent.*

White was halfway between the bathroom and the connecting doors when the door of Veronica's hotel room opened. Two men barged in. The first one, dressed in a dark business suit and armed with a silenced pistol, immediately swept the room left. White fired his pistol twice, a double tap to the assailant's center mass, just as the man's weapon was bearing on him. White switched his aim a bit to engage the second shooter, who had come in behind the first one. The second shooter, sensing motion to his left, had already started to pivot in White's direction. But before the shooter could even swivel his head to face the threat, White fired two rounds into his torso. The shooter gave a muffled cry of pain and shock, the impact of the bullets flattening him against the wall. But he was still holding on to his pistol, clearly doing his best to bring it up toward White, who was now less than ten feet away. White squeezed the trigger and shot him in the face. The man slid down the wall, a smeared trail of blood glistening behind him.

White stepped over the second shooter and walked to the first man he had shot. He was still alive, but not for long. White picked up the man's pistol and tucked it in his waistband. He opened the door, which had closed behind the men, and stepped into the hallway. His pistol at the high ready, he scanned for additional threats. Three people were out of their rooms, probably wondering what the commotion was all about. One lady was wearing a white hotel bathrobe and holding a glass of white wine in her hand. A few doors farther down the corridor, a man was holding a woman in his arms. White retreated to the relative safety of Veronica's room and closed the door.

"XJD-31, this is Vigil-One. Shots fired. I have two suspects down in Flower's room," he said.

"XJD-31 copies. We heard everything. Help is on the way."

White looked at the first shooter. At least one of his rounds had hit the assailant in the lungs. The man was coughing up bright red blood. He looked up at White and tried to say something. White reholstered his pistol, grabbed the man's wrist, and rolled him to his stomach. White drilled his knee into the injured man's back and handcuffed him. The shooter yelled out in pain.

White went to the door, wanting to keep an eye on the hallway to ensure a position of dominance. His hand was just inches from the door handle when he heard the locking mechanism whirl.

CHAPTER TWELVE

The Ritz-Carlton
San Francisco, California

Van Heerden hugged the wall as soon as he heard the two double taps. He thought about racing down the hall to Hammond's room to help his men, but the hotel room door had probably closed on its own, costing him the element of surprise. He would need to be very careful and time his entry perfectly. He kept his silenced pistol close to his leg as he cautiously continued down the corridor.

To his immediate left, a door suddenly opened. He brought his pistol up, aiming it directly at a woman's head. Right behind her, dressed in a white T-shirt and blue jeans, was a man holding two glasses of red wine. He looked at Van Heerden, his face frozen in shock. Van Heerden's pistol bucked once. Without so much as letting out a cry, the man fell backward, toppling to the floor. The woman opened her mouth to scream, but Van Heerden knocked her out cold by slamming his pistol hard against the side of her head. He caught her with his left arm as she fell. To his right, a few doors down the corridor, another woman exited her room. She didn't look in his direction. She was wearing a bathrobe and holding a glass of white wine. Her hair was wet, as if she had just come out of the shower. Van Heerden was about to step inside the room when he saw a man wearing a tuxedo briefly peek into the hallway. As far as Van Heerden could tell, the man had come out of Hammond's room. Was he the missing bodyguard? Van Heerden thought so, helped by the fact that the man was wielding a pistol. The woman in the white bathrobe shrieked at the sight of the gun and scurried inside her hotel room, slamming the door behind her.

Van Heerden looked at the woman in his arms. He thought about killing her, but somehow it felt wrong. He didn't mind killing when needed, but there were grounds for mercy here. She was no longer a threat to him. He carried her into the room and laid her down on the bed.

"Albert, from Barry," came from his man in the lobby.

"Go for Albert."

"The agent just took off at a sprint toward the staircase," Barry said.

That was to be expected. Surely the bodyguard in Hammond's room had sounded the alarm. Knowing that his window of opportunity was fast closing, Van Heerden moved into action.

"If you can do it safely and without being seen, take him down in the staircase," he ordered.

"On my way," Barry replied.

"Then I want you to exfil," Van Heerden said.

It took a second more than it should have for his man to reply. "What about Chuck and Daniel?"

"Status unknown. Just do what you're told. Albert out."

Van Heerden walked purposefully toward Hammond's room, his pistol at his side. He stopped a few feet away from Hammond's door and listened. Someone yelled. Could one of his men still be alive?

There was no way for Van Heerden to slip silently into the room. The door was the sort that was impossible to open quietly. The locking mechanism was going to emit a humming sound as soon as he slid the key card in and out.

Van Heerden swore silently. If he entered the room, his chances of a clean escape were almost nonexistent. Still, there was a possibility he could redeem himself in the eyes of his employers if he killed

Hammond. But the real reason Van Heerden had already decided to go in had zilch to do with what his employer wanted or didn't want. Like him, Chuck and Daniel were former Recces. That no person made it on their own through selection had been hammered into them since their first day of training. They were a team. They won together, or they failed together. Van Heerden wasn't about to leave anyone behind.

CHAPTER THIRTEEN

The Ritz-Carlton
San Francisco, California

White, who had moved behind the door the moment he had heard the locking mechanism start its cycle, saw a long silencer appear in the gap between the door and its frame. He smashed the door into the man's forearm. He heard a grunt, but the gun didn't fall to the floor. White's right hand reached for his own pistol, but the intruder shoved the door open, pushing White against the wall behind him. The intruder swung his gun toward White, who stepped in and kicked it away just as it fired, its round flying less than an inch above his right shoulder. Before the intruder could take aim again, White lunged at him, his hands wrapping around the man's wrists.

White recognized the intruder as the man he'd seen holding a woman in the hallway a few doors down. They were about the same height. The man had silver hair, deep-set eyes, and frown lines etched into his forehead. He was older too. But strong. White drove his knee repeatedly into the man's groin, to little effect. A few silenced shots hammered into the ceiling, and White wasn't sure whose finger had pressed the trigger. Feeling his hands weakening, White abandoned thoughts of snatching the man's pistol away from him. Instead, his left hand moved quickly to the Street Beat Spyderco knife at his side. The blade slid from its polymer sheath easily. White lashed out from left to right across the man's forearm, slicing flesh. The intruder dropped his pistol, and White tried to kick it away as it fell. He missed.

The intruder headbutted White on the nose, causing him to tear up in pain. White switched the knife to his right hand and lunged again, this time aiming at the man's throat. But it was as if the man with the silver hair had been waiting for this exact move. He sidestepped the blade and grabbed White's right wrist with his left hand. Using White's momentum, he brought him around in a circular motion before suddenly stopping and reversing direction with his entire body. White's frame went one way while his arm went the other. White felt his elbow and wrist joints almost snap at the torsion exerted on them. He dropped the knife and landed hard on his back. Not wasting any time, the silver-haired man began to throw punches. Stinging pain exploded on the right and left side of White's head. White had to do something, but he didn't even have the force to bring his arms up to protect himself.

His only objective was to stay conscious—or alive—long enough for the rest of his team to arrive. He hoped Veronica had locked the door of the bathroom as he had asked her to. On the verge of losing consciousness, his brain registered blood mixed with the bile of failure. And shame. Lots of shame. Then there was just the feeling of floating at the bottom of a black hole.

CHAPTER FOURTEEN

The Ritz-Carlton
San Francisco, California

Veronica silently cursed. What the hell had just happened? Was this attack random, or was it targeted? Two minutes ago, the man she loved was asking her to marry him. Now, she was hiding in a bathroom.

Damn!

There were so many questions bouncing in her head. It took a conscious effort to push them away. She had to focus. She took several deep breaths to calm herself and regain control of her mind. It worked. Despite her heart pounding in her chest, her hands were steady. She held the Bishop blade tightly, ready to pounce at anyone crazy enough to breach the bathroom's door. She had been locked inside the bathroom for less than one minute. Her first move after retrieving the knife was to kick off her heels.

So far, she had counted five shots. Two double taps, followed by a single shot. It had taken everything in her not to come out of the bathroom. The last thing she wanted was to distract Clay.

Someone yelled out in pain. She stopped breathing. Was it Clay? Had he been injured? Did he need her? What was she supposed to do?

She had to do something. There was no way she could stay hidden any longer. She quietly unlocked the door and opened it a crack, just enough to peek out. Her eyes picked up three persons in the room. Two were dead, or seemed to be, and one was alive.

Clay.

She was about to call his name when the hotel room door opened. For an instant she thought reinforcements had finally arrived, but her relief was short lived. A tall man she had never seen before fired at Clay at almost point-blank range. A blink of an eye later, they were fighting over control of the gun. Silenced shots were fired into the ceiling, and white plaster powder cascaded to the floor.

Should she intervene? Before she could make a decision, a small knife appeared in Clay's hand. He slashed at the man. The gun tumbled. Then everything happened in a blur. One moment Clay was on the offensive, the next he was on his back with the intruder on top of him, punching him in the face repeatedly with both hands. Hot rage engulfed her, and Veronica hurled herself at the man with the silver hair, her hand firmly wrapped around the handle of the knife. In four strides she was on him, and the blade came down in a deadly arc. She aimed for his neck, but the man must have felt her presence because he started to turn to his left. He gasped for air as the knife entered his back just behind his left shoulder. His body stiffened, and he let out a guttural scream that startled Veronica. He got up but staggered left and right as he tried to remove the knife from his back. Incapable of reaching it, he looked at her, his deep-set eyes the appearance of hell itself. She stepped backward as he stumbled toward her. Her back hit something.

The window, she thought, as the man kept moving in her direction. She frantically looked around for something to use against him, but his hands grabbed her by the neck. His fingers fastened around her throat, squeezing her flesh, choking the life out of her. Veronica kicked at his shin, but her strike didn't carry much power. She pounded at his arms, tried to scratch his eyes, but to no effect. Already her strength was leaving her. Even in his wounded condition, the man was too strong for her. Her chest was burning, and black dots swirled at the edges of her vision.

She went limp. All the rage and anger inside her wasn't enough to move her body. How was it possible that a moment of pure magic could be transformed into absolute horror? For the first time in her life, she could feel death breathing down her neck.

And it terrified her.

Suddenly, she was with Clay again. He was on one knee in front of her, holding in his hand the most beautiful engagement ring she had ever seen.

I'm no saint, and I'm no hero. I'm just a man who loves you.

As her last conscious thought drifted away on a wave of pain, a tear slowly rolled down her cheek.

CHAPTER FIFTEEN

The Ritz-Carlton
San Francisco, California

White's entire face hurt, making it difficult for him to breathe. He felt as if he was coming up from deep underwater, rising sluggishly to the surface. He opened his eyes. His vision was blurry. Everything was unfocused. He couldn't make out anything clearly. Even the sounds were muffled. Fuzzy movements to his right made him turn his head. A searing pain shot through his jaw and eye socket. He groaned. He blinked several times, and his vision cleared enough for him to see.

The man with the silver hair had White's Bishop blade embedded in his back. More worrisome was the fact that he had his hands around Veronica's neck. He was holding her up, pinning her back against the window. Her legs were thrashing madly, her feet two or three inches from the floor. The icy terror that raced through White's veins was suddenly replaced by a tsunami of adrenaline. He forced himself up and rushed the assassin, dropping him rearward with a sharp kick to the back of the knee. The man let go of Veronica's neck and tried to elbow White with his right arm. White anticipated the move and blocked it easily with his forearm while simultaneously giving a good shove at the Bishop blade with the palm of his left hand, pushing the blade even deeper into the man's back. White heard him growl in agony.

Not wasting any time, White wrapped his right forearm around the front of the man's neck and his left forearm across the back of it. He then locked his right hand into the crook of his own elbow, pinioning the man's neck in a viselike grip. The man was tough and resilient, more than White could ever have imagined given the knife in his back. He tried to pull White's arm away from his neck. It was a futile effort. He then pitched forward and attempted to pull White over, but he was getting too weak. White squeezed his bicep even tighter, cutting off the man's flow of blood and oxygen. It should have been over by now, but the man continued to struggle for another thirty seconds before he finally stopped moving.

Drenched in sweat and out of breath, White let him go. A few feet in front of White, Veronica started coughing. She looked at him with glassy red eyes, holding her neck. White glanced around. A few feet away from the bed, the man's silenced pistol lay next to the diamond engagement ring. He slipped the ring in his pocket and placed the man's gun in the bathroom sink. Drawing his own pistol, White ejected the half-spent magazine and inserted a fresh one before holstering it again. He then headed to the coffee maker and ripped the electric cord off it, which he used to tie the assassin's hands behind his back. Pulling his pistol out, White walked back to Veronica and knelt down next to her.

"You okay?" he asked, keeping his eyes on the door and his pistol in the low-ready position.

"I . . . I think so," Veronica said, her voice faltering. "You?"

"Yeah," he replied, barely moving his mouth. His tongue was swollen, and his jaw was killing him.

Still, he had to let his team know what was going on. As far as he was concerned, this was just the beginning. A second wave of attackers could breach the door at any time. But before he could contact the mobile communications unit, Vigil-Three's voice came in through his earbud.

"Vigil-One, this is Three," the agent said, his voice barely loud enough for White to hear.

"Go for One."

"I've been shot in the back, but I got the bastard."

White's breath caught in his throat. "What's your location?"

For God's sake! How many of them are they? White thought, waiting for Vigil-Three's reply.

"I'm . . . on the landing between the second and third floor. West-side staircase. The bullets hit the vest. I'm good, I think."

"Good copy, Vigil-Three."

White waited for XJD-31 to jump in, knowing they were listening. Hadn't they heard Vigil-Three's plea for help?

"XJD-31 from Vigil-One," White said, more than a little irritated with how the mobile communications unit was managing the situation. "Did you get Vigil-Three's last? He needs assistance, and I need agents to secure safe passage for Flower."

"We copy, Vigil-One. Please note that the local police are now on site and that I've lost comms with Vigil-Two, Four, Five, and Six. Stand by for more info."

White couldn't believe what he was hearing. *What kind of clusterfuck is this?* he asked himself, knowing that this shitshow was partially his fault. No, that wasn't true. It was *all* his fault.

He glanced at Veronica, whose cheeks had thankfully started to regain some color. "I need you to go back in the bathroom," he said to her.

"No fucking way," she replied, stunning him. "I'm done hiding. Let the fuckers come."

White watched her in admiration as she removed the Bishop knife from the assassin's back in one swift motion. White heard the man moan, but nothing more. He didn't move or speak. Just a low moan of pain. White reached for the small of his back and handed Veronica the pistol he had seized from one of the gunmen.

"You remember how to use one of these?" he asked.

Veronica didn't respond, but she popped the magazine out, checked how many rounds were left, and slammed the magazine back into the pistol's grip. She then assumed a good firing position and used the bathroom's doorframe to partially conceal her location. White moved to the connecting doors and did the same. Despite everything that had happened, a painful smirk appeared on his cracked lips. Veronica had saved his life. There was no question about it. She had definitely inherited her father's tenacity and resolve, but she was also a fearless, intrepid woman of her own. With Veronica, there was no imitation of any sort, no artificial emotions or gestures. Everything she said or did was genuine.

"Thanks for saving my life," he said, just loud enough for Veronica to hear him.

"Don't mention it," she replied the same way. "But don't ever forget it."

He had no intention—none whatsoever—of forgetting anything that had happened that evening. In that very moment, he swore that he would find whoever had put a target on Veronica's head and hunt him, her, or them down to the ends of the earth if he had to.

"Clay?" Veronica called out. "You still have that ring of yours?"

He looked at her, confused. "Are you kidding?"

"I saw you pick it up," she said. "C'mon, send it over. Quickly."

White dug into his pocket with his nongun hand and pulled out the diamond engagement ring. He lobbed it to her. She snagged it cleanly midair.

"Ask me again," she said.

"Now? You want to do this now?" Had she lost her mind?

"Ask the damn question, Clayton. I'm old fashioned."

"Veronica Hammond, will you marry me?"

While still holding her pistol, Veronica unceremoniously slipped the engagement ring onto her own finger. "Yes, I will."

White didn't know if he should laugh or cry.

"I'll be honest, this is not exactly how I expected things to turn out," he said.

"Me neither, but here we are," she replied. "If we don't make it out of here, I want the whole world to know we were together when it went down."

White looked at his new fiancée. Her makeup had streaked down her face, and her eyes and nose were red. Dark bruises had already started to show up on her neck, but Veronica still looked amazing. He would do anything for her.

White could hear people running in the hallway, just outside their rooms. Then everything became quiet. He knew what was going on. Bad guys were stacking on both sides of their doors, waiting for the order to breach.

"Here we go," White said, once again pressing the emergency button on his radio. "Get ready."

For the benefit of the mobile communication unit, White continued, "This is Vigil-One, we're in Flower's room and about to be overrun."

This time, whoever was manning the radio responded right away.

"Stand down, Vigil-One. Stand down. Local law enforcement has secured the immediate vicinity of Flower's room and the staircases. Acknowledge."

"This is Vigil-One. I acknowledge," White replied, holstering his pistol and signaling to Veronica to bring hers down. "Flower is safe. I say again, Flower is safe."

CHAPTER SIXTEEN

Oxley Vineyards
Kommetjie, South Africa

Having lost interest in the glass of sauvignon blanc he had poured himself, Oxley had pulled a bottle of Bowmore twenty-five-year-old single malt from the shelf. The smell of dark fruits was instantly recognizable, as was the coastal smokiness he loved so much.

Oxley was slowly working on his second drink when one of his encrypted phones rang. There was only one person who had this number. Krantz. Oxley turned on the light and got up from his leather chair. Throwing his head back, he downed the rest of the scotch. The liquor hit the back of his throat and didn't stop burning until it reached the pit of his stomach. He refilled his tumbler and picked up the phone.

"Talk to me, my friend," he said.

"Things aren't looking good in San Francisco," Krantz said, his voice as steady as ever. "She's still alive, and Van Heerden has been taken into custody."

Oxley's face contorted in anger. "Is there any way for you to intervene?" he asked.

"Not at this time."

Oxley took a long, deep breath. Like Oxley, Krantz wasn't one to shy away from a fight, no matter how bad the odds were. If Krantz didn't feel there was something he could do to stop the situation in San

Francisco from turning to shit, there wasn't anything else for Oxley to do but take a step back and regroup.

"How many of Van Heerden's men are left?" Oxley inquired.

"Exact number is unknown for now," Krantz replied. "At least two of them made it to the staging area after completing their objective."

"Can you take care of them?" he asked.

"It shouldn't be a problem."

"What about SkyCU Technology?" he asked, his thoughts moving to the next stage of the operation. "Are you ready to proceed?"

"I've been conducting surveillance on the location and on the employees. I'm ready to go."

Oxley hesitated. There were significant risks with proceeding with their backup plans, but after Van Heerden's fuckup, it was his only way to buy himself some time. He made his decision.

"Start with the cleanup in San Francisco, then go to Palo Alto," he said to Krantz. "Report back when you're done."

CHAPTER SEVENTEEN

The Ritz-Carlton Hotel
San Francisco, California

Abelard Krantz examined the scene before him. It was mayhem. There were emergency lights flashing everywhere. Fire trucks, police cars, and ambulances were parked all around the hotel. Krantz could even hear a helicopter in the distance. A few minutes ago, right before he had called Oxley, he had observed two paramedics carrying a stretcher with a man fastened to it. Despite the oxygen mask strapped to his face, Krantz had recognized Van Heerden. Two men dressed in dark suits, who Krantz assumed to be Secret Service or FBI, joined Van Heerden and the paramedic in the back of the ambulance.

Van Heerden had come highly recommended. In fact, Krantz had used his services under another alias a few years back. He had found Van Heerden to be professional and goal oriented. Most of his men were former Recces, not the cheap labor other mercenary outfits employed. It was a shame today's operation had turned into such a nightmare.

Krantz wished Oxley had given him the authorization to play a bigger role in the operation, but his boss had been unyielding to his pleas, fearful of how Alexander Hammond would retaliate if he were able to prove their involvement.

And here we are, Krantz thought, frustrated by the knowledge that he was now the one stuck with the cleanup.

A crowd of curious onlookers had gathered around the main entrance of the hotel, their faces twisted in a tangy mix of curiosity and craving as they took pictures of the scene with their smartphones. Krantz watched in disbelief as one young couple took a selfie with a fire truck in the background. It looked to Krantz as though they were mostly people who had come out of nearby restaurants and apartment buildings, seeking a few likes for their Instagram accounts. Still, people with high-resolution smartphones were dangerous. It was time for him to earn his keep.

———

As he entered the underground garage, Krantz pulled the nondescript baseball cap lower over his forehead to shield his eyes and face from the surveillance cameras. There were only a few dozen cars left scattered throughout the parking structure. His late-model Jeep Cherokee was still where he had left it, which was a small miracle since smash-and-grab automobile thefts and break-ins had reached epidemic levels across the city. Krantz slid into the driver's seat, his holster digging into the small of his back. He started the engine, his mind thinking about his next step. He had two options. Both were messy. One was definitely less dangerous, but the odds of getting caught were slightly higher.

Krantz pulled out of the parking garage and was immediately caught in traffic, thanks to all the emergency vehicles blocking the routes around the Ritz-Carlton. He had anticipated such a move from law enforcement and had parked five blocks away. Clearly that hadn't been far enough. Up ahead, he could see a traffic bottleneck and several police cars. A roadblock. And there was no way to get around it.

Slowly, at least, the traffic was moving. It took less time than Krantz had expected to reach the roadblock, and as he drove past the first police car, he understood why. The cops weren't stopping every car, only a select few. A uniformed police officer shined his flashlight into Krantz's vehicle before waving him through. Krantz accelerated away, relieved he hadn't been stopped and the car searched. It would have been difficult to explain why he was carrying explosives in the trunk of his rental car, though most cops wouldn't even know what they were looking at.

Krantz entered an address in the navigation system of the Jeep Cherokee and followed the directions to his desired place—Van Heerden's men's staging area.

———

Located in one of the less desirable neighborhoods of San Francisco, the staging area was a medium-size apartment usually rented to criminals or unsuspecting college students looking for a cheap place to spend a night. Krantz had secured it through a popular online marketplace.

He parked the Jeep Cherokee down the street, but close enough so that he could keep an eye on it as he went to do his business. He killed the engine and climbed out of the vehicle. He opened the trunk and grabbed his backpack.

It was easy to see why the apartment didn't fetch more than eighty dollars a night despite being within the boundaries of one of the world's most expensive cities. The streets around the building were filthy and smelled of decay and waste, the light drizzle from the overcast sky incapable of dispelling the offensive odors. Trash, discarded dirty diapers, and empty liquor bottles littered the entrances to run-down, crumbling buildings. Ragged shelters of cardboard and tin had been put up in every alley.

Krantz shook his head in disbelief as a pair of rats ran past him, scurrying through split-open garbage bags. He wondered how the most powerful and prosperous nation on earth could allow such a terrible thing to happen to its citizens. In Krantz's mind, it was an affront to human dignity. But it wasn't his fight.

He spotted the getaway car Van Heerden had purchased for his men. It was an old, light gray Honda sedan. The kind of car that didn't draw attention in a neighborhood like this, although Krantz was pretty sure that, left unattended, the wheels would be gone within days. There was nobody else in the street, but it was possible that eyes were watching him as he made his way to the front of the car. Krantz took from his backpack what he needed and then lay on his back next to the front bumper. He quickly installed a red filter on his penlight and rolled to his side, holding the small light in his mouth. Then he went to work.

———

Back in his vehicle, Krantz turned on his smartphone and waited for it to boot up. He then scrolled through his contact list and pressed one of the numbers.

"Who's this?" a man answered, his strong South African accent evident.

"This is Phoenix," Krantz said. "Identification is Romeo-Five-Five-Six. Confirm."

"Confirmed. This is Erik. Identification is Victor-Six-Five-Five."

"Confirmed," Krantz replied. "Are you with Frank?"

"Yes, but I can't reach Albert."

"Understood. Albert has been taken into custody," Krantz said. "You gentlemen need to begin your exfil now. Follow the third protocol. You know which one this is?"

"Stand by," the South African mercenary replied.

Krantz knew they had cheat sheets. They weren't supposed to, but these types of guys always did. They were shooters, not spies. Krantz and Oxley had built different exit protocols. They were primarily for the safe withdrawal of Van Heerden and his men, but also for unfortunate scenarios like the one they presently found themselves in.

"Got it," the man replied thirty seconds later.

"You have the keys for the vehicle?"

"Frank found them on a small hook under the bathroom sink."

"Perfect," Krantz said. "These keys are for an old, light gray Honda parked a few hundred feet west of your apartment building."

"If Albert is out of commission, who's gonna pay the second half of our fee?" the mercenary asked.

"Let's focus on getting you guys out of the country first," Krantz replied. "Since our arrangement was with Albert, you'll have to give us your wiring instructions."

"Give me a minute," the mercenary said.

The man must have placed his hand over the phone because Krantz could only hear muffled voices in the background, but he knew exactly what they were arguing about. Seconds later, he was proven right.

"Frank and I want to get a cut out of the other guys' payments."

Krantz's lips curled in a defiant sneer. "That wasn't part of our agreement—"

"Then change the fucking agreement," the mercenary spat, interrupting him. "Or we're coming after you."

If the two South African mercenaries had been in the car with Krantz, they would have seen his coal-dark eyes dance with cruel amusement. He had given these two way too much credit. Van Heerden would have never renegotiated the terms of an agreement while under stress, especially trapped in hostile territory. These two guys were well-trained brutes, but poker players they were not, and they held none of the good cards. Oxley had made the right call.

"I understand," Krantz replied, waiting just long enough to give the mercenary the impression he had indeed considered his offer. "Very well. Send me the instructions at the number appearing on your phone, and I'll see that you get your money by the time you reach your first waypoint."

"Good," the mercenary grunted in satisfaction.

"One more thing before you guys take off," Krantz said. "Did you leave the two SUVs where you were supposed to?"

"Yes, but they're still dirty."

Krantz knew what the mercenary meant. The bodies of the Secret Service special agents they had murdered were still in their respective vehicles, and they hadn't wiped clean their fingerprints.

"Understood. I'll take care of it," Krantz said. "But you need to go now before the authorities cordon off the entire area."

"We'll call from our first waypoint, Phoenix. Don't you forget our money."

Krantz dropped the phone into the inside pocket of his leather jacket and tossed his baseball cap on the passenger seat. These two twats were caught in the middle of a cyclone, and they were threatening the only person able to get them out. Not that Krantz had any intention of helping them, but they didn't know that.

Krantz kept an eye on the rearview mirror of the Jeep Cherokee, looking at the main entrance of the building. It took the two men less than five minutes to pack up their stuff and exit onto the sidewalk. They scanned their surroundings before taking off in the direction of the Honda. Krantz lost them a few seconds later, their dark silhouettes disappearing behind a large panel van. But it didn't matter. He'd know soon enough if he'd done a good job or not.

The ground under the Jeep Cherokee shook as the Honda exploded in a brilliant flash, sending a pillar of fire into the night. The old car lifted off the ground and came to rest upside down in the middle of the street, a burning heap of twisted metal.

Krantz suppressed a smile. Clearly his demolition skills were stale. He had used way too much explosive on the Honda. If he'd been back in training and this mission had been an assessment, his SAS instructors would have failed him.

And rightly so, he thought, driving off.

CHAPTER EIGHTEEN

San Francisco, California

White slowly rubbed his face, trying to massage away the numbness. As he waited for the paramedic to return, he thought again about how courageous Veronica had been to come out of hiding to defend him. She had unequivocally, and heroically, saved his life. If it wasn't for her, he would have been punched to death.

Despite the number of pills the paramedic had given him, the beginning of another headache was gnawing at his temples. The muscles in his neck were tense and sore, and his back was killing him. With a groan, he got up from the chair he'd been sitting in for the last fifteen minutes and carefully stretched his back. The hotel room he'd been ordered to stay in was similar to his own on the fifth floor, minus the connecting doors. The FBI agent in charge had made it clear to White that he wasn't permitted to leave the room. A quick phone call to the special agent in charge of the Secret Service San Francisco field office had confirmed that White was to abide by the FBI directive. White had also been relieved of his service pistol. It had been placed in an exhibit bag along with his spare magazines, Spyderco knife, and radio. At least he'd been able to sneak back into his room to get his ankle holster and snub-nose revolver from his safe.

"We're just following protocols," one of the FBI agents had said, his discomfort apparent. "Sorry about that."

White understood. Thank goodness Veronica was safe. Shaken, but safe. He took a few steps toward one of the windows. He parted the curtains and peered out the window at the activity below. Emergency vehicles ringed the perimeter of the hotel. Police cars, fire trucks, and at least half a dozen ambulances were on scene. Behind them, news vans were parked on the sidewalk opposite the hotel. Hundreds of onlookers had also gathered, most of them with smartphones in hand. The hotel had become like a movie set.

Or a morbid tourist attraction, thought White. In all fairness, that was to be expected. This was the kind of news that eclipsed everything else. What he didn't appreciate was the fact that he was being kept in the dark. With his radio now in evidence, he had no way to contact his men. The FBI had let him keep his personal phone, but nobody had replied to his texts or calls.

Growing more restless by the minute, White grabbed the television remote and turned on the flat screen. As he flicked from one channel to another, he realized that each channel was more or less using the same news footage. Commentators were arguing among themselves. One of them, a man White recognized as a former Secret Service agent who'd been let go due to an accidental weapons discharge inside the White House, was thumping his fist on a desk, his too-long mustache moving in concert with his upper lip.

White turned off the television just as there was a knock at his door. There was a click, and the door opened. A medium-size, stocky man sharply dressed in a navy-blue suit entered. He had a broad forehead, a graying crew cut, and sharp blue eyes. He offered his hand to White.

"Alan Summers," the man said, introducing himself. "I'm the SAC of the field office here in San Francisco."

White shook the man's hand. "Yes, sir. I believe we spoke on the phone."

"We did," Summers said, looking around the room, his eyes stopping on the two small empty bottles of vodka on the night table.

"To take the edge off?" he asked, turning his attention back to White.

White shook his head. "They're not mine," he said truthfully. It was the paramedic who had added them to his coffee, but it wasn't White's job to denounce him.

Summers didn't seem to care if they were or not. White presumed the SAC had more than enough on his plate already. Summers gestured to the two armchairs near the window. "May I?" he asked.

White took a seat, doing his best to look calm despite his internal turmoil. Summers was about to give him some news about Veronica and the rest of his team. He leaned forward and rested his elbows on his knees. He studied Summers's face for any clues. The man looked weary, like someone stretched to the breaking point by emotions. It didn't bode well for White.

From his jacket's breast pocket, Summers took out a recorder and placed it on the small table next to him. He pressed one of the tiny buttons. White raised an eyebrow at him.

"I need to record this for accuracy," Summers explained.

White grabbed the recorder and turned it off. "No. You don't," he said.

"What are you doing?" Summers asked. It was clear he hadn't anticipated White's resistance.

"Before I answer any of your questions, I want you to tell me how my team's doing. I've waited long enough."

"Shit, man," Summers said, lifting his hands in surrender. "Didn't the FBI tell you?"

A small amount of bile crept up into White's mouth. "Tell me what?"

Summers hissed out a lungful, and his shoulders sank. "They're all dead. All of them."

White felt as though he'd been kicked in the balls by a mule. His breath left his lungs in one long whoosh. That wasn't possible. There was no way this could be true. He had spoken to Vigil-Three, a young special agent named Lester, less than one hour ago. Lester had told him the rounds had hit his vest. And what about Marcus? What about the drivers? White tried to speak, but no sound came out. The inside of his mouth had turned into a desert. He tried again.

"I spoke with Lester—"

"Yeah," Summers cut in. "Lester died on his way to the hospital. Apparently he'd been shot three times. Two rounds hit his vest, but a third one entered his lower back."

"But I spoke to him," White insisted. "He told me he was fine."

"I don't know what to tell you, Clayton," Summers said, his eyes watering. "I really don't. I knew Lester. He was a good kid."

"And Marcus?" White asked, his voice a murmur.

"Shot and killed in the elevator," White replied. "The local police also found the body of a guest of the hotel next to Marcus. A young man. He was stabbed in the back of the neck."

"Jesus," White said, his head throbbing with pain.

"Both drivers were shot and killed while behind the wheel," Summers continued. "Bullets to the head. They never knew what hit them. Because of the GPS trackers installed in the vehicles, we were able to locate them both in an underground parking garage in a nearby neighborhood."

White felt empty inside. It was as if he had lost his soul. Summers got up from his chair and walked to the minibar. He grabbed four of the miniature liquor bottles and placed them on the small table. One of them tipped over and rolled toward the side of the table. White caught it before it fell. It was a small bottle of Jack Daniel's. Summers was holding one too.

White twisted the cap off and downed it in one gulp. Summers did the same with his. White placed the small recorder on the table, next to the remaining bottles, and looked at Summers. Summers slipped the recorder back into his pocket. Then he grabbed another bottle, unscrewed the cap, and gave it to White. He repeated the same process for himself.

"Okay, tell me what happened," Summers said as he leaned back in his chair. "I'm listening."

And, with a heavy heart, White did. He didn't leave any details out. Not even his relationship with Veronica.

CHAPTER NINETEEN

Naval Air Station Fort Worth, Texas

The rumble of the wheels hitting the runway woke Veronica with a start. There was another bump followed by the squeals of tortured rubber. She felt the breaking effect as the air force pilot reversed the thrust of the engines. The plane rolled for less than a minute before turning off the runway and taxiing toward a large, well-lit hangar. She looked out the window but didn't recognize the place. It resembled a military airfield more than a runway in a major American city.

Seated to her right was one of the Secret Service agents from the San Francisco field office. She had met him for the first time a few hours ago when he and six other agents had rushed her out of the hotel and escorted her to the government-owned Gulfstream sitting idle for her at the San Francisco International Airport. He was a big man, built solidly with thick arms and wide shoulders, but with kind brown eyes. He smiled at her and said, "We're at Naval Air Station Fort Worth, ma'am. Right outside Dallas, in case you're wondering."

"We're in Texas?" she said.

"Yes, ma'am."

Veronica didn't recall falling asleep, only that she had felt emotionally and physically spent upon boarding the aircraft. The last thing she remembered was asking the agent where they were going. Texas hadn't been his answer.

"What are we doing here?" she asked.

"Your father wants to see you," the agent said, fishing a pack of gum out of his pocket.

She'd had no idea her father was in Texas.

The agent took a piece of chewing gum for himself and held the pack out to Veronica. Her mouth tasted as if she'd licked an ashtray. She figured that was why the agent's eyes were almost pleading with her to accept.

"Thank you," she said, taking two sticks. She unwrapped them and popped them in her mouth. She almost spat them out, so intense was the watermelon flavor.

"I like them a lot," the agent said, chewing his gum hungrily and handing her a bottle of water.

She forced herself to swallow the sweet chemical substance in her mouth and then drank a third of the bottle, washing the watermelon taste away.

"Have you heard from Special Agent White?" she asked between two more sips of water.

"Nothing more than what we already knew when we left San Francisco," the agent replied.

"What about the rest of my protective detail?"

The agent's jaw tightened, and the lines on his face spoke of a burning rage. "I don't know," he said, turning his face away from her, as if he knew she could read right through him.

She gently touched his arm. "Please," she said. "I need to know."

He nodded. His eyes were dry, but there was a grief in them that scared Veronica. She feared what he was about to say next.

"They didn't make it," he said. "They were all murdered."

Veronica's mouth opened, but she couldn't say anything. Instant guilt overwhelmed her, choking the words in her throat. She pressed her lips together. *Oh my God. This is insanity.*

Until a moment ago, and despite all the evidence pointing to the contrary, she hadn't been totally convinced that she'd been the actual target of the attack. Now, with all her protective detail but Clayton dead, there couldn't be any doubt. *But why?* she asked herself. *Why?* She was an archaeologist with little or no influence outside the archaeological circles she operated in. She did have a significant social media footprint, but there was no way anything she had ever posted could have led to an attack on her life.

Could it be because of her father? She didn't see that either. Her dad wasn't even the vice president yet. She knew he used to be the commanding officer of JSOC. Could that be it? Terrorists coming after him through *her*? She wasn't naive. She was well aware of what JSOC did. Not all the operators assigned to JSOC were like Clay. A bunch of them were real killers, sent deep behind enemy lines to exterminate America's adversaries. She understood the need for that, but, on the other hand, it would be immature to think their enemies wouldn't fight back the same way.

It made her nauseous to think that she had fought Clay about the number of men he wanted to bring along. She had even threatened to relinquish protection if he continued to push for a bigger protective detail, afraid of what her academic friends would think of her. These folks didn't live in the same world her dad and Clay did. It was *their* night, and she hadn't wanted to make a big show, or to draw too much attention for the wrong reason. Her insides were churning, and for a moment she thought she was going to be sick. She took a deep breath to quell the feeling.

"You're okay, ma'am?" the agent asked. "I'm sorry, I shouldn't have said—"

She raised her hand. "No, thank you. Thank you for what you do . . . what's your name, again?"

"Jeremy, ma'am. Jeremy Myers."

"Well, thank you, Special Agent Myers," Veronica said. "And I'm sorry for the loss of your friends and colleagues."

"We'll get whoever did that," Myers replied through clenched teeth as the plane slowly came to a stop inside the hangar.

Veronica nodded. Clay had promised her the same thing.

Outside the plane, she saw a Humvee with flashing orange emergency lights leading a small motorcade of three identical black SUVs.

Vice President-Elect Alexander Hammond had arrived.

Bottle of water in hand, she got up from her seat, squeezed past Myers, and walked to the back of the Gulfstream to use the lavatory, her stomach heaving with each step. She locked the door behind her and pressed her back against it. She wasn't ready to see her father. Not yet. The faces of the agents who'd been killed at the Ritz-Carlton were the only things occupying her mind. She felt hot tears behind her eyelids. She hadn't known the agents well, yet they had sacrificed their lives for her. They had given up everything, absolutely everything, in order for her to live. What kind of men did that? She wasn't worthy of such sacrifice. She clamped her eyes shut, emotions caught in her throat, warm tears rolling down her cheeks.

"Heroes do that," she whispered to herself. She wiped the tears away angrily, as if she was mad at them for their audacity at falling.

I should have taken the time to learn more about them, about their families, she thought. *I didn't even know most of their names.*

She had taken them for granted. And it was true for Clay too. It wasn't until today that she had truly realized how much he meant to her. She was an idiot. How had she been so blind? She looked down at the ring on her finger and lightly touched it. She wished he was here now, with her.

Veronica glanced at her reflection in the small mirror above the sink. She grimaced at the darker patches of skin around her neck. Her eyes were puffy and sad. Her brown hair hung limp around her shoulders. She turned on the water faucet by pressing the blue and red buttons and then squirted the cheap soap into the palm of her hand. She scrubbed her hands, picking at some imaginary dirt beneath her nails. When the water stopped, she repeated the process. Then she washed her face and tied her hair into a bun, pushing away a few strands from her eyes. On her left, above the roll of toilet paper, was an alcove with courtesy bags stacked on top of each other and secured with a blue rubber band. She grabbed one of the bags and yanked the zipper open. Inside were a toothbrush, a minuscule tube of toothpaste, a pair of earplugs, a small bottle of hand sanitizer, two Tylenols, and a condom.

She opened the Tylenol packet, put the two pills in her mouth, and swallowed them with some water from her bottle. She then brushed her teeth and drank more water. By the time she was done, she was feeling much better, but angrier too. She needed answers, and by God she was going to get them.

When she came out of the lavatory, there wasn't anyone left on the plane.

Except for her dad.

CHAPTER TWENTY

Naval Air Station Fort Worth, Texas

Veronica's father enveloped her in his arms and didn't let go for a long time. When she looked at him, she could see that tears had collected in his eyes.

"I'm so happy you're okay, Vonnie," Alexander Hammond said. He kissed her on the forehead, just as he used to do before tucking her into bed when she was still a child.

Veronica was genuinely happy to see him. Since she was a kid, she'd been the apple of her father's eye, and until very recently, she'd always enjoyed a close relationship with him. She wouldn't have become the woman she was now if it hadn't been for her father's love and unyielding support. Despite being absent from home a lot due to the relentless pace of the deployments, he'd managed to have her back when it counted the most. The only hiccup had been recently, when he'd started expressing his strong opposition to anything even remotely connected to Drain. She'd attributed some of it to the stress of the presidential campaign and his natural worries for his family's safety; she'd hoped his objections would fade, but now she tensed, prepared for his chastisement.

"They told you what happened?" she asked.

Her dad's face hardened, and his eyes grew dark. "Yes," he said. "I was briefed."

He motioned for her to take a seat across from him, which she did. He unbuttoned his suit jacket and loosened his tie before sitting down. "There's a whole bunch of people who want to speak to you," her father said. "And time is of the essence here."

She expected as much. "I know," she said.

"We caught one of the attackers alive," he said, a brief smile appearing on his lips. "The one you stabbed in the back."

The man with the silver hair. Veronica shivered at the thought. She could still see him punching Clayton's face, his fists like pistons. She remembered vividly plunging the knife into the man's back and the noise it made when the blade hit bone.

"You did well," her father said, placing a comforting hand on her knee. "You saved Clay's life. You know that, right?"

Veronica guessed that was true, but by then Clayton had already killed two intruders. "He saved mine, too, Dad," she replied.

Her dad nodded. "Yeah, I'm aware of what happened in the room, Veronica. All of it."

She didn't like the tone her dad had used to say that. She looked straight at him, her head cocked slightly to one side, her eyes narrowing. Her dad pointed at the engagement ring on her finger.

"Is that for real? Did this really happen?"

She was momentarily caught off guard, but decided not to play defense. Clay would probably get some heat because of it, but with everything that had happened and the way he had ultimately saved the day, she didn't think she would put him in a bind by admitting that much to her father. She clasped her hands together and leaned toward him. "Yes, it did, Dad."

Her father dipped his chin, looking disappointed. "I was afraid of that," he said.

"What do you mean?"

"Clayton admitted the same to a Secret Service investigator," her father said. "He's been placed on administrative leave pending the results of a full investigation into today's events."

Veronica wasn't sure what it all meant. "Why? That doesn't sound good."

"Because it isn't. Odds are he'll get fired from the Secret Service. He may end up facing charges too."

She was taken aback by her father's words. It didn't make sense to her. Why would he face charges? Their relationship was forbidden by some regulations within the Secret Service code of conduct, but charges?

"I don't think I understand," she said.

"Really? C'mon, Veronica," her father snapped back. "How long has this been going on?"

She had rarely seen her father so confrontational, at least with her. Clearly she had misjudged the entire situation. "I'm not sure what you want to hear," she said. She quickly understood this wasn't an acceptable answer.

"You have to be kidding me," he said, slapping his hand on his thigh. "I don't want you to tell me what I want to hear, I want to know the damn truth. Do you realize how much trouble Clay is in?"

She was starting to. "A while," she admitted. "Just before you ran for office."

Her father pinched the bridge of his nose and closed his eyes. He sighed heavily and then said, "And you didn't feel like telling me? Why?"

"Oh, I don't know, Dad, maybe because I'm a thirty-six-year-old woman? I don't need to run things past you. You get that, right? You're not my commanding officer, and I'm certainly not one of your soldiers."

She watched as her father's mouth clamped shut, his face turning beet red. But his eyes remained soft. "You were almost killed, Vonnie," he whispered a moment later. "I almost lost my little girl. Didn't I tell you to drop this Drain mobile app? That nothing good would come out of it?"

"Seriously? What in hell does Drain have anything to do with this?" Veronica blew out a breath in frustration. "Why are you constantly fighting me on this? Drain had nothing to do with what happened tonight. How could it?"

"You really can't see it, Veronica? Think about it for one minute," her father said, traces of anger and disbelief apparent on his face. "Traveling around the world to remote archaeological sites."

"And?"

"For Chrissake! Don't you realize how vulnerable this makes you? You barely escaped with your life tonight, and you were in the middle of San Francisco, surrounded by security."

Veronica looked away, thinking of the Secret Service agents who'd been killed. By wanting to push ahead full speed with Drain, was she being selfish? Maybe her father had a point after all.

Hammond continued. "I know excavating sites is exciting, and important work too," he added. "But put yourself in my shoes, Vonnie. In a few weeks I'll be vice president of the most powerful country in the world, and having you trek around the globe constantly is an opening for our enemies."

She turned her eyes back to him. "So you want me to buckle down, stay home, and forget about *my* dreams? Am I getting this right?"

A soft smile appeared on her dad's lips. "Maybe just for a couple of years."

She shot daggers at him, and his smile froze on his face.

"Maybe just for a couple of years?" she repeated with pure disdain. "Wow. How stupid do you think I am?"

Veronica saw her father's spine straighten and his shoulders stiffen. She had hit a nerve. She pushed on.

"You're gonna be vice president for four years, Alexander," she said, knowing how he hated when she called him by his name. "Maybe eight if you win reelection. And I know the presidency is next on your list. Mom told me."

Hammond cleared his throat. "You and your mom are my everything," he said, his voice warm and sincere. "Everything I do, I do it for you, and for people and families like us all over this great country of ours. You know that, yes?"

A true politician, she thought, but knowing there was some truth in what he was saying. Maybe she'd been a little unfair with her dad, too quick to rebuke. She took one of his hands in her own and squeezed it.

"But that won't work for me, Dad," she replied. "You're asking me to put my life on hold for eight to twelve years. Does that seem fair to you?"

Her father sighed heavily. "Of course it isn't, Vonnie," he said, startling her. "It's not right for me to ask you to put everything aside for me. But will you at least consider postponing the release of the new version of Drain until next year? It would give us some time to figure how to work out your protection with the Secret Service."

For a man who had run the most secretive and lethal entity of the United States military, her father didn't seem to grasp how the corporate world worked.

"I can't promise you that," she replied. "SkyCU has spent a fortune on Drain. They'll push the app out as soon as it's ready."

"I see," Hammond replied with a certain sadness in his voice.

"But," Veronica added, once again squeezing his hand. "What I *can* promise you is that I'll postpone my own travel until we can figure out how I can do so safely. What about that?"

Her father laid his other hand on top of hers and gave her half a smile, but it was forced.

"Sure," he said, standing up.

She thought he would have been thrilled with her proposition. She couldn't see what was wrong with it. Drain would be out, but she wouldn't be traveling until she received the go-ahead from the Secret Service. She didn't understand his guarded reaction.

"I want you to spend the night here on base," he said. "I've instructed half of my protective detail to take care of you. You'll be safe here, I promise."

"I appreciate that, Dad, I really do, but I can't stay here. I have a meeting in Palo Alto tomorrow."

"Well, Veronica, you'll have to cancel. You're staying here for now," he replied dryly. "Tomorrow morning, investigators from the FBI and the Secret Service will speak with you about what happened in San Francisco."

She nodded. There was no point in arguing further. She had her laptop with her and would connect with her team at SkyCU remotely if she had to.

"I'll check in with you tomorrow," he said, heading toward the door.

"Dad?"

He stopped and turned to face her.

"About Clay," she said. "Can you—"

"There's nothing I can do to help him," he said, cutting her off.

"That can't be true," Veronica said. "You're about to become the vice president of the United States."

"And that's exactly why I can't do a thing."

"Oh, c'mon, Dad, that's bullshit," she said. "I wouldn't be here with you right now if it wasn't for Clay. And he's my fiancé. Please do something, at least about the charges you talked about."

Her father shook his head slowly. "If you had come to me twenty-four hours ago, I would have been in a position to help. Clayton would have been reassigned. Now that the investigation has started, my hands are tied."

Veronica rolled her eyes. "I have a feeling you're saying this because you're ticked off Clay didn't come to you first. Because he didn't ask you permission to marry me."

"No, Veronica," he said, his tone turning paternalistic, as if she were still a little girl. It made her blood boil beneath her skin. "I'm angry because by acting the way he did, notwithstanding how he handled himself once the shit hit the fan, he compromised his team and jeopardized the security of the person he was sworn to protect. And in this instance, it was you. My only daughter. He needs to face the consequences."

She stared at him long and hard, not recognizing fully the man standing in front of her. She could feel that her father wasn't being completely straightforward with her. For a fleeting moment, there was an expression of regret on his face. Then he turned away and strode out of the aircraft.

———

Alexander Hammond was fuming as he climbed back into his SUV. His daughter had no idea the shit her goddamn Drain application was stirring. Why did everything these days have to be crowdsourced and crowdfunded? Some technology was better off staying controlled by those who knew how to use it, not available to the masses.

Hammond didn't remember the last time he'd been under such pressure.

"Where to, sir?" his driver asked.

"Back to my plane," he replied. "We're headed to San Francisco."

Hammond grabbed his phone and quickly typed a message to General Tom Girdner, a longtime friend and associate who was now the provost marshal general of the United States Army. Hammond had always wished he wouldn't have to go ahead with this, but his stubborn daughter had left him no choice.

He tapped the send button. His phone rang almost immediately.

"I'm listening, Tom," Hammond said.

"I just received news that we have eyes on Clayton White, sir."

"Okay, good work. Ask your guys to pick him up and have them bring him to a hotel somewhere in the city." Hammond looked at his watch. "I'll meet White in about four hours. Did you get my last message?"

"Yessir," Girdner confirmed. "The men are already staged not too far away from the target building. Just in case you called."

"Thanks, Tom."

"I thought we'd put this all to bed six years ago. I'll call you again once I hear back from the team," Girdner said before ending the call.

Leadership required hard decisions, and as much as he'd hated going along with the assassination of Maxwell White, he'd known what he was doing was for the good of the country. But he couldn't help but think about what it now meant for his daughter. There was so much Veronica didn't know about him, and if she ever came to learn what he had just agreed to, it would obliterate their relationship.

Forever.

CHAPTER TWENTY-ONE

Palo Alto, California

Krantz wasn't a tall man, but the width of his rowing shoulders made him appear taller than his five-foot-eight stature. His hair was dark brown, like his scruffy beard. His powerful body moved with the athletic grace of a man confident in his physical strength as he jogged across Independence Avenue and bumped into the young man he'd been following for the past ten minutes.

"I'm so sorry," Krantz said as he smoothly slipped his right hand into the man's jacket pocket while tapping the man's shoulder with his left. "That's on me, my friend. I should have looked where I was going."

The young man looked confused and pissed at the same time, but he didn't say anything. Even as he was walking, Krantz had noted that the man's eyes had been glued to his phone nonstop for the last minute or so. From the stupefied look on his face, Krantz guessed that the man was watching the news and had just learned about the attempt on Veronica Hammond's life.

"Have a good one," Krantz said, waving the young man goodbye and pocketing the key fob he'd taken from him.

For the Palo Alto operation, he had changed into a pair of dark jeans and had thrown a leather jacket over a black turtleneck. Holstered on his right hip was a .45-caliber Heckler & Koch USP Compact Tactical. Two spare magazines were secured in magazine pouches on his left side. Since the ammunition for the pistol was subsonic, the gun was extremely quiet, especially when used in conjunction with a suppressor like the one Krantz carried in his jacket. The rest of the equipment he would need to complete his mission was in the black backpack slung over his shoulder.

He had parked the Jeep Cherokee he'd rented one block south in the parking lot of a busy café near West Middlefield Road. He had spent the last four days scouting the area and conducting surveillance and countersurveillance on the eight employees of SkyCU Technology. In addition, he had installed four miniature sticky surveillance cameras whose feed he could watch from an app on his smartphone. It allowed him to keep an eye on the comings and goings, even from his motel room a couple of miles away.

Palo Alto was the backup operation. Krantz had known Oxley long enough to know the man wasn't into half measures. Veronica Hammond might have been the brain behind Drain and the one with the influence to push for its global adoption, but SkyCU Technology had designed and distributed the app. Getting rid of Veronica would have been a major setback, perhaps enough to postpone the upgraded app's official release indefinitely—but it wasn't guaranteed. That was why he was in Palo Alto now. To take care of the what-ifs.

Krantz's phone vibrated in his pocket. It was his mobile surveillance app. He tapped on the notification and watched the second-to-last SkyCU employee exit the building. This employee would walk to the next block and catch a bus to San Jose, where he lived in a three-bedroom condo with his mother and sister. Krantz looked at the time. In another ten minutes, the last employee would, in turn, leave the office and walk to his car. If Krantz had been unsuccessful at lifting the key fob from the young man he had bumped into, the employee taking the bus would have been his plan B. There was also a third option in case the first two failed, but it required a more permanent solution with the last employee.

Krantz picked a bench that offered him a good view of his target building. Though he wasn't a smoker, he pulled a pack of Marlboros out of his breast pocket and lit a cigarette. He puffed on the cigarette but didn't inhale its toxic smoke. He casually but methodically studied the windows of the businesses across the street. He was looking for anything out of the ordinary that would tell him he was under surveillance or that the FBI was on to him. Krantz didn't believe they were.

Right on schedule, he watched the last employee exit the building. Satisfied federal agents weren't about to pin him to the ground, and that the SkyCU offices were now empty, he tossed his cigarette into a storm drain.

It was go time.

SkyCU Technology occupied half of the third floor of a three-story white rectangular building. The main entrance to the building was through a pair of double doors facing the street. Apart from SkyCU, the commercial space was home to a pair of real estate agencies that shared the first floor and a computer repair shop that occupied the entire second floor. Thanks to his surveillance cameras, Krantz knew the building's doors locked automatically after six o'clock and that a key fob was needed to unlock them. There was parking in front for customers, and a slightly smaller lot at the back for the employees of the businesses. Both parking lots were well lit, but there were no more lights visible in the windows of any of the building's businesses.

Krantz stayed away from the streetlights and well within the shadows of the tall palm trees bordering the sidewalk as he approached the edifice. As he walked by the last palm tree, he removed the sticky miniature surveillance camera he had fixed on the trunk three days ago. Krantz used the stolen key fob to enter the building and stopped by the hand-sanitizer station positioned next to the elevator's doors. With a flick of his hand, he removed another miniature camera, this one magnetically attached to the stand of the Purell dispenser. Krantz entered the staircase and climbed to the third floor. He didn't encounter anyone on his way up, nor did he see anybody in the third-floor corridor. Not taking any chances, he walked the entire length of the hallway and checked that the door of the vacant commercial space was indeed locked.

There were two more sticky surveillance cameras in the building. One was by the red fire hose cabinet attached to the wall near the elevators. Krantz had angled it in a way that permitted him to see the elevator doors and the entrance to SkyCU. The second one was inside the elevator, wedged in the right back corner at knee height. He would pick them both up on his way out, but for now he wanted to keep them operational to provide an extra layer of security.

The building didn't have its own alarm system or surveillance cameras, but SkyCU Technology did. After checking the hallway once more to make sure no one was going to surprise him, Krantz removed a set of lock-pick tools from his backpack. He took a moment to study the five-lever deadlock before selecting the right pick. Ten minutes later, he had the door open. Krantz slipped inside and closed the door quietly behind him and locked it. He heard the beeping of the alarm before he saw the panel. He grabbed a small screwdriver from his lock-picking kit and unscrewed the face of the alarm system panel. He pulled off the plastic cover and dropped it into his jacket pocket, then grabbed a small black device from his backpack.

The device, no bigger than a smartphone, had four twelve-inch-long wires sticking out of its front end. Krantz connected three of the wires to the terminal of the alarm system panel and powered on the unit by flicking a switch on the side of the device. The beeping stopped.

The room was dim, but the light coming in from streetlights was enough for him to see by, thanks to the eight windows facing the street.

At first look, and in contrast with the exterior of the building, the office was modern and beautifully decorated. Off to the left-hand side of the space was a pod of offices. The middle of the office space was occupied by a bunch of video arcade machines, the biggest flat-screen television Krantz had ever seen, an enormous L-shaped chocolate-colored leather couch, and what seemed like a dozen or so video game remotes plugged into the floor. There was also a Ping-Pong table and an espresso bar. On the right side was a large conference room enclosed on three sides by floor-to-ceiling glass walls.

Krantz stepped farther into the office and saw what appeared to be a solid wood door at the far end. As he had predicted, the door was locked with an electronic lock activated by a keypad fixed to the wall at the side of the door. From his backpack, he pulled out a white box and placed it over the keypad. Ten seconds later, numbers began to roll on a small readout in the center of the box. One by one, solid green numbers replaced the rolling ones. When he heard the electronic lock click, Krantz gently pushed the door open.

Bingo, he thought as he looked inside the server room.

The server room's square footage was about the same as the conference room's. There were three rows of racks holding boxy black servers covered in blinking LED lights. These were the dedicated servers for SkyCU Technology. This was where the company stored its plans and research data. It took a minute for Krantz to locate the actual file server. It was at the end of the third rack. The file server was hardwired to ten high-capacity hard drives. Krantz assumed each of them was in turn linked to another server for backup and data redundancy and then redirected once more to the cloud for safekeeping.

It didn't matter. The thumb drive Oxley had given him had come from the Guoanbu, the Chinese intelligence service. It would do what it was supposed to.

Krantz plugged the thumb drive into one of the ports and waited. For a moment, nothing happened, and he wondered if he had missed a step. He'd been promised the device was plug and play, which suited him fine since he wasn't the most technology-savvy guy around. He was about to pull the thumb drive out when an array of orange lights lit up its back. There was nothing left for him to do but to wait for the lights to turn green.

Then his phone vibrated. And he knew he had a problem.

———

Krantz's two remaining miniature surveillance cameras had detected movement. He unlocked his phone screen and watched, trying to decide if there was indeed a threat. It would have been a more difficult call to make if there had been only one man in the elevator. But not only were there two men inside the elevator; there was also a third man standing next to the entrance of SkyCU Technology. Krantz reached for the silencer in his pocket and screwed it onto his pistol. He double-checked he had a round in the chamber and exited the server room at the same time the two men exited the elevator. Any tiny hope he had about being overly paranoid vanished when the two men teamed up with the one who'd been standing guard next to the SkyCU Technology door.

Now that the angle was better, Krantz could see what the three men looked like despite the grainy image. He wasn't happy with what he saw. Krantz had spent almost fifteen years with the SAS. Studying faces and evaluating threats was a big part of what he did for a living. He knew what special operators looked like, and these three guys weren't it. Their hair was trim, their bodies fit, but they just didn't have the demeanor of apex predators.

Cops. That was the word that popped into Krantz's head. That thought brought more questions. Had they followed him? Possible, but unlikely. He'd been careful. But now wasn't the time to wonder how he'd found himself playing defense. Now was the time to figure a way out.

He glanced at his phone again. One of the men had a lock-pick gun in his hand, but none of them had a real weapon out.

Strange, Krantz thought. If they knew he was inside the office, they would surely come in with their guns drawn, right? Why hadn't they done that?

Bloody hell. What's going on here?

Krantz took a long, deep breath to steady his nerves and to oxygenate his brain. The door would open in a matter of seconds. He had to be ready. He took position behind the espresso bar, aiming his silenced pistol at the door. He heard the low humming of the pick gun. Krantz waited patiently in the darkness, steady in his firing position. He had the time to count to ten before there was a faint jingling of metal as the lock turned. The grinding hum stopped, and the door opened, letting the light from the hallway into the office space.

Krantz squinted at the light as the first man entered the office, but he didn't move. He waited for the other two men to enter. Once they were all inside and the door closed, Krantz fired. His shot caught the first man in the head just as he was about to switch on the lights. He dropped instantly. Krantz's next two shots hit the second man center mass, while his fourth shot, fired less than one second after his first, entered the last man's right eye. Krantz was about to change magazines when the man he had shot in the torso slowly rolled to his side and reached for something behind his back. Krantz reengaged immediately and dispatched a final round into the side of the man's head. Krantz ejected the magazine and inserted a fresh one, pocketing the other.

The first man he had shot was on the floor, facing down. Krantz rolled his body over.

He wasn't prepared for what he saw.

These men weren't cops. They were military.

The dead man had two wallets in his pockets. One contained a North Carolina driver's license, three credit cards, all of them matching the name on the driver's license, and about two hundred dollars in cash. The second wallet contained a CID special agent badge and a military identification, once again matching the driver's license. The

CID—Criminal Investigation Division—was the United States Army command responsible for investigating felony crimes and serious violations of military laws within the army. In addition to the two wallets, Krantz found a smartphone, a set of keys, and a SIG Sauer P228 pistol.

Krantz swore under his breath. What in hell were those guys doing in Palo Alto? Before he could search the other two, he heard multiple sirens approaching from two different locations. He had to go.

Now.

He quickly picked up his five spent brass and took a picture of each man's face with his phone. He then raced back to the server room and was relieved to see that the lights at the back of the thumb drive had turned green. That meant that the malware had done its job and had infected the servers, the cloud, and the entire backup system. Another hour or so and it would all be over for the young start-up. All SkyCU's data would be expunged, as if the Drain app and whatever other projects they were working on had never existed. This was also true for whoever had downloaded Drain. The mobile app would be wiped out from their device the next time they tried to open it while connected to the internet.

Oxley would be pleased. Krantz didn't know for sure how long Drain would be out of commission, but he was confident it would be enough to give Oxley the time he needed to fix the mess off the Arabian Peninsula.

Thirty seconds later, Krantz was out of the building and was walking toward his Jeep Cherokee. His heart almost stopped when two police cars sped past him. They had turned off their sirens, but their emergency lights pierced the night as harshly as their sirens had a minute ago. They continued down the main avenue, away from the SkyCU Technology building.

CHAPTER TWENTY-TWO

San Francisco, California

White had his hands stuffed in his pants pockets as he swiftly crossed the street toward an all-night coffee shop. The skies were dark, and the air was chilly and heavy with the scent of oncoming rain. The weather fit his mood beautifully.

A chime dinged as he entered the coffee shop. He shut the door softly behind him. Beautifully finished bookshelves lined the back wall, and small round wooden tables with chairs were placed throughout the store, with the occasional comfortable-looking, worn armchair thrown in. A couple of uniformed police officers sat at one of the tables, each sipping from a white mug. One of them turned to look in his direction. White waved at him.

"You okay, pal?" the officer asked, looking at White with suspicious eyes.

"Long night, brother," White said, approaching the lone employee standing behind the counter.

"It certainly looks like it," the second officer chimed in. "You need medical attention?"

White chuckled, but his smile quickly turned into a grimace. His whole face still hurt like hell. "Not much they could do," he replied.

The cops shrugged and continued working on their coffees. The young man behind the counter politely greeted him with a smile, but

White could see he was happy that the two police officers were there. White wouldn't be surprised to see him offer unlimited refills to the officers for as long as the man with the messed-up tuxedo and beat-up face was inside the coffee shop.

"A large black coffee," White said. "And a bottle of water."

"Anything to eat?"

"I wish," White said between clenched teeth. He was pretty sure he wouldn't be able to eat anything but liquid food for the next day or so.

"Sorry?" the young man said. "I didn't hear what you said."

"Nothing," White replied. "Just the coffee and the water, please."

White chose a barstool facing the street and carefully took a sip of his steaming coffee, feeling the bitter acidity wash over his tongue and gums. He swallowed, enjoying the lingering taste of the roast in his mouth, which didn't do much to soothe his dark mood.

White sighed. What had started as the best day of his life had turned into the worst nightmare. His colleagues—his friends, really—were dead. And his career with the Secret Service was virtually over.

White had been fully aware that his position within the VPPD—the Vice President's Protective Division—had ruffled more than a few feathers among certain more senior special agents who had been waiting years to go on the detail. Following his graduation from the Secret Service Academy, the Service had assigned White directly to the Protective Intelligence Division—PID—instead of having him spend his first four to six years in one of the Secret Service's field offices investigating credit card fraud, identity theft, or currency counterfeiting. Fortunately for White, who truly had no real interest in these types of investigations but would have been ready to pull his weight and do his time for a chance to one day join "The Show," somebody in human resources had concluded that White's exemplary military records and advanced medical training would be put to much better use if he was assigned to the protective division. After White had put in only two years with the PID, Alexander Hammond had pulled a few strings to have him transferred to the VPPD, where he became the detail's DSAIC—or deputy special agent in charge. A great deal of resentment and jealousy had been generated by his quick ascension and his direct access to Hammond.

One evening, just a few nights after her dad had officially joined the presidential ticket, Veronica had told him she had overheard other special agents talking among themselves about him. White, who'd always been confident in a leadership role and had never felt the need to please every single one of his subordinates for fear of not being liked, hadn't probed further.

"Aren't you curious to know what they're saying about you?" she'd asked, pushing him gently.

He'd shrugged at the question. "It wouldn't change anything, Vonnie," he had finally replied. "I do my best every single day, and I challenge my team to do the same. It's true that I expect a lot from them, both on an individual level and as a group, but I like to believe that this creates positive peer pressure where members of my team support and encourage each other."

She had thrown him a man-melting smile and said, "Keep talking, I like your voice."

"The thing is," he'd continued, serious, "we're all in this together. Members of the team who are stronger in one area are helping the others who are weaker."

"So everyone's a teacher and a learner," Veronica had said.

"Exactly. You never stop learning," he'd replied, nodding at her. "My point, Dr. Hammond, is that whatever they say or think about me won't change the way I interact with them. I'll continue to treat them fairly and with respect."

While he spoke, Veronica had poured two glasses of her favorite Barolo. She'd handed him one, which he had accepted.

"That means you won't care that they all think you'll be the next assistant special agent in charge of the JJRTC?"

That had startled him. "It's flattering, but ridiculous. I'm not qualified," he'd replied, rejecting the idea. The JJRTC was the James J. Rowley Training Center, also known as the Secret Service Academy. It was a good posting, and one known to be a springboard for higher office within the organization. But he wasn't interested in a desk job. And never would be.

White took another sip of his coffee.

In the distance, a bolt of lightning split the night sky. Seconds later, heavy drops of rain hit the windows of the coffee shop. The few pedestrians brave enough to be out at this maddening hour were hurrying down the sidewalk, doing their best not to step into a puddle. White looked at his phone. Still no reply from Veronica. He resisted the urge to text her again. He'd done so too many times already. He had tried to call, too, but they had all gone directly to her voicemail. He missed her, but he was mostly worried. He was still shaken by what had happened at the Ritz-Carlton, and it hadn't been his first rodeo either. The wars in Iraq and Afghanistan, and then his Secret Service training, had prepared him well for these kinds of situations—as much as one can be prepared to take another man's life, that is. But for Veronica, a brilliant archaeologist who'd spent most of her life sheltered from violent experiences, today's events must have been traumatizing.

That said, she had conducted herself with courage and valor he had rarely seen in a civilian. Not that civilians didn't possess those traits; they simply didn't have the training to respond adequately to life-threatening scenarios.

And her courage almost cost her her life, White reminded himself. *She almost died trying to save me.*

He didn't know what he would have done if he had survived and she had not. Cold shivers ran up and down his spine, and he almost dropped his coffee mug. He put it down and opened the bottle of water, tilting it to his lips.

His phone vibrated against the scuffed wood of the table. Veronica's number showed on the screen.

"Veronica?" he asked. "Are you all right?"

"Hey, baby. I'm okay," she said. "Sorry I didn't get back to you sooner. My phone was off. Where are you?"

Relief flooded through him. "Don't worry about it. It's so good to hear your voice," he replied. "I'm still in San Francisco. And you?"

"Fort Worth," she said. "My dad's here too. I think that's why they diverted the plane here. He wanted to see me."

White knew the place well. "Until we know what's going on, it's the right move. You'll be safe there."

"Yeah, I guess," she said. "They put me in a house on base. Half of my dad's protective detail is here with me. They're on four-hour shifts, I think. They're using the guest bedroom as their break room."

"They'll take care of you," White said. "They'll even cook for you if you ask them."

"Really?"

"No, but I would."

He heard her laugh, which was good news. But he still worried about her.

"How are you doing, Vonnie? Really."

He heard her take a deep breath. "I don't know, Clay. It's weird. I feel like I should be shaken, and I am, but not as much as I thought I would be, or should be. Does that make any sense?"

"Not everyone has the same reaction to traumatic events, especially like the one we've been through together," White said. "And nobody recovers the same way either."

"I . . . I feel fine, but my mind . . . my mind has a really hard time accepting we've lost so many. Every time I close my eyes, even if it's only for a second, I . . . I see them. And I feel the weight, Clay. And it's fucking crushing me," she said, her voice breaking in a sob.

He hated not being with her. He felt completely powerless. He wished there was something he could do to make her feel better, but listening was all he could offer her for the time being.

"What you've been through tonight is way outside the range of normal human experience," White said, remembering saying exactly the same thing to a Marine he had rescued in Iraq. The young Marine had been the only survivor of a helicopter crash that had killed his entire squad. "It's normal to be confused, Vonnie."

"I'm just . . . so damn angry."

"Whoever did this, I swear I will do everything in my power to make them pay. I know the Secret Service and the FBI will talk to the surviving member of the assault team the minute he wakes up," White said.

"The man I stabbed in the back?"

"Yes," White confirmed. "He'll talk. We'll know the truth soon enough."

They remained silent for a while, and then they both started to say something at the same time and laughed.

"You go ahead," Veronica said, sniffing.

"Listen, Vonnie, I have to tell you something," White started. "The Secret Service—"

"I already know," she replied, cutting him off. "My dad told me. You're suspended, aren't you?"

White cocked his head. Veronica's mood had suddenly flipped, sounding almost happy at this unfortunate turn of events. "You don't seem too upset about it," he said.

"Well, are you?"

White wasn't mad at the Secret Service. They were within their rights to suspend him. He would have done the same if he'd been in charge. "I think we both knew this could happen," he said.

"My dad thinks you'll get fired, Clay."

"I won't fight them if it comes to that."

"Good," she said.

"Good? You're serious?" White chuckled.

"You do know that if you aren't a Secret Service special agent anymore, it means we get married sooner, right?"

Of course he knew. But until a couple of minutes ago, he hadn't been convinced that their somewhat uncanny engagement was valid. He wouldn't have blamed her if she'd decided to give him back the ring. What would they say to their friends, and even to their future children, about how their engagement went down? It would be a crazy story, and one that wouldn't necessarily bring back joyful memories.

"I think I'll need to speak to your dad first," White said. "And I'd love to propose to you again, if you don't mind. Properly this time."

"Maybe it could be a bit more romantic too?"

"I'll try, but no promises."

"Deal," Veronica said.

"Your turn. What was it you wanted to say?" White asked.

"I just wanted to put you on speaker as I grabbed my laptop. But I have it now."

"I thought you'd want to go to bed by now," White said.

"I already slept on the plane. I need to link up with SkyCU's servers for a minute or two. I need to check a few things before tomorrow's meeting."

"You can't risk that," White replied, surprised she'd even consider attending the meeting. "Can't you postpone?"

"My father insisted I stay in Fort Worth for the time being," she replied. "I'll connect with the team remotely."

White heard her groan. "What's up?" he asked.

"I'm trying to access my SkyCU account, but I keep getting kicked out. I can't log in."

He heard the clicking of her keyboard and mouse pad in the background. It was a sound he knew all too well. Veronica often worked in bed late at night, and all that typing and clicking more often than not put White right to sleep.

"That's weird," she said. "It's never happened before."

"Maybe they're updating their systems," White suggested. "Is the mobile app working?"

"Updating the servers wouldn't prevent me from logging in," she replied, her tone impatient. "And yes, I was just on Drain. It's working."

Noting how aggravated she seemed to be, White asked, "Anything I can do from here? I can stop by their office if you want. I have the time, you know, now that I'm unemployed."

His attempt at humor fell flat. "I'm not kidding, Clay," she said, her tone dead serious. "I have a bad feeling about this."

"What's going on?" White asked, suddenly alert.

"You know my dad has been against Drain from the start, right?"

"He did mention it to me once or twice," White replied. "He's afraid of you traveling the world without adequate protection."

"Well, that's just it," Veronica said. "I think that isn't the entire story."

White had no idea where she was headed with this. The Secret Service agent in him kind of agreed with her dad. It would be difficult to protect Veronica twenty-four seven if she spent months overseas at a time.

"His point about your protection is valid," White offered. "Especially after San Francisco, I think—"

Veronica cut him off. "I know. I already told him I wouldn't travel until I get the all clear from the Secret Service."

"Then it's settled," White said.

"I thought so, too, but when I mentioned that the new version of Drain would launch anyway, his whole demeanor changed. He wasn't happy."

That didn't make much sense to White. "Did he tell you why? I'm sure there's a good explanation."

"No, but I can't help but wonder if he has anything to do with me not being able to access the servers."

"No. No way, Vonnie. That seems too far fetched," White said. "I know your dad, honey. Why would he care if the revamped mobile app launches or not?"

"That, Clay, is exactly what I'm wondering. I have to find a way to get back to California. I'll call you later."

"What? California? You can't," White said. "We don't have enough information about tonight's attack, Veronica. Listen to your dad and stay in Texas for a little while. It's the best way to keep you safe, okay?"

There was no reply. "Vonnie?"

White looked at his phone. His fiancée had hung up on him.

CHAPTER TWENTY-THREE

Oxley Vineyards
Kommetjie, South Africa

Oxley, who was now on his fourth drink, had been more than a little anxious to hear back from Krantz. So when his phone rang, he picked it up right away.

"Please brighten my day, Abelard," he said. "How did it go?"

"No issues in San Francisco. Van Heerden's men have been silenced."

At last some good news, Oxley thought. "What about Palo Alto?"

"Palo Alto was interesting, to say the least," Krantz replied. "The start-up is done for, like you asked, but I was interrupted by three special agents from the CID. They broke into SkyCU while I was still inside."

Oxley stopped breathing. The CID? "I assume you left them there?"

"Correct."

"How sure are you they were really from the CID?" Oxley asked, running his fingers through his hair.

"Their military identification cards looked legit," Krantz said. "I took pictures of their faces. I'll send them to you."

In a burst of rage, Oxley threw his tumbler across the room. It smashed against a bookcase, missing by less than a foot the expansive aquarium his wife had gifted him for his fifty-fifth birthday, showering glass, ice, and single malt on the hardwood floor. This entire operation was rapidly degenerating into a full-scale fiasco.

He needed to regain control over his emotions. Oxley prided himself on his ability to remain calm, whatever was thrown at him.

"Please do," he told Krantz, wondering what the CID presence meant. There was no way Hammond could have identified Oxley's involvement in the attack on his daughter so quickly. Then another possibility occurred to him.

From the corner of his eyes, Oxley noted movement. It was his wife. Adaliya had entered the study without knocking, a worried look on her face.

"I'll look into our options and get back to you with a new set of instructions," Oxley said, gesturing Adaliya to stay put, afraid she could step on broken shards of glass and hurt herself. "For now, I want you to get the hell out of San Francisco and find a place to hunker down until I contact you again."

"Understood."

"Let me know if you need anything, my friend," Oxley said. "I'll be in touch."

Oxley placed the phone on his desk and looked at the only woman he had ever loved. As always, he found it difficult to avert his eyes once they were set on her. Adaliya was a tall, slim, and vivacious woman in her forties who always carried herself with practiced elegance. She had long, curly black hair and dark, sparkling eyes. The plush white bathrobe she had wrapped around her contrasted with her dark skin. She was leaning against the doorframe, her hands deep in the pockets of her robe.

"What happened here?" she asked, contemplating the wet mess on the floor. "That better not be one of the tumblers my brother gave you."

"Come this way," he said, his fingers drawing a path around the broken glass.

Oxley slouched back into his leather chair, letting his head fall forward and using his hand to massage the back of his neck.

"Let me take care of this," his wife said, taking over.

Oxley closed his eyes, enjoying his wife's warm touch on his skin. The primary mission had failed, but at least Krantz had taken care of SkyCU Technology. The unforeseen presence of three CID agents disturbed him. The more he thought about it, the more Oxley was convinced the CID agents were there for the same reason Krantz had been. To neutralize Drain. Although Alexander Hammond himself didn't have much sway with the CID anymore, Oxley knew someone who did. Tom Girdner. Another American general who had contributed to CONQUEST.

It was more than worrying.

Oxley's only connection to Van Heerden was through Krantz; the mercenary had no idea it was Oxley who had been financing the operation, and it was unlikely Van Heerden could give the authorities any information beyond Krantz's alias. The thing he knew for sure, though, was that Van Heerden's failure came with a high price tag.

Oxley had had to burn through most of his contacts within the intelligence community to get the information he needed to prepare the San Francisco operation. He had always known there would be a thorough investigation of tonight's event. He had also accepted that there was no way all his paid assets were going to get away from this scot-free. But it had been a calculated risk. The loss of paid assets would have been worth it if Veronica Hammond had been killed, but with the utter failure of the mission, Oxley had forfeited valuable resources with not enough to show in return. On the contrary, Oxley's problems had only grown worse because of Van Heerden's botched operation.

Anyone could have been responsible for the attack on Veronica. Hammond had made enough enemies during his military career to warrant such action being taken against him. ISIS, Al-Shabaab, Al-Qaida, you name it. They all wanted him dead. Oxley couldn't think of a better way to exact revenge on one's enemy than to kill his daughter. Taken separately, the San Francisco and Palo Alto events couldn't lead to Oxley. Combined, though, they brought out a much different outcome.

Alexander Hammond was no fool. He would learn of Oxley's involvement.

"Shit!" Oxley shouted.

Even though Hammond hadn't been sworn in yet as vice president of the United States, he was still a formidable adversary with plenty of powerful allies. Oxley would need to be very careful moving forward and pondered the benefit of reaching out to Hammond personally. Maybe they could find a compromise? Should he come clean and plead his case?

Definitely too soon to do that, Oxley thought, shaking his head. Forcing him to give up Maxwell White's flight plan had been the right thing to do at the time, but it had destroyed whatever bond, if any, he had ever shared with the American general. There was no trust left between the two men.

"What's wrong, my love?" his wife asked him, a whisper in his ear. "San Francisco didn't pan out the way you wanted it to?"

Oxley twisted his head and looked at his wife. There were no secrets between them. None whatsoever. Besides Krantz, she was the only person he trusted unconditionally. Adaliya was his life partner, the mother of his children, his lover, best friend, business partner, and confidante. It was as if she always knew what he needed at a specific time. Sometimes it was brute honesty, sometimes empathy, but more often than not, listening was the key.

Oxley's dad, now long deceased, had chastised him for waiting so long to get married. Oxley had simply not wanted to make the same mistake his father and mother had made. His five children with Adaliya were treasures to be cherished.

He had met Adaliya in Kenya, while conducting training scenarios with the Kenya Defense Forces. Britain's Ministry of Defence had long maintained a cooperation agreement that allowed British soldiers to train in hot conditions on rugged terrains. Adaliya, a criminal lawyer, had been hired by the British government to defend two SAS soldiers under Oxley's command accused of assaulting a Kenya Air Force general. Oxley had fallen for her immediately. Her laugh and mischievous smile had enchanted him. He had no idea what an accomplished woman like her had ever wanted to do with a poor soldier like him, but she had stirred his soul in a way he had never thought possible. At the end of the trial, where she had successfully defended the SAS troopers, she had given Oxley her number in London.

Once he was back in Britain, he had called the number, half expecting a cashier from the local grocery store to pick up. To his utmost surprise, it had been Adaliya's voice at the other end of the line. A week later, he had proposed to her with a £500 engagement ring. They were married the next month.

"It didn't go well," Oxley admitted. "Van Heerden has been taken, and Veronica Hammond is still alive."

"And the technology?" Adaliya asked.

"Still a clear and present danger to us, I'm afraid. But I managed to buy us some time."

"Enough to take care of our problem in the Arabian Peninsula?"

"We'll see. I hope so," he said.

The clock was ticking.

Oxley shifted in his chair. He was exhausted, but not tired for some reason. He felt Adaliya's breath close to his ear.

"You're stressed out," she said. "Let me take care of you."

He exhaled, letting her hands take charge. In seconds, the pounding in his head subsided, but she continued, running her fingers across his forehead and along his eyebrows, then down his cheeks and by the unshaven skin of his jaw. She leaned over, and her lips touched his cheek. That's when he turned his broad shoulders and grabbed her. She gasped as he lifted her in the air from his seated position. He gently dropped her on his lap and pulled her close, lacing his fingers with hers, savoring the perfect and familiar fit of their hands together. For a moment, he pretended that everything was all right: that Veronica Hammond was dead, that the Palo Alto incident was just a bad dream, and that the transaction with Le Groupe Avanti was going to go through without a hitch.

But then reality caught up with him, and he knew that in order to fulfill his promise to his wife, he would need to wage war against Alexander Hammond.

CHAPTER TWENTY-FOUR

San Francisco, California

White looked at his screen incredulously. Why had Veronica hung up on him? He had tried to call her back twice, but she hadn't picked up. She'd been distraught by the fact that she couldn't gain access to the SkyCU servers. And had she really suggested that her dad might have something to do with it?

Even though Veronica hadn't asked him to go, maybe it wouldn't be such a bad idea to stop by the SkyCU office in Palo Alto. It wasn't like he was going to get any sleep anyway.

His phone rang. Veronica's number didn't appear on the screen. Disappointed, he pressed the green button to accept the call. "Who's this?" he asked, his voice harsher than it should have been.

"Your future father-in-law, or so I just learned. And please, drop that acerbic tone, son. Won't work with me."

Stunned, White almost snapped to attention in his chair. "Mr. Vice President-Elect," he said. "My apologies, sir."

"Not feeling too sorry for yourself, are you?" Alexander Hammond asked.

"No, sir. Not for myself," White said sincerely. "Only for the guys I lost today. And their families."

"Yeah, of course," Hammond said. "I knew them all. Not a lot, but enough to know they were good men."

"They were," White said. An image of his friend Marcus Thompson laughing out loud while holding his two kids in his massive arms popped into his mind. Then it was immediately followed by an image of Marcus with his brains blown out, his body in a heap on the floor of an elevator. The events of the last few hours had taxed the very depths of White's soul. The situation seemed almost unreal. When he had left the air force, he never expected to have to shoot someone again.

"I'll make you this promise, Clayton," Hammond said, cutting through White's thoughts. "I'll make absolutely sure that the Secret Service will be there every step of the way to support the families of the fine men we lost today."

If any other politician had spoken those words, White would have rolled his eyes, knowing they meant well but would never follow through. But since they came from Hammond, the man who had run JSOC for years, White knew he could take it to the bank.

"Thank you, sir."

"We need to talk," Hammond said.

White winced. He'd known this moment would come. Hammond was going to give him shit for proposing to his daughter without having the decency to ask him permission prior to doing it. And he'd probably threaten to kill him for the sheer audacity of proposing to Veronica while on duty, which could have cost his daughter her life.

"Agreed," White replied. "Let me first—"

"In person, Clay. I want to speak to you face to face."

"Veronica told me you were in Fort Worth, sir," White replied, confused. "I'm still in San—"

"I know where you are," Hammond interrupted. "I'm on my way to you. I'll be in San Francisco in a few hours. In the meantime, I want you to listen to the CID warrant officers who are about to pay you a visit."

Hammond hung up before White could reply. Did Hammond just tell him CID special agents were on their way? White looked at his watch. It was almost two in the morning. He was drinking the rest of his now-cold coffee when the chime on the door rang and two men entered. The first was tall and burly, with close-cropped blond hair and hollow cheeks. The other was shorter, had skinny legs but overdeveloped arms and shoulders. They were both wearing dark slacks and sport shirts with windbreakers.

"Special Agent Clayton White?" the taller man asked.

White turned his head to his right and looked at the two uniformed police officers. They had both placed their coffee mugs on the table and were watching the scene. White noted they had slid their chairs slightly back from the table in order to give themselves some room in case they needed to move in a hurry.

"Who's asking?" White said, getting up from his stool.

"I'm Warrant Officer Ashby from CID, sir," the man said. "We were told we would find you here."

White saw the shorter CID agent nod at the two uniformed police officers as he stopped by the counter to order something.

"You pinged my personal phone to locate me?" White asked.

The warrant officer shrugged and said, "Our orders are to take you to a hotel so you can freshen up. Vice President-Elect Hammond will be here in a few hours. You really took a beating, didn't you?"

"The other guy is in even worse shape," White replied. "Why did the vice president call on CID to do this? This is out of the ordinary, isn't it?"

The shorter of the two CID agents came back with a cardboard tray holding three coffees and a paper bag containing either a muffin or a couple of biscuits. "If I had to take a guess, I'd say it's because the Secret Service and FBI have their hands full. Good morning, sir," he said, after White nodded. "I'm Warrant Officer Tim Folsom. Coffee?"

"I'm good, but thanks anyway," White said.

"Our commanding officer told us the order came to him directly from General Girdner, the provost marshal general," Ashby added. "He specifically asked us to take care of you."

"We made a short list of hotels that had vacancies," he said, handing his phone to White. "You can pick the one you want. And we have clothes for you in the vehicle."

White looked at the list on the screen. "Any of those will be fine, gentlemen," he said. "But can we make a quick stop by Palo Alto first?"

"That's a bit out of the way, isn't it?" Folsom asked. "What's so important in Palo Alto?"

"SkyCU Technology," White replied. "Vice President-Elect Hammond's daughter works there."

CHAPTER TWENTY-FIVE

Naval Air Station Fort Worth, Texas

Veronica ignored Clay's incoming calls. She needed to do this on her own. She had shared her concerns about her father with him, but she had felt some resistance on his part. She didn't blame him. Clay's complete trust in her father wasn't uncommon. She had seen it before among officers who worked with her dad. Alexander Hammond was the kind of man people wanted to follow into battle.

She scrolled down her contact list until she found the number she was looking for.

Noah Larson. He was a software engineer at SkyCU. Though Noah was still in his twenties, he was one of the most gifted people Veronica had ever worked with. Without him, she doubted Drain would have launched.

She glanced at the clock on the wall and hesitated. Should she wake him up? Was she being crazy?

Maybe tonight's attack had indeed thrown her off her game. Clay had told her this could happen. Why was not being able to log in to the servers suddenly such a big deal to her? Couldn't she wait until morning like any reasonable person would?

No way, she thought. *If something's wrong, Noah will be glad I called him.*

He answered on the first ring.

"Veronica! I've been worried sick," he said, not showing any signs of fatigue. "How are you?"

She had kind of forgotten that the assault at the Ritz-Carlton was all over the news. It was normal her team would be anxious to hear from her. She should have reached out to them sooner.

"I should have called, Noah, I'm so sorry—"

"Nonsense! I'm just glad to hear your voice. I'm the one who should have called, but I didn't want to intrude, you know? I'm sure there's a lot going on, right?"

"I'm doing well," she said. "But I need your help. Have you tried to log in to our portal or servers recently?"

"Not since I left the office. I've been glued to the television. Why?"

"I can't access anything from my end, and I'm wondering if that's the case for the rest of the team too."

"Is Drain working?"

"It was last time I tried," she said. "Let me check again."

Veronica put Noah on speaker and looked at her screen, her finger hovering over the location the thumbnail for Drain should have been. It wasn't there anymore. It had disappeared.

She swiped to the next screen. It wasn't there either.

Had she deleted it by mistake? She tried to access Drain indirectly through an app store, but it wasn't available. It was as if Drain had never existed. *What the hell's going on?*

"I can't find Drain, Noah," she said, her anxiety rising. "Look at the app."

She heard Noah curse under his breath, which did nothing to attenuate her fear. "Talk to me, Noah," she pleaded.

"I don't understand. I've never seen something like this before," he said, his voice panicky.

"What are you seeing?" she asked, hearing the sound of his fingers typing on his keyboard.

Then Noah gave out a deep, throaty yelp, quickly followed by another curse. "We've been hacked. Holy shit, Drain's gone!"

"What? How's that even possible?" Veronica asked, stunned.

"It's not. It's not possible," Noah replied. "Unless . . ."

"Unless what, Noah?"

"Unless someone gained physical access to our servers in Palo Alto and wiped them. And who would want to do that anyway? Drain isn't a threat to anyone—it's a freaking archaeological application!"

Veronica's mouth and throat suddenly turned into sandpaper. Her hands became clammy.

Noah didn't notice she'd fallen silent. "I need to head to the office now to assess the damage. I can't do that remotely."

His words brought her back to reality. "No!" she shouted. "Don't go."

"Why the hell not? What's going on, Vonnie?" There was a pause. "Do you know something about this? Does it have something to do with what happened to you tonight?"

"I . . . I don't know, Noah," she replied honestly. "But I don't want you to take any unnecessary risks, okay? Just in case. Please."

She heard him exhale. "I'll need to call the others. They need to know what's going on."

"Of course. Please do," she said, but Noah had already hung up.

She rubbed her moist hands on her jeans. Was it a coincidence that SkyCU had been the victim of a cyberattack the same day someone had tried to kill her? She had a feeling that both occurrences were linked. That meant that her father wasn't behind the problems logging in to SkyCU.

Thinking her father would go that far to disrupt her work on the app had been a stupid idea from the start. No wonder Clay had been dismissive.

What's wrong with me? she asked herself. The only thing her dad ever wanted was to keep her safe. Right?

CHAPTER TWENTY-SIX

Palo Alto, California

White was the first to spot the rectangular white three-story building that housed the offices of SkyCU Technology. The start-up's website specified that the business was located on the third floor. The main entrance was through a pair of double doors facing the street.

"It's right there to our left," White said.

Ashby, who was driving the unmarked sedan, slowed down.

"What are you looking for?" Folsom asked. "It's quiet. All the lights are off."

White was pleased to see nothing extraordinary going on around the building. At least it wasn't on fire. Quiet was good.

"Do you mind dropping me off?" he asked. "I'll do a quick walk-around; then we can all be on our way."

Ashby turned the sedan around and parked next to the curb. "There you go," he said, switching off the engine.

"I'll just be a couple of minutes," White said, opening the car door. "Thank you."

White climbed out of the vehicle and stepped onto the palm tree–lined sidewalk. There were two exterior parking lots connected to the building. A large one was in front and to the left, while a smaller one was at the back of the building. Both were well lit and deserted, with the exception of a dark-colored SUV. No lights were visible in any of the windows. White walked leisurely around the perimeter of the building, looking for any signs of a break and enter. He didn't find any.

He almost didn't bother walking to the main entrance to try opening the double doors. Surely, they would be locked. He glanced toward Ashby and Folsom, who were both leaning against the hood of the sedan, smoking cigarettes. He motioned to them he was almost done. White branched off to his right and headed toward the entrance. Behind the double doors, a faint light emanated from the foyer. Nothing seemed unusual or out of place. There was a small note at the side of the door reminding the tenants to use their key fob after 6:00 p.m.

White nevertheless pulled the door handle and was stunned when the door swung open. He examined the locking mechanism. It was a standard commercial electronic lock. It didn't look like it had been forced open. Inoperative power locks were usually caused by either a wiring or mechanical problem. He glanced behind him at the two CID agents, hoping to let them know he was going inside, but they weren't looking in his direction.

White stepped inside the foyer and pressed the call button for the elevator. Since he was already inside the building, it wouldn't take much of his time to check the third floor. Who knew? Maybe if he was lucky there would be a SkyCU employee working late who wouldn't mind letting him in?

White rode the elevator to the third floor. He stepped off into a darkened corridor. In front of him was a small sign with plenty of space to name all the businesses that occupied that floor. For now, SkyCU Technology seemed to be the only tenant. White found its entrance door in no time. He was about to knock when he noticed that the deadlock had been tampered with, as if someone had used a lock-pick gun to break it.

White pulled his snub-nose .38 revolver from its ankle holster. Then, with his left hand, he turned the knob and gently pushed the door open. The interior was dark, with barely enough light for him to see. He slipped inside the instant there was enough space for him to go through. His right foot immediately hit something, and he almost fell forward. He looked down.

Shit! His feet had bumped into a dead man. White's heart rate spiked, and he stepped to his left, getting away from the doorframe. His back scratched against something.

The light switch, he thought. He used his left hand to flip it. The light came on. Two more bodies were on the floor. There was no need to check for a pulse to know they were dead. Each of them had been shot in the head, although one of them had also been shot twice center mass.

White rapidly cleared the sleek and modern office, including the large conference room enclosed by three floor-to-ceiling glass panels. Deeper into the office space, there was a solid wood door with an electric lock controlled by a keypad. White guessed this was where the servers were located.

Damn it, he thought. *Veronica was right to worry.*

White returned to where the bodies lay and holstered his revolver. He took his phone and dialed 911 to report the incident. He identified himself to the dispatcher and also informed her that there were two armed CID agents in a government sedan parked in front of the building. After he hung up, White crouched next to the man he had tripped over and frisked him. He found a SIG Sauer P228 pistol, a smartphone, and a black wallet.

White opened the wallet and did a double take. It contained a military identification card and a CID special agent badge. He then looked at the smartphone.

GIRDNER—4 MISSED CALLS.

What the fuck's going on?

White swiped up, but a numeric keypad appeared on the screen. The phone was locked. Without thinking, he pocketed the dead agent's phone. He was about to move to the next body when the door behind opened and Ashby and Folsom appeared, their guns pointed right at him.

CHAPTER TWENTY-SEVEN

Palo Alto, California

White slowly raised his hands over his head, his mind racing. Were Ashby and Folsom in on it too? With his .38 snub-nose revolver safely tucked inside his ankle holster, there was no way for him to draw it before being shot dead.

"Step away from them, Clayton, or I swear to God I'll shoot you in the face," Ashby said.

White obeyed and took a few steps back. He slowly turned fully toward the two CID agents. They looked sick and distraught, and not sure about what to do next.

"What happened here?" Folsom asked, his eyes bouncing between White and the dead men. "Please tell me you didn't do this."

"Listen to me really carefully, guys," White said, making absolutely sure not to make any sudden movement. It was easy to see that the two CID agents were on the edge. It wouldn't take much for them to shoot him by mistake. "I found the three of them exactly like this. They were dead when I came in."

"Do you know who they are? Have you seen them before?" Ashby asked, his pistol still pointed at White's torso.

"I've never seen them before. I have no idea who they are," he lied.

White almost asked Ashby if *he* knew them, since they were CID. But he kept his mouth shut.

"Call the police," Ashby said to Folsom. "Tell them we're at the—"

"I've already called the police," White said. "And if you pay attention, you'll hear the sirens."

There were indeed police sirens in the background. Lots of them.

Ashby and Folsom holstered their pistols, which, combined with the fact that they had themselves suggested calling the authorities, told White they truly had no idea what had happened here. He brought down his hands.

"How did you know to come here?" Ashby asked.

"As I said, this is the company Veronica Hammond works with. I just thought I'd check it out."

"So, this is definitely connected to the attack at the Ritz," Folsom said. "It has to be."

White didn't reply directly; instead, he asked if he could go outside to let the city cops know where to go.

"I'll come down with you," Ashby offered. "Tim's gonna stay here to secure the scene."

Folsom gave him a thumbs-up.

White and Ashby remained silent as they rode down the elevator. White still couldn't believe that the three dead men were CID agents. There were no scenarios in which that made sense.

Then he remembered the smartphone in his pocket, and he realized that wasn't entirely true.

CHAPTER TWENTY-EIGHT

Twenty-four thousand feet over New Mexico

Alexander Hammond fought to keep his calm in front of the five members of his protective detail who had boarded the small government jet with him, but the effort required was immense. He had to keep his mind clear. There were a lot of moving pieces to juggle. The attack on his daughter had stunned him. He hadn't seen it coming. At all.

And up until he had boarded the plane and received a call from General Tom Girdner, he had no idea who had been behind the attempt on her life. Girdner's call had changed all that. Expecting a brief account of the off-the-book operation he had asked Girdner to take care of after his failed talk with Veronica, the provost marshal general's report had shocked Hammond to his very core. The three CID agents Girdner had tasked with setting fire to the SkyCU Technology office had been killed before they could execute their plan.

And, of all people, it was Clayton White who had found their bodies.

Hadn't Hammond asked Girdner to pick White up and bring him to a hotel? What was White doing at SkyCU in the first place?

Hammond took a deep breath, but it did very little to calm his nerves. How could the easiest of tasks have turned into a goddamn train wreck? Hammond didn't much believe in coincidences. Someone had beaten him to the punch in Palo Alto. Someone whose goal was the same as Hammond's, but who was willing to go even further to achieve it. There weren't that many people who had so much to lose that they would benefit from Veronica's death and the demise of the start-up she was associated with. In fact, he could think of only two.

Himself. And Roy Oxley.

That cockroach of a man has everything he needs to take me down, and that includes what I did to Maxwell White, Hammond thought. *And that can't stand.*

Hammond's past was catching up to him, and if he didn't act quickly and decisively, it would engulf him and torpedo his vice presidency before it had even started. Even worse, there was nothing guaranteeing that Oxley wouldn't have another go at Veronica. That meant Hammond had to crush Oxley first. It was a question of survival.

And what about Clayton White? *What the hell was he thinking, proposing to Veronica while on duty?* It was so unlike White to have acted this way it blew Hammond's mind.

White was arguably one of the best special agents ever to work for the Secret Service; he had Maxwell's sense of dedication and single-mindedness. If anyone but White had been inside the room with his daughter when the intruders barged in, Hammond and his wife would be planning Veronica's funeral.

Nevertheless, he was going to let the inquiry into White's behavior run its course. He wouldn't intervene. And, contrary to what he had told his daughter, it wasn't because he couldn't or didn't want to. It was because having White on administrative leave suited his purpose perfectly.

The fact was, Hammond needed White's services—and he wouldn't be able to use him if he was under the authority of the Secret Service. Vice president-elect or not, there was only so much he could do without arousing suspicion. He wasn't the commanding officer of JSOC anymore. His soon-to-be position as vice president, although in theory more powerful and influential, didn't allow him the same flexibility. He would have to get used to that.

He was confident White still had no idea that his father's death was anything more than it had appeared at the time, and that was something Hammond could use to his advantage now. Still, guilt assailed him. Not only because he was about to manipulate Clay, but because what he'd been forced to do to Maxwell still haunted him.

When it came to CONQUEST, at least Hammond had the deniability of wartime if the program and its atrocities ever became public. It would be a scandal, but it was unlikely he'd be tried for war crimes. But if the public learned that he'd been complicit in the murder of a fellow American officer . . . he would be crucified.

Hammond unbuckled his seat belt and walked to the minifridge. Coming back to his seat, he looked at the members of his protective detail. Two were playing cards, one was sleeping, and the other two were reading paperbacks.

"What are you guys reading?" he asked, opening his Perrier.

One of the agents showed him the cover of his book. "*Open Carry*, by Marc Cameron, sir. It's about a US marshal conducting an investigation into the disappearance of three people in Alaska. This guy can write, sir."

"You're from Alaska, aren't you?" Hammond asked, but he already knew the answer. "His descriptions are pretty accurate?"

"Yes, sir. Vividly so."

Hammond's phone vibrated in his pocket. He excused himself and went back to his seat.

"Hammond."

"General Girdner, sir," the provost marshal general said. "My phone is secure."

Hammond covered the speaker with his hand. "Gentlemen," he said to the five Secret Service agents. "I need ten minutes."

The special agent who'd been reading the Marc Cameron book woke up his buddy, who'd been sleeping in the seat next to him, with a quick elbow jab, and then they both joined the other three at the front of the plane.

"What's up, Tom? Any more news coming from Palo Alto?"

"Reports indicate that Drain is down. In fact, it's been completely wiped out."

That was the first bit of good news Hammond had heard all day.

"You were right, sir," Girdner continued. "Whoever took down our guys had the exact same objective we did."

"We both know who's behind this, Tom."

"Roy Oxley."

"Right."

"May I ask what you have in store for Clayton White?" Girdner asked.

Hammond frowned. He didn't like to be quizzed by his subordinates. "Why is that of any importance to you?"

"Do I need to remind you that we're six weeks away from inauguration? Both our necks are on the line here, Alex," Girdner said.

"And do I need to remind you that Oxley tried to assassinate my daughter?" Hammond hissed back through clenched teeth. "Are you asking me to let this go?"

"Of course not," Girdner replied, his tone apologetic. "I'm just trying to put things in perspective. I don't want this thing with Oxley to escalate any further than it needs to. Oxley is dangerous, and resourceful."

"Even more reason to go after him now. Oxley is a bully, Tom. We can't let bullies run the schoolyard."

It took a moment for Girdner to reply, but when he did, Hammond saw that his friend had put two and two together.

"That's why you need Clayton White," he said. "You're going to send him after Oxley."

"Clay's gonna get the job done," Hammond assured him. "I know how he operates."

"You're playing with fire," Girdner warned him. "If Clayton learns what you did to Maxwell, he'll—"

"He won't," Hammond growled. "And don't ever mention this to me again. Understood?"

Girdner's reply was curt. "Anything else, Mr. Vice President-Elect?"

"Don't get fancy with me, Tom, or you can kiss your nomination goodbye," Hammond replied before he ended the call.

During CONQUEST, Girdner, then a brigadier general, had been the commanding officer of the Army Corrections Command. His assistance had been needed when it came to the actual design of the interrogation program. Girdner was due to retire at the end of the month, and it wasn't a secret that the president-elect, under the advice of Hammond, was going to nominate him as secretary of defense. Hammond didn't think Congress would object to a waiver for Girdner under the National Security Act of 1947—the law that stipulated that the secretary of defense had to be a civilian well removed from military service.

Hammond and Girdner had always seen eye to eye. Trust had never been an issue between them. Hammond hoped it would stay that way.

CHAPTER TWENTY-NINE

Naval Air Station Fort Worth, Texas

Veronica was getting desperate for information. She had tried calling Noah, but he hadn't answered his phone. Same thing for the other members of her team.

Why aren't they taking my damn calls? she fumed. She was seriously considering escaping her protective details. She needed to head back to California to assess the damage to Drain. She couldn't stand being kept in the dark.

She had already spotted where one of the Secret Service cars was parked. She had seen Special Agent Myers climb out of it. Myers, who had been seated next to her on the plane, had left the keys on the kitchen counter before heading toward the guest bedroom for his four-hour break. It would be child's play for her to grab the keys and slip out of the house through the bathroom's window. Leaving the military base unnoticed would be drastically more challenging. She was still working on her plan when her phone chimed with a text message.

It was from Clay.

Three CID agents were found dead inside the offices of SkyCU.

Just when she thought the situation couldn't get worse, it did.

What were they doing there?

Instead of texting back, Clay called her.

"Where are you?" she asked him as soon as he was on the line.

"Just outside the SkyCU building," White replied. "I'm the one who found them."

Veronica didn't know what to think. There was too much unanticipated information coming in at the same time. "What were you doing there?"

"After our last conversation I decided to stop by," White explained. "You sounded so worried I thought I'd give you a bit of comfort by checking out the place."

"Was anyone else hurt?" she asked, suddenly worried about her teammates.

"No. Just the three CID agents," White said.

"Drain is gone," she said, hearing the tension in her voice. "Completely wiped. Noah told me the only way to do that was by someone downloading malware directly onto our servers."

"You mean in person? Here at the SkyCU office?" White asked.

"Correct," Veronica confirmed. "Do you think that's what the CID agents were doing there?"

Why was she thinking about her father again?

"There's no way to know for sure, I'm afraid, but if I was a betting man, I'd say that they were probably there to secure the place, not to wipe Drain off your servers."

"Who killed them, then?" she asked.

"My guess? Whoever installed the malware," White replied. "And before I go, does the name Girdner ring a bell?"

"Tom Girdner? I don't know him personally, but if you're talking about the provost marshal general, yes. I know of him. He's one of my dad's friends. Why?"

"Why? The provost marshal general is in charge of the CID, right?" White said. "I just wanted to confirm. I'll call you back as soon as I have more concrete news."

Clay's hesitation hadn't lasted long. Just a beat, really. But she had noticed it. And she didn't like it. For some reason, her fiancé hadn't been totally straightforward with her.

CHAPTER THIRTY

San Francisco, California

White rolled out of bed and yawned. He looked at his watch. He'd slept for less than an hour. Ashby and Folsom had driven him back to San Francisco once the police had taken his statement. They had checked into a hotel and called it a night. His last conscious thought before falling into a dreamless sleep had been of Tom Girdner.

White had never met the general, but he had heard good things about him, mostly from Hammond. Like Hammond, Girdner was supposedly a straight shooter. His name had been mentioned in the news recently as a possible pick for secretary of defense in the next administration. Since he was a friend of Hammond's, that made sense. What didn't make sense was that the phone White had seized from the dead CID agent had registered no less than four missed calls from Girdner, all of them prior to White finding the bodies. There had been no more calls since then.

There were two things White had difficulty understanding. The first was why a CID special agent would receive four calls directly from the provost marshal general. General officers didn't call warrant officers, especially in the middle of the night. They just didn't. The second issue White was struggling with was the way the missed calls showed on the CID agent's phone. It read *GIRDNER—4 MISSED CALLS.*

Unless he was wrong, that meant that Girdner had either made the calls from his personal phone or that the CID agent had already logged into his contact list the specific number Girdner had called from. Which kind of led back to the first issue.

To complicate things a bit further, Ashby and Folsom had also mentioned at the coffee shop that it was General Girdner who had called their commanding officer to request their assistance in dealing with him. White wondered if it would be a wise idea to mention his concerns to Hammond. Maybe Hammond could shed some clarity on why Girdner had sent CID agents to the SkyCU Technology office?

Reaching his arms toward the ceiling, White performed a quick three-minute stretching session to get his blood moving, before completing two series of push-ups, sit-ups, and burpees. Once he was done, he examined the clothes the CID agents had gotten for him. In addition to the underwear, there was a pair of blue jeans, a white collared shirt, a navy-blue light jacket, and a pair of brown boots. That would have to do.

For someone who had slept for less than sixty minutes, White felt surprisingly refreshed. He headed to the bathroom and turned on the shower. He wanted the water as hot as he could stand. Using the razor and toothbrush from the courtesy kit the CID agents had given him, he quickly shaved and brushed his teeth. The skin on his face was still tender, but at least the colors hadn't gotten worse. With a pair of sunglasses, he'd look okay. He spent five glorious minutes under a powerful stream of hot water. Planting his outstretched hands against the tile wall in front of him, White leaned forward and brought his head down. He let the scalding water loosen his tensed muscles and massage his back and neck.

Once out of the shower and wrapped in a towel, White turned on the television to see if there were new developments. He watched the news as he got dressed. The clothes he'd been given were a bit too large for him, by maybe a size or two, but they were comfortable, and the boots fit perfectly. He had just turned on the coffee maker when someone knocked on his door. He looked through the peephole and recognized Warrant Officer Ashby. The CID agent was holding two large coffees in unbranded paper cups.

"Come in," White said, opening the door.

Ashby entered and looked at the coffee maker, which had started percolating, and handed White one of the coffees. "This one isn't crappy," he said. "I got it from the lobby. It's surprisingly good."

White tasted the hot drink, enjoying the burst of subtle flavors. He wasn't a coffee snob by any means, but the air force had taught him the benefits of a good cup of joe. He drank it black because most of the time he didn't drink it for the taste. One of the best coffees he'd ever had he had drunk from a tin cup in Afghanistan. One of the PJs had concocted it himself. The brew had been as thick and black as motor oil. And White had loved it, especially the slapped-in-the-face effect it gave him.

"Hammond will be here in about ten minutes," Ashby said. "Then me and Tim are off."

White nodded and shook Ashby's hand. "Thanks for the coffee," he said.

"Yeah, no problem," Ashby replied, opening the door. As he was about to exit, he turned toward White and said, "They say you killed two guys and stabbed another one in the back, and that you're the one who saved the vice president-elect's daughter. Is that true?"

The question caught White off guard. "Between you and me, Veronica Hammond played a huge role in saving her own life," he said.

Ashby looked at him for a moment and then said, "She does look kind of badass, doesn't she?"

White smiled and thanked the CID agent once more for the coffee. Once Ashby had left, White picked up his phone from the night table and typed a text to Veronica.

About to meet with your father. Love you.

Her reply was instantaneous. WHY???

He said he wants to talk to me face to face. I'll text when we're done.

White placed his phone in his jeans pocket and drank a few more sips from the paper cup as he watched the news. The anchor was saying that the authorities hadn't yet identified the perpetrators of the attack at the hotel, which wasn't surprising. The FBI and Secret Service would do their best to delay any information that could be detrimental to their investigation. Keeping the media at bay was going to be a full-time job—an impossible task, really. White knew how the game was played. A senior FBI or Secret Service official, usually one with only a few months left before retirement, would leak something juicy in exchange for future consideration for a contributor job with the network.

He was considering topping up his paper cup with some of the coffee from the coffee maker when there was a knock at his door. Before he could reach the door, it swung open and two Secret Service agents entered. Both wore dark suits, white shirts with no ties.

"Hey, boss," one of them said. "He's on his way up."

Before White had a chance to say that he wasn't the boss anymore, the other agent spoke into the microphone at his wrist and let the rest of the protective detail know the site was green and that Angler was clear to enter White's hotel room. *Angler* was the code name the Secret Service had assigned to Alexander Hammond. Since Hammond's love for fishing was notorious, White thought the name fitting.

"Thanks," White said. "You guys came directly here from the airport?"

The agents nodded and stepped out of the room to take positions outside. A few seconds later, Hammond came in. The door shut behind him, and he looked at White.

"Holy shit, Clayton," he said, dropping the briefcase he carried on the bed.

"It's not as bad as it looks, sir," White said.

Hammond looked around the room, saw the coffee maker, and poured himself a cup using one of the hotel mugs. Hammond added a couple of creamers and some sugar. White watched him take an experimental sip.

"As you can imagine, there are a lot of things I want to discuss with you," Hammond said.

"I understand, sir," White replied.

"But there's only one thing I'll say about yesterday's tragedy." Hammond's eyes were dark and unreadable. They were neither friendly nor aggressive. Just intense. "I'm glad you were next to her when it happened. And for that, I'll always be grateful."

That wasn't what White had expected him to say.

"Thank you, sir," he said after a few seconds.

"But let me be crystal clear about something, okay?"

Here it comes, thought White, realizing he had stopped breathing.

"It was a stupid move to propose while on duty," Hammond said. "I don't know what you were thinking, or why you'd think that could fly, but I'm not gonna intervene in any way to rescue you from this mess. You're on your own, and frankly, I think you deserve to be fired."

White had never expected Hammond to interfere with the investigation, nor would he have asked for it. There was nothing in his statement White disagreed with.

"Yes, sir."

Hammond took a long sip from his mug, and then said, "That doesn't mean I won't speak highly of you at the inquiry."

"Thank you, sir," White replied. Had Hammond just offered him an olive branch?

"As for Veronica, and as much as I'm disappointed by the way you chose to proceed, I think you guys are perfect for each other."

It was as if an enormous weight had been lifted from his shoulders. White was relieved to know he wouldn't have to fight Hammond over marrying his daughter. On any other day, that would have been enough to lift his spirits to new heights. But not today.

"Means a lot to me, sir," White said, extending his hand.

Hammond shook it. He then picked up his briefcase and sat in one of the armchairs around a small table. He pulled out a sheaf of documents and invited White to sit in front of him.

"Now that we've cleared all our personal stuff out of the way, let's talk business." He slid the documents across the table. "But first, you'll need to sign those."

White rapidly looked through the paperwork. "A nondisclosure agreement?" he asked, confused.

"You're wrong, Clay," Hammond said. "This is your ticket to go after the person who tried to kill your fiancée."

CHAPTER THIRTY-ONE

Oxley Vineyards
Kommetjie, South Africa

Oxley watched his wife's fingers fly over the keys of her laptop. She'd been at it for an hour, only stopping occasionally to sip from the can of energy drink at her side, calling up file after file from the SkyCU Technology servers they'd successfully hijacked.

"You're sure they won't be able to trace it back to here?" Oxley asked for the fourth time.

Adaliya stopped typing and looked over to him, clearly annoyed with the disruption. "Seriously? How many more times will I have to tell you? It's impossible," she replied, flexing her hands and fingers over the keyboard. "Every bit of data has been uploaded to an untraceable third-party cloud."

Adaliya arched her back and stretched her arms above her head. Oxley moved in behind her and started massaging the base of her neck.

"Keep talking," he said, trying to understand.

Adaliya let her head drop forward and said, "The instant Krantz's device infected the main server, it was game over for them. And even if they could somehow find the lines of malicious coding associated with the malware, they'd have no way of knowing where it came from since the attack came from within their own server. If we had hacked into their system through regular means, my answer would be different."

That part Oxley had no problem understanding. It was the other chunk of information with all the technical terms he had difficulties with.

"Tell me again about the part that worries you, and please, make it simple for me," he said.

His wife gently removed his hands from her shoulders and turned her head to look at him. Oxley didn't want to give her the impression he didn't fully grasp what she had already explained to him, but her smile told him she knew. He wasn't fooling anyone. Then her face changed, and she said, "I have a feeling I'm not the only one accessing the raw data and the design files of the new Drain application."

"All right. What makes you say that?"

"The inner class isn't protected, Roy," she said, her fingers once again hovering over the keys. "The default level of access control to the data field isn't what I thought it would be. See?"

Adaliya pointed her right index finger to a line of code in the middle of her screen. She tapped on it to emphasize her point. Oxley had absolutely no idea what he was looking at, but he trusted his wife. She'd learned how to code during her first pregnancy and had only gotten better since then. She had even configured a couple of mobile applications that were still being used by her previous law firm.

"That's the issue I'm having," she said. "There are three access-modifier keywords. This particular one is public. It's not private or protected."

"And that means what, exactly?" Oxley asked, leaning toward the screen.

"What it means for us is that this data field, the one specific to the Drain mobile app, can be accessed by anyone with access to the malware."

"The Chinese MSS," Oxley said, talking about the Ministry of State Security, China's intelligence service.

"That's what I think, baby," Adaliya said.

Oxley wasn't angry or surprised. It would have been naive of him to think the MSS hackers hadn't built a sophisticated back door into their malware to exploit. In the last ten years, the Chinese government's reputation for hacking had become legendary. It was a numbers game, really. China's top 2 percent of programmers—their best—were greater in number than the entire profession in the United States, England, and Canada combined.

Oxley had no special love for the Chinese government. In fact, he more often than not thought of them as hostile to his business interests. Oxley considered himself a patriot. He wouldn't willingly allow the Chinese spies access to information or technical data he felt could compromise the security of Great Britain or, to a certain extent, the United States. Sure, Drain was a revolutionary tool for archaeology enthusiasts, but Oxley highly doubted there was any actual groundbreaking technology behind the application. The technology used for the application already existed. The novelty of Drain was in its implementation. It was the first mobile app to utilize crowdsourcing and satellite images to discover new archaeological sites or shipwrecks. It was a user-friendly application that people could use during their lunch break at work.

Anyway, it was too late to do anything about the back door into the malware—not that Oxley or Adaliya would have known how to block the exploit anyway. The Chinese had gained access, which in Oxley's opinion was a very small price to pay to ensure that the updated Drain mobile application would be delayed long enough for him to clean up the site off the Arabian Peninsula. Once the Chinese government realized there was nothing in Drain they didn't already know or hadn't stolen before, they would switch their attention to something of more value.

"Now that we've secured the data, what do you want me to do with it?" Adaliya asked.

"Erase it," Oxley replied. "Delete it all."

———

Oxley thought about offering his help to Adaliya, but there was something particularly sexy about watching his wife go through the motions of preparing dinner. It helped soothe the unrest inside him too.

A preemptive move against Alexander Hammond was the right play. The more he thought about it, the more convinced he became. Knowing Hammond, the man would retaliate. He wouldn't let the attempt on his daughter's life go unpunished. But Hammond was a hard target. He was well protected. With the attack on Veronica, the Secret Service would certainly raise the threat level against him, making it almost impossible for Krantz or a third party to breach the layers of security surrounding him. Oxley didn't want to have to look over his shoulder for the rest of his life. He had to find another way to get to Hammond, and an idea had just started to form in his mind.

He wanted to ask his wife for her opinion, but he didn't dare interrupt her, so he just watched Adaliya singing and moving her hips as she seasoned the meat. He took two wineglasses from a cabinet and grabbed the decanter into which he had poured a bottle of Oxley Winery Pinotage. By the time he handed his wife a glass, she was done rubbing the meat with the spices and the fresh herbs she had cut from the garden earlier in the afternoon and had just set the filet mignon in the pan. They touched their wineglasses together, then swirled the red liquid around their glasses before they inhaled the pinotage's aroma. They then examined the wine's legs—the streaks that trickled down the side of the glass after the wine was swirled. They both sipped, swishing the wine around their mouths before swallowing.

"So?" Oxley asked, looking eagerly at his wife. "Are we there yet?"

He watched her repeat the process. "It's good, but it's not ready."

"Yeah, I know," he said, disappointed. The minute the wine had touched his tongue, he had known the wine wasn't ready. "Pierre has his work cut out for him."

"You think he's the right man for the job?" Adaliya asked.

Oxley cocked his head, sensing a hesitation from his wife. "Why do you ask?"

She smelled her wine again, then swirled it once more around her glass. "I'm not sure, Roy. There's something about him. A vibe."

"He has a stellar résumé," Oxley said. "He worked at some of the best restaurants in Los Angeles and San Francisco."

"I know," retorted Adaliya. "I'm well aware of his credentials."

"And," Oxley continued, smiling at her, "he knows how to run a winery. We need this to work."

His wife sighed, which was never a good sign.

"Listen, I know what you're saying, honey," he said, trying to make amends. "I have my doubts about him too. I'll put a team on him for a few weeks, okay? Until we're sure he's legit. How does that sound?"

"We're so close. We're so damn close," she reminded him. "I want us to cover all angles. That's all."

"I know," he said, thinking about all the major social development projects they would be in a position to financially support once they received the funds from Le Groupe Avanti.

Adaliya had already recruited local innovative millennial entre-preneurs to lead hard-impacts programs in underserved settlements in and around Cape Town. Despite the relatively small amount of money Oxley had poured into the projects thus far, the equivalent of US$5 million, Adaliya had seen some meaningful changes. It didn't take much to empower the families living in the settlements. They just needed a fair shot and the tools to succeed.

He and Adaliya were the future of South Africa. Their five children needed them to succeed. The South African people needed them to succeed.

"This is bigger than us, my love," Adaliya said.

Oxley nodded, and they clinked their glasses.

Adaliya sipped the wine and cringed. "Oh God, I was really hoping this would be much better."

Oxley chuckled and took her glass and threw its contents into the sink. He did the same with his. He grabbed two beers from the fridge.

She smiled at him. "What's our next move?"

"I'm gonna call Krantz and ask him to do one more thing for me while he's in the States. And . . ." He took a deep breath.

"What is it?" she asked, raising an eyebrow.

"I want you and the kids to move back to London," he said.

Adaliya made a face. Clearly she wasn't thrilled with the idea.

"Please, do it for the kids," Oxley pleaded. "Out of an abundance of caution, of course."

"You think Hammond will strike back? At us?"

Oxley took a swig from his beer. "Unlikely," he said, deciding not to share his true feelings with her.

"But you still want us to leave our home," she said, a certain sadness creeping into her voice. "I know you, Roy Oxley," she continued. "You wouldn't ask if you didn't feel threatened."

She was right, of course. Hammond had successfully run countless black operations at JSOC. He had mastered the art of operating in the shadows. CONQUEST was the perfect example. Oxley couldn't predict exactly how Hammond would come for him.

"It will be much easier to protect you and the kids in London, Adaliya. And, more importantly, Hammond wouldn't dare run an op against us on British soil. That would be madness."

That seemed to convince her. Her legal mind was now at work, probably calculating the odds of an American covert operation in London and coming to the conclusion that they were nil.

Oxley gently grabbed his wife's forearm. She seemed to hesitate for a moment but walked into his embrace. He wrapped his arms around her and held her in silence.

"Okay, I'll go to London," she said after a while. "For the kids."

He breathed a sigh of relief. He looked into her eyes reassuringly and said, "Thank you. I'll join you guys as soon as I can."

She shook her head. "Finish what you've started, Roy," she said, her voice hard and cold. "Do *whatever* you must. Then, come back to us."

He buried his face in her hair, knowing it might be a while before he had the chance to watch her cook again. "Okay," he said. "I will."

CHAPTER THIRTY-TWO

San Francisco, California

White signed the papers Hammond had pushed his way.

Never before in his career had White been asked to sign such legal documents. As a combat rescue officer assigned to JSOC and then as a Secret Service special agent, he was expected to keep confidential and delicate information to himself. He would never willingly compromise himself or expose his protectees, his colleagues, or his country to danger. White had proven himself capable of keeping his mouth shut, and Hammond knew that. Which made the need to sign this nondisclosure agreement quite unusual. But if signing these documents allowed him to hunt down whoever had tried to kill Veronica, White was all for it.

"I know this is somewhat peculiar, but you'll understand why this was needed," Hammond said, putting the papers back into his briefcase.

White looked at Hammond with a *Now what?* expression. Hammond sat back in his chair and crossed one leg over the other. Even seated, the man had a commanding stature. A few months ago, at the vice presidential debate during the campaign, Hammond had destroyed his adversary. But he had done so with finesse, using strong policy points instead of attacking his rival personally. In White's opinion, it was during this debate that the American people learned what he had himself known for years. Hammond was an intransigent but charismatic man with an imposing physique and an even more imposing reputation. When he spoke, people listened. White wasn't immune to that.

"Years ago, at the height of the war on terror, the United States government, in collaboration with its British and Australian allies, commissioned a special unit tasked with investigating corruption within the upper echelons of the coalition forces. The operation, known only to a select few within the three governments involved, was code-named CONQUEST. Your dad was in charge of the US component of the operation."

That was news to White. His dad had never mentioned this to him. But from what he knew about Maxwell, this was exactly the kind of thing his father would have been involved with.

"On the British side, the man responsible was a former SAS operator turned MI6 agent named Roy Oxley," Hammond continued.

"I never heard the name," White said.

"I'm not surprised. Oxley keeps something of a low profile, but if you know where to look, you'll find that he has his fingers in many pies."

"What kind of pies?" White asked.

"Money laundering and international terrorism."

White was taken aback. How could a former SAS operator entrusted with investigating corruption have ended up supporting terrorism?

"Am I missing something, sir? I just don't see this happening."

Hammond suddenly grew solemn. White watched him take a deep breath.

"Your father had him arrested for corruption," Hammond said, looking straight into White's eyes. "Oxley was kicked out of MI6, and criminal charges were brought against him."

White's heart skipped a beat. He had a feeling Hammond wasn't done. He was right.

"Oxley was prosecuted in a secret military tribunal. A week into the trial, the military judge ordered the charges dropped."

"Why?"

"Nobody knows for sure, Clay," Hammond replied, looking away. "Nobody really knows."

White could tell Hammond wasn't being totally up front. "But?"

Hammond sighed. "Though I can assure you I never believed it myself, Oxley's defense lawyer convinced the judge your dad had fabricated evidence."

White sat back in his chair and shook his head from left to right. "Nonsense," he said. "I don't believe it."

"Neither do I," Hammond repeated. "But Oxley was released from custody nonetheless."

Okay. So Oxley had felt betrayed and had turned against the Americans because of Maxwell. What White didn't understand was why Hammond was telling him this. A second later, Hammond dropped his bombshell.

"I believe it was Oxley who brought your dad's chopper down, Clay," Hammond said.

Hammond's statement was so far out of left field that for a moment, White didn't react. Maxwell's chopper had been shot down by the Taliban. Hammond had told him so himself. He remembered Hammond entering his hospital room in Germany wearing his dress blues. They had talked for a few minutes about White's time in Iraq and about Veronica; then Hammond's face had turned ashy white, and he had told him about his dad. White remembered Hammond's words vividly.

"His helicopter was shot down south of Bagram by the Taliban two days ago. There were no survivors."

But there was something else White remembered. He recalled how convinced he was that Hammond had lied to him about the Apache helicopters catching up to the Taliban. How the Apaches had mowed down all the Taliban fighters responsible.

Yes, it was all coming back to him. It all made sense now.

White looked at Hammond. "You lied to me, sir. You came to see me in Germany. And you lied right to my face." It was a statement, not an accusation.

"I didn't lie, Clayton," Hammond said. "I didn't tell you the whole truth."

"What's the goddam truth, then?" White asked, keeping his overwhelming desire to punch Hammond in the head in check.

"The Taliban fired the RPG, but it was Oxley who told them about your dad's routine and the routes his helicopter usually took out of Bagram. We think the Taliban had numerous teams positioned alongside these routes, waiting for the right moment to strike."

"Why are you telling me this now, six years later?" White asked. "Why couldn't you tell me the whole story then? What changed? I swear to God, you better have a good reason."

Hammond slowly nodded. "If I could go back in time, Clay, I would. Trust me on this."

"Answer the damn questions," White warned him.

Hammond raised his hands in surrender. "I was ashamed, Clay. We knew Oxley was coming after your dad. But we didn't do enough to protect him. I didn't do enough. I failed him, and I failed you."

"And you failed my mom too," White said.

"I know," Hammond confessed. "Poor Carolyn."

White's mother had never been the same after Maxwell's death. She'd been a champion during the funeral, and White had thought she was doing okay, but a few months later, she'd fallen into a deep depression. White had sold the family house and had rented her a nice and bright apartment a few minutes' walk away from his own in New Haven. He'd visited her several times every week, oftentimes staying for dinner. Heather, Hammond's wife, also stopped by often, a gesture White had been grateful for. Then one day, his hands full of grocery bags, he had found his mother lying on the floor. The medical examiner had called it an overdose. White had disagreed. His mom had died of overwhelming grief.

"I should have had the courage to tell you then, Clayton. I'm sorry."

White stared into Hammond's eyes; they were red rimmed with regret.

"Okay," White said. "I believe you. So why are you coming forward with this now?"

"Because Roy Oxley orchestrated the operations against Veronica. The one at the Ritz, and the one in Palo Alto," Hammond said.

White sat straighter in his chair. That Oxley sonofabitch had stolen his mom's happiness. And now he wanted to steal Veronica from him?

No fucking way, White thought.

"Why Veronica? What does she have to do with all of this?" he asked.

"Nothing, except that she's my only daughter," Hammond replied.

"Then what have you done to him to warrant his wrath?"

"Because I was Maxwell's commanding officer, Oxley came to me for help when your dad recommended that charges be brought against him. I refused to even listen to him."

White took a moment to digest what Hammond had said. Then he changed the subject. "Did you send the three CID agents to Palo Alto?"

"A friend of mine did, as a favor."

"General Girdner?"

"Yes," Hammond replied. "After the attack at the Ritz, I thought it would be prudent to send someone to secure the SkyCU office since it's one of the places Veronica visits often. Clearly I was right to think so, since the CID team was ambushed."

"Someone must have been waiting inside," White said. "They were all shot in the head, but one of them had also been shot twice in the chest. All of it before they could even draw their own firearms."

"Oxley is resourceful, and dangerous." Hammond said. "He won't stop until he gets what he wants."

"Veronica."

"Yes," Hammond conceded. "Veronica."

"So what do you want me to do, sir?"

"Oxley currently lives in South Africa," Hammond explained. "Among other business interests, he owns and operates Oxley International Shipping Lines. Does Le Groupe Avanti ring a bell?"

"The French shipping company?" White asked.

Hammond nodded.

"I've seen their blue container ships in ports around the world," White said. "They're hard to miss."

"Well, listen to this," Hammond said. "I've learned that Le Groupe Avanti is seriously considering buying Oxley International Shipping Lines for a considerable sum. I'm talking about a ten-figure deal here."

White considered this. "You think he'll use the money to finance terrorism?"

Hammond placed his elbows on the table and leaned forward. "Either that or another operation on US soil, like the Ritz-Carlton one."

"Am I heading to South Africa?" White asked.

"I want you there ASAP. I need you to do a reconnaissance and to establish a pattern of life on Roy Oxley. Once you've done that, you'll have the opportunity to participate in the takedown."

"A takedown?" White asked, raising an eyebrow.

"His assassination."

White didn't even flinch. He was glad Hammond had asked him to do that. In White's book, this wasn't murder. This was a legitimate operation against a clear and present danger to the United States.

"Is that why you won't push for my reinstatement with the Secret Service, sir?" White asked.

"It is."

"Okay, then," White simply said.

Hammond nodded. "I'll be your only contact," he said. "You won't be talking about this to anyone else. For the first phase of the operation, you'll be operating with limited support. Understood?"

"Yes, sir."

Hammond opened his briefcase, from which he pulled out a cell phone.

"I want you to take this," he said, pushing it toward White. "It's the best the NSA had readily available. It's totally secured. There are two numbers already programmed."

"Yours and who else's?" asked White.

"Someone I trust, and who'll be able to provide you with some guidance once you're in South Africa."

White inspected the device from every angle. It was black and looked like a regular cell phone, but it was much heavier. "Who else knows about this?" he asked.

"For now, no one."

"What if my supervisor tries to—"

"I've already taken care of it," Hammond said. "As of zero six hundred this morning, you're the new special envoy to the vice president-elect. Congratulations."

"So, does that mean I'm officially done with the Secret Service?"

"For now, but my office pays better anyway," Hammond said, looking at his watch. "You'll receive what's equivalent to a deputy director salary."

White remained silent, stunned at how quickly his situation had changed in the last twelve hours. White ran his fingers through his hair, contemplating the situation he found himself in. He had promised Veronica he'd find whoever was responsible for yesterday's attack. This was his chance. Working directly for Hammond gave him the flexibility required to execute the mission. And there was that significant bump in pay too. He did have a wedding to pay for.

"What's the next step?" White asked.

Hammond beamed and tapped him on the shoulder. "You're a good man, Clay," he said. "Here's what I suggest we do."

CHAPTER THIRTY-THREE

San Francisco, California

One hour later, White was still stunned by his conversation with Alexander Hammond. He had to give it to Hammond, though; the man had played his cards well. By forcing White to sign a nondisclosure agreement prior to their conversation, his future father-in-law had placed him in an unsustainable situation. The fact that he couldn't discuss with Veronica what he'd learned from their meeting made him sick to his stomach. Hiding things from one's fiancée wasn't the best way to keep a strong and healthy relationship. White understood that in the interest of national security some things had to be off limits to civilians—that was simply common sense. But what made him uneasy about the troubling intelligence Hammond had revealed to him was that it directly involved Veronica.

Knowing Veronica was in Fort Worth protected by his former Secret Service colleagues reassured him. Though he couldn't share with her any specific details about his mission to South Africa, Hammond had allowed him to contact her to give her a quick sitrep.

"Hey, baby," she said, answering her phone on the first ring. "Weren't you supposed to call me back once you had more concrete news?"

He had indeed promised her that. "That's why I'm calling," he said.

Veronica laughed. "And here I was thinking you were calling because you missed me."

"There's that too."

"Tell me how your meeting with my dad was."

"Not nearly as bad as I thought it would be," White lied. "He offered me a job. It comes with a nice pay bump."

"Did you take it?"

"Well, my first thought was that if we want a two-hundred-person wedding and enough money left over for a honeymoon in Bali, the right call was to take the job."

He heard her chuckle again. Her laugh reminded him how terribly he missed her, how permanent his hunger for her had become, and how difficult it was going to be to keep stuff from her.

"I had Bora Bora in mind, but okay. Bali's a good idea, I suppose," Veronica said.

"Whatever you desire the most, Vonnie," he said. "Who says we couldn't do both?"

"Sure, with that big pay raise of yours. Why not?" Then her voice turned serious. "What does he want you to do to earn it?"

"Mostly investigative stuff," White replied, doing his best to keep whatever he said to her as close to the truth as possible. "I think I'll be traveling quite a lot, though. I hope this won't be an issue."

White heard her slight intake of breath. "You already have a mission, don't you?"

"I'm leaving in a few hours."

"Any chance you can stop by Fort Worth on your way?" she asked wistfully.

"No, but I'll be back in a few days. And I'll have my phone with me."

"All right, then. What about the concrete news you wanted to talk to me about?"

"Your dad and Tom Girdner have absolutely nothing to do with the problems you have with Drain. The same is true for the issues with the servers."

"Well, that's great news, I guess," she said with a guarded tone. "You seem convinced."

"I am."

"I'm thrilled for you, Clay. But I still have my doubts. You didn't see my father's face when I told him the updated version of Drain would come out whether he wanted it or not."

White didn't want to end the call arguing with Veronica. If he were in her shoes, maybe he'd think the same way since she didn't have access to the intelligence he had.

"Can we talk about it when I get back? I'd like you to run me through the conversation you had with him one more time."

"Okay, we'll do that, Clay," she replied a couple of seconds later. It was her way to let him know she wasn't pleased about the consensus they'd reached. "We'll talk when you get back."

170

PART THREE
TWO DAYS LATER

CHAPTER THIRTY-FOUR

Arlington, Virginia

Abelard Krantz needed much more than the twenty-four hours he got to conduct a thorough reconnaissance of the upscale neighborhood he found himself in. Unfortunately, time was of the essence. The clock on the Ford sedan's console said it was just past eleven o'clock. The sun was shining directly into the vehicle, making the inside temperature too high for comfort. Thankfully, clouds were rolling in from the east, moving like a swarm of grasshoppers, rapidly covering the blue sky. The tall trees lining both sides of the street were gently swaying in the wind, their leaves stirring.

Though the street wasn't particularly busy, there was still enough traffic that Krantz's sedan—a rental car he'd procured with an alias—didn't draw any undue attention. With his monocular pressed against his eye, Krantz confirmed that there were still two cars parked in the driveway of General Girdner's Victorian-style residence. The general's wife, a petite, fit brunette with short hair, had arrived around ten o'clock, wearing colorful yoga pants and a tight-fitting pink T-shirt. She had spent a couple of minutes talking with her neighbor before entering the house through its main door. When General Girdner had returned thirty minutes later with two grocery bags in hand, he had parked his Lincoln SUV next to his wife's sedan and disappeared inside the house. Exactly six minutes later, the automatic garage door had slid open, and

Girdner had reappeared with a green water hose. Krantz had watched him plug the hose into a manual sprinkler before once again returning inside his home, leaving the garage door open.

Krantz didn't believe the Girdners had anyone living with them. Their kids were all adults now. Krantz had confirmed all this online, thanks to social media. Grandkids were a possibility, but he doubted it. Earlier in the day, just a few minutes after sunrise, he had flown his drone over the neighborhood and made a couple of medium-altitude passes over the general's house. Back in his car, when he watched the videos, he hadn't noticed anything indicating that young kids were present in the household. He hadn't seen any dogs either.

He glanced once more at the clock. It was time to go. Krantz double-checked that he had everything he needed in his backpack and climbed out of the vehicle. He locked the rental car and walked toward the general's house, keeping an eye out for nosy neighbors or anything else out of the ordinary.

Girdner's garage door was still open, and the manual sprinkler was still watering the front lawn in a circular motion. The general was making it way too easy. Krantz took one last look around to make sure nobody was paying him too much attention, then walked up Girdner's driveway and entered the garage. The interior was tidy and smelled like a mix of gasoline and freshly cut grass. On the right was a beautifully restored vintage Harley-Davidson. It was in pristine condition. On the motorcycle seats were a pair of stylish helmets and matching leather gloves.

Realizing his eyes were lingering way too long on the Harley-Davidson, Krantz forced himself to snap out of it.

Get your head in the game, he told himself. Still a tad jealous, Krantz climbed the four interior steps leading to the door connecting the garage to the living quarters. He eased his pistol out of his holster and screwed the sound suppressor onto the end of the weapon.

He tried the handle. Unlocked.

Krantz froze in place. Was he being played? Or watched? Who would be stupid enough to leave his garage door open and access door unlocked? Krantz reminded himself that for Girdner this wasn't a war zone, or even hostile territory. This was his home. His neighborhood. He had lived in this house for a few years now—five to be exact, if Krantz was to believe the old real estate listing he'd found online—and had gotten himself overly comfortable with a false sense of security, trusting that nothing bad could happen to him or his wife. To Krantz, that kind of mentality wasn't compatible with being in the military. The only explanation was that Girdner had only seen combat from afar. The general's reputation was as a gifted bureaucrat, but he wasn't a warrior. He wasn't like Krantz, or Oxley.

Krantz pushed the door open an inch, waited, and pushed it another two inches. No matter how old the house was, these connecting doors always seemed prone to creaking. This door was no different. Just before Krantz had enough room to slip inside, the hinges squeaked. He stopped breathing and counted to ten. When he didn't hear anyone, he entered what looked like a mudroom, his pistol extended in front of him. He eased the door shut behind him.

The savory smell of meat, onions, garlic, and spices cooking together set his stomach rumbling. The small mudroom led to a hallway, and as he entered it, he made an effort to remember the photos he'd seen from the real estate listing.

To the left along the hallway was the dining room, and Krantz heard the chatter between two people sharing a meal. Wanting to clear as much of the house as he could before confronting the general, Krantz made a right into the hallway. He hugged the wall, his pistol up and at the ready. The first door to his left was open. It was an unoccupied powder room. He continued past an empty bedroom and a small office. There was only one more room left to check on this side of the hallway. Krantz would have bet ten bucks it was the laundry room. A dull noise was coming from within. It sounded as if the clothes dryer was on.

Krantz was less than three feet away when a small woman in her mid-fifties, dressed in purple nursing scrubs and sneakers, came out of the room holding numerous sets of clean sheets in her arms. Embroidered over her breast pocket was the name of a well-known cleaning company.

Shit. The goddamn housekeeper, Krantz thought.

The woman froze in shock, completely immobilized by the sight of the gun aimed at her head. She opened her mouth to scream. Krantz fired two suppressed shots into her heart at point-blank range before any sound could come out of her mouth. The linen fell to the floor, but Krantz was able to catch the woman's body as her legs collapsed under her. He eased her to the ground and pivoted 180 degrees toward the opposite end of the hallway, his pistol leveled, ready to fire at anyone who might have heard something and decided to investigate. One minute later, after no one showed up, Krantz concluded that the tumbling items in the dryer must have covered the sound of his muffled shots. Keeping his pistol in his right hand, he grabbed one of the woman's arms and dragged her into the laundry room, leaving a streak of blood on the hardwood floor.

With one side of the hallway clear, Krantz moved more rapidly. The hallway opened into a large living room to his left, and a formal dining room on his right. He couldn't see farther without breaking cover, but he assumed the kitchen and another smaller dining area were beyond the dining room. He heard someone laugh and the sound of utensils hitting plates. Krantz scanned the living area and spotted the staircase leading to the second floor. He briefly considered skipping clearing the second floor but decided not to take the chance. Even if the general or his wife heard his footsteps, they would believe they came from the housekeeper.

He moved swiftly, but as silently as possible, across the living room. The well-worn hardwood floor had recently been polished to a dark shine. To his right was a stone fireplace with built-in bookcases and shelves on either side, on which various photo frames with pictures of

Girdner's family were proudly displayed. Three modern-looking high-back sofas were arranged around a large square cocktail table facing the fireplace.

Krantz began moving up the narrow wooden steps to the second floor. The stairs creaked slightly, but the carpet runner hushed the sounds of his shoes. He stopped a couple of steps short of the second floor, listening for noise coming from any of the four bedrooms. Nothing. Once he'd checked each and was satisfied no one else was in the house, Krantz hurried back down to the ground floor.

He made his way to the dining area and peeked around the wall. Seated at a square table set next to a three-sided bay window, General Girdner and his wife were halfway through a lunch of steaks and steamed vegetables. A nearly empty bottle of white wine sat in the middle of the table.

Girdner was the first to see him. To the general's credit, he didn't panic, but his jaw sagged open in surprise. The same couldn't be said for his wife. Following her husband's gaze, she looked behind her, her eyes immediately moving to Krantz's suppressed pistol. She leaped to her feet and backed away from the table, knocking over her chair in the process. Krantz didn't react. He didn't move a muscle. He simply kept a stable firing position, his pistol pointed at her husband. The woman tried to keep a brave look on her face, but she was beyond terrified.

"Abelard Krantz," Girdner said through clenched teeth.

His wife's gaze moved slowly from Krantz's pistol to her husband. "You know this man?"

Krantz detected a mix of anger and bewilderment in her tone, which made him smile. "Your husband and I are old friends," Krantz said.

That didn't seem to make her feel any better. In fact, her lips started trembling and her knees were shaking badly.

"What's your name?" he asked.

"W . . . w . . . what?"

The poor woman was so shocked her nervous system was shutting down.

"Your name," Krantz repeated.

"Oh . . . it's . . . uh . . . it's Barbara."

"Before you faint and hit your head, Barbara, why don't you take a seat?" Krantz suggested. "Pick up the chair, sit down—and please, finish that delicious-looking meal of yours."

Moving like a robot, she did as she was told. Once she had retaken her seat at the table, Krantz asked, "Is there anyone else in the house?"

"No," was the immediate response Barbara provided.

Girdner raised his hands and said without hesitation, "That's not true. Our housekeeper is here somewhere. Probably in the laundry room."

Krantz nodded to him, relieved that the general was in a cooperative mood. Looking at Barbara, he said, "Your husband just saved your life, Barb. You should thank him."

Barbara didn't react. She just sat there, looking straight ahead, a dazed look on her face. It was as if she had swallowed half a dozen powerful painkillers. Girdner grabbed his wife's still shaking hand and turned his head toward Krantz, his brows knitting together.

"Please," he begged.

"I haven't asked anything yet," Krantz replied. "But you don't need to worry about your housekeeper; she won't surprise us."

Girdner swallowed hard. His Adam's apple bobbled.

"Does she know?" Krantz asked, pointing at Barbara with the tip of his pistol.

Girdner shook his head. "She doesn't, I swear."

"I believe you, General," Krantz said. "There's no need for you to swear your life on it."

Krantz placed his black backpack on the table, accidentally knocking Barbara's wineglass over. It hit the floor and shattered on impact. Barbara jumped in her chair. A short cry of anguish escaped her lips.

"It's just wine, Barbara," Krantz told her, as if she was acting like a child. "Everything's gonna be okay."

Krantz grabbed her husband's glass and put it in front of her. "Take his. I'm sure he won't mind. Right, General?"

Girdner looked daggers at him.

"If eyes could kill," Krantz said, resisting the urge to pistol-whip Girdner.

Barbara's face had turned bright red, with tears flowing down her cheeks. From his backpack, Krantz pulled out a set of Bose headphones and a cell phone. He checked the Bluetooth connection between both devices and handed Barbara the headphones once he had confirmed it was working.

"Put them on," he said. Barbara didn't move.

Krantz sighed. "Tell your wife to put them on, or I'm gonna put a bullet in her throat."

"Honey? Honey?" Girdner said, trying to get his wife's attention. "Please put the headphones on. Please?"

Krantz stared at her. Barbara had entered some kind of trance. He'd seen that before in regular army units. Soldiers sometimes acted this way after living through a near-death experience. Krantz pointed his pistol at her, but once again Girdner intervened. He stood up and took the headphones in his hands, gently placing them over his wife's ears. Once he'd retaken his seat, Krantz used the cell phone to play music. He increased the volume until he could actually hear a little bit of the classical playlist he had selected.

"Thank you," the general said.

Krantz grinned. "Of course, General. As I said to your wife, we're old friends, aren't we?"

"Sure, but what the fuck is this all about?" Girdner asked, his tone changing now that his wife couldn't hear him.

For the first time since he'd interrupted the general's lunch, Krantz caught a glimpse of the man he once knew. For a moment, he had thought the general hadn't aged well, that he had gotten a bit too soft. But this wasn't the case. Girdner, like so many other military men, had two different personalities. His family and professional lives were two separate entities. Now it was the general who was speaking. The family man had retired to his quarters.

"What do you think?" Krantz asked. "You think this is a social visit?"

"Did you kill my men at the SkyCU office?" Girdner asked.

"You know I did, Tom. It was a simple case of bad timing, I'm afraid," Krantz replied truthfully. "It was supposed to be a quick in-and-out operation for me. And it was, until your team showed up. What were they trying to accomplish, by the way?"

"Don't play dumb with me. You know exactly why they were there. Are you here to kill us, Abelard?" Girdner asked with a straight face.

"That's not my preferred option, General," Krantz replied. "Hopefully, once I leave your house, the only dead person will be your housekeeper."

Girdner opened his mouth as if to say something but opted otherwise.

"Truth is," Krantz continued, "I'd like us to work together."

"Us?" Girdner asked. "You mean with you and Oxley?"

Krantz nodded. The general seemed to think about this for a moment, and then said, "I wish Roy had contacted us first before going after Hammond's daughter."

"That time has come and gone, General," Krantz said. "Can we move forward?"

Krantz wasn't about to discuss Oxley's decision or thought process with Girdner. This wasn't why he was in Arlington. He wasn't here to make small talk or justify anything. Krantz had shared his concerns about the Ritz-Carlton operation with Oxley, but he'd been overruled. At heart, Krantz was a soldier. All his life he had served other people's interests. And that was fine. He was okay with that. He'd long ago accepted his position in the food chain. Oxley was a great man, and a good leader. By cutting Krantz into his deal with Le Groupe Avanti, Oxley had once again proven to Krantz he'd made the right choice by joining forces with him years ago. If Oxley had made a tactical mistake going after Veronica Hammond, Krantz saw it as his duty to fix it.

"I can," finally replied Girdner. "But I'm not sure Hammond will."

"What kind of retaliation is he planning?" Krantz asked, watching the general's facial expression for any signs of deception.

Girdner put his elbows on the dining table and locked his hands together, his expression torn between fear and deep thought. Krantz was aware of what he was asking of Girdner, so he didn't push. Barbara was still seated ramrod straight in her chair, but the tears had stopped.

"If I tell you what I know, and Oxley escapes Hammond's retaliation, can we finally put our differences to rest now that Drain has been shut down?"

"That's why I'm here," Krantz lied. "That's the plan."

"I'll tell you what I know, Abelard. Then I want you to get the hell out of my house."

Krantz allowed a small smile to cross his lips. "Of course."

CHAPTER THIRTY-FIVE

Cape Town, South Africa

Pierre Sarazin stared at his menu as though it was his first time at the restaurant. Even that simple task had become a challenge. He was glad he had kept himself in shape all these years because he didn't think his heart would have survived the pressure he was currently under if he hadn't. His life was getting more complicated by the minute under the heavy load of his constant lying.

Alexander Hammond had warned him about Roy Oxley, and so had the Direction Générale de la Sécurité Extérieure, or DGSE, France's main intelligence agency tasked with acquiring secret political, military, and economic information from foreign sources. It was getting so damn hard to keep all his lies straight that Pierre's heartbeat was consistently over 110. Even the drop-dead gorgeous view of Cape Town he had from his table did nothing to quell his anxiety. He signaled the waiter and ordered a dozen oysters and paired it with a glass of crisp chenin blanc. When the wine arrived, he closed his eyes and took a small sip.

For years Pierre had used his cover as a sommelier to conduct industrial espionage operations in the United States. There had been almost no risk involved, and the intelligence he had fed to his superiors at the DGSE had made him a rising star within the spy agency. During the last ten years, he'd been promoted four times due to the value of the intelligence he had provided. Targeting visiting foreign officials, American business leaders, and even celebrities dining at the high-end restaurants he'd been working at had been easy and almost danger-free. Compared to the bits of intelligence some of his colleagues risked their lives to collect from unreliable sources, Pierre's intel was always solid.

That was, until three years ago, when by mistake he'd tried to break into Alexander Hammond's phone. At the time, Pierre hadn't been familiar with Hammond, but he had recognized one of the people he'd been dining with: US Senator Peter Shelby, one of the most influential senators in the US Senate and the current chair of the US Senate Select Committee on Intelligence. In retrospect, Pierre should never have attempted to hack into such a prominent politician's phone, but his track record had been flawless, and he had never come close to getting caught. It would have been a fantastic achievement—one the instructors back at the National Academy for Intelligence in Paris would have talked about for decades. All he had to do was stand within one meter of the senator's phone for thirty seconds and let the device the DGSE Technical Directorate had given him do its work. The device was preloaded with bootable software that could break through most four- to twelve-digit screen-lock passwords quickly. Once the screen was unlocked, the device would upload a key-sniffer application to the target's phone that would link directly to a server Pierre kept in his condo. From there, a listener application and a reverse shell would be installed on the targeted phone, giving Pierre and the DGSE unlimited access.

Pierre had honestly believed his stratagem had worked, as it had so many times before. It wasn't until he returned home after his ten-hour shift at the restaurant that he realized how wrong he was. Hammond and two men dressed in dark clothing and carrying silenced pistols were waiting for him in his living room.

"Close the door and lock it behind you, will you, Pierre?" Hammond asked him. Something in the man's voice told him there was no point trying to run away.

"Who are you and what do you want?" Pierre asked, calculating his odds of success in reaching for his pistol under the kitchen sink.

"Clever stuff, Pierre. Really. Quite clever," Hammond said. "It would probably have worked if you'd targeted the good senator's phone instead of mine. How long have you been spying for the French government?"

Despite his best efforts to appear unruffled by the situation, Pierre was terrified. His direct-action training was long forgotten. With the exception of his martial arts classes and regular visits to the gun range, he didn't have the fighting spirit he once possessed.

"Who are you?" he asked, having renounced the idea of going for his pistol.

"I'm General Alexander Hammond. I'm the commanding officer of JSOC."

Pierre was familiar with JSOC. In fact, it was common knowledge that the DGSE's Action Division had worked in close collaboration with JSOC on occasions when French and American interests coincided. Pierre gestured toward an open bottle of Bordeaux sitting on his marble kitchen countertop.

"May I?" he asked.

"Sure. As long as you're not reaching for the gun you keep under the sink," Hammond warned him.

After pouring himself a glass, he took a seat across from Hammond.

"What now?"

"How long have you been at it, Pierre?"

"Long enough," he replied, his heart beating at an alarming rate. "Am I under arrest?"

"Do these gentlemen look like police officers to you?"

Though their faces were partially hidden, the two men at Hammond's side had the demeanor of military personnel, probably tier-one operators. The kind of men who wouldn't think twice about putting a bullet in Pierre's brain if given the order to do so.

Pierre shook his head.

"What does that tell you, Pierre?"

"That I'm not under arrest," he replied, taking an extralong sip from his glass.

Hammond's lips curled into what could be loosely interpreted as a smile.

"Sure thing. But it should tell you something else too," Hammond replied, his tone serious but nonthreatening.

Pierre didn't feel the need to elaborate any further on the meaning of the men's presence. They all knew what would happen if he didn't cooperate. Pierre understood that if an arrest was an option, it would have been the FBI knocking at his door, not the JSOC commanding officer flanked by two Special Forces guys. The way he saw it at the time, three options were in play. The first was the morgue. He guessed that his second option wasn't much more joyful. Being kept in a secret prison for decades wasn't on his list of things to do. Because he was a member of an ally's intelligence service, he feared he'd be considered an extrajudicial prisoner with no right to a fair trial. The third option, the one he had hoped Hammond would suggest, was worth considering.

Pierre willingly opened the door. "What can I do for you, General?"

This time there was no misunderstanding. Hammond smiled at him.

———

Pierre's oysters sat untouched in front of him, but his wineglass was empty.

He had been employed by Oxley Vineyards for a little over three months, and he hated it. The winery employees were competent enough, and the wine could actually become drinkable in a few years, but Roy Oxley scared him shitless.

He wasn't sure if it was because he'd been in the game for too long, or because his previous assignments in Europe and in the United States had been so much less risky, but he was seriously considering retiring. He didn't think the DGSE would mind. Of course, they'd offer him a bonus of some sort to keep him on, but they would ultimately let him go. His pension wasn't a fat one, but he'd saved enough to live comfortably. His handlers at the DGSE had initially been startled when Pierre told them he was moving to South Africa to work in a vineyard. But at the mention of Roy Oxley, they had suddenly become quite eager for him to start in his new position and had even congratulated him for his initiative in seeking employment at one of Oxley's businesses. The financial transaction between Oxley International Shipping Lines and Le Groupe Avanti was something the French government was apparently very interested in.

Pierre's deal with Hammond was simple. From day one, he had been allowed to continue whatever he'd been doing for the French government, with the exception of spying on American citizens. Foreign nationals were, of course, fair game as long as Pierre forwarded to Hammond all the material he uploaded to his masters at the DGSE. In exchange for Pierre gaining Oxley's trust, Hammond had promised not to kill him—and a fat bonus. It had seemed like a fair deal to Pierre.

Since his arrival at Oxley Vineyards, Pierre had had limited contact with Oxley, but the few times they had talked, his gut had told him Oxley was suspicious of him. Oxley wasn't one to give his trust to anyone, and Pierre had a feeling he was already walking on eggshells. Both the DGSE and Hammond had provided him with files on Oxley. Oxley wasn't someone to take lightly. And neither was his henchman, Abelard Krantz, another former SAS operator turned "businessman." Krantz might be wearing expensive suits during board meetings, but Pierre had a feeling the man was a murdering psychopath. His steady, never-wavering voice that seemed always stuck on the same note did nothing to change Pierre's assessment of him.

While he could understand the DGSE's interest in Oxley, particularly due to the upcoming sale of Oxley's shipping line to a French shipping company, he wondered what Oxley meant to Hammond. He'd spent quite a bit of his free time during his first two weeks in South Africa trying to figure out the link between the men, but it had been a dead end. Then, two days ago, Hammond had contacted him. His request wasn't difficult, but it was certainly unusual.

Pierre unlocked his phone and scrolled down to the picture he had saved in a special folder. He zoomed in on the man's face. He'd never seen him before, nor had he any idea who Clayton White was, or even why he was coming to Kommetjie.

What he did know was that Hammond had already deposited a large sum of money in his Cayman Islands bank account. He'd asked Pierre to acquire a weapon.

And to be ready to support White in any way he could.

CHAPTER THIRTY-SIX

Arlington, Virginia

"You remember Maxwell White?" Girdner asked, pouring himself some more wine.

"Of course," Krantz replied, glancing at Barbara. The poor woman was still looking straight ahead, but now her lips were moving. Krantz wondered if the woman had truly lost her mind.

"Maxwell White's son, a former air force officer, is now the head of Veronica Hammond's protection detail."

That caught Krantz's attention. "Maxwell's son is a Secret Service agent?"

"That's what I just said."

"Was he at the Ritz-Carlton?"

"He's the one who saved the day," Girdner replied. "If it wasn't for him, Veronica would be dead. His name's Clayton White."

Krantz had never heard the name before. He was startled that a lone Secret Service agent had been able to stop Van Heerden's well-trained mercenaries. Something didn't compute here. A piece of the puzzle was missing.

"Did you say this Clayton White was a former air force officer?"

Girdner sat back in his chair, leaving his wineglass on the table. He gave Krantz a knowing smile, as if he knew what Krantz was thinking.

"Yes, that's what I said," Girdner confirmed. "What I should have also mentioned is that Clayton White isn't some kind of desk jockey or flyboy. He isn't like me. He's like you."

This was the last thing Krantz expected Girdner to say. "Like me?"

"Clayton White is a former combat rescue officer," Girdner explained, once again reaching for his wineglass. "He spent years in Iraq and Afghanistan attached to tier-one units."

"Okay. So what does Hammond have to do with White?"

Girdner seemed to hesitate, so Krantz casually extended his arm so that the tip of the suppressor at the end of his pistol was inches away from Barbara's head. That seemed to motivate Girdner.

"Hammond is sending White to Kommetjie."

"To kill Oxley?" Krantz asked incredulously. "One guy?"

Girdner lifted both his hands in the air. "Shit, I don't know. Maybe. Hammond never fully reads me in."

There was a note of panic in the general's voice, which told Krantz he was probably telling the truth. What was Hammond thinking? Sending one man to take down Roy Oxley was outrageously stupid, no matter how good the assassin was. Again, something didn't add up. Hammond wasn't an idiot. Far from it.

"When is White leaving?"

"He's already left," Girdner replied. "He's due in Cape Town in a few hours, I think."

With his left hand, Krantz reached into his backpack and grabbed his encrypted smartphone. He powered it up and waited for the phone to acquire a good signal. Once it did, he dialed Oxley's number and brought the phone to his ear, leveling his pistol at Girdner.

"How's Virginia?" Oxley asked.

"The food's crappy," replied Krantz, completing the code they had agreed upon to signal he wasn't calling under duress.

"Good. Talk to me."

"Hammond's sending Maxwell White's son to Kommetjie. Name's Clayton White. He's due to land in Cape Town in a few hours."

There was a brief pause at the other end of the line as Oxley processed what Krantz had told him.

"Very well, then," Oxley said. "Good job. Now get back here. I have a feeling we'll get busy real soon."

"Understood," Krantz replied.

"And please, my friend, take care of the good general for me," Oxley said, ending the call.

Girdner looked like he was going to be sick. He had suddenly turned very pale. Krantz wondered if the general had heard Oxley's last instruction. What Girdner said next answered that question.

"There's no reason for you to kill us. Think about it."

Krantz was surprised that he was still listening to the general, that he hadn't already killed him and his wife. For some reason, murdering them didn't feel right. Girdner hadn't betrayed Oxley. Plus, Krantz had given him his word.

If he killed Girdner and his wife, there would be no end to it. Hammond would never rest until Krantz and Oxley were six feet under. By letting Girdner and his wife live, could Hammond interpret this as a gesture of goodwill on Oxley's part? Could it somehow cool things down just a little? Should he call Oxley back and try to convince him to back down? For a moment, Krantz brought his pistol down.

And that's when Barbara Girdner made her move.

Taking Krantz completely by surprise, Barbara soared to her feet and dove over the table, a steak knife in her right hand. Krantz realized what was happening a fraction of a second too late. For the first time in his life, he had made an unforgivable tactical error. She had played him all along, biding her time for the right moment to strike. For some reason, Krantz's eyes moved to Girdner, and judging by the face he made, the general was as surprised as Krantz by his wife's sudden attack.

Barbara crashed into Krantz with astonishing velocity, pushing him back several feet as she landed on the floor flat on her stomach. Krantz didn't realize she'd stabbed him in the chest until he felt the blood gushing out of his wound. He staggered back, looking in disbelief at the steak knife embedded to the hilt in his chest.

He felt no pain. Odd.

Barbara was in the process of getting up when Krantz shot her in the top of her head. She collapsed not far from his feet without a moan. The general screamed as he leaped forward, his arms outstretched in front of him. By the time Krantz turned to face him, Girdner was almost on him. What should have been an easy shot suddenly wasn't. Krantz's arms had become heavy, and his legs weren't working right either. Krantz fired just as Girdner slammed into him, sending Krantz crashing backward into the kitchen island and his pistol clattering across the hardwood floor.

Then the pain came. And it was searing. It was as if a cold steel rod had been forced through his chest. His breathing became shallow and ragged, and there was a peculiar wheezing sound at each short inhalation he took. Krantz knew what it meant. The knife had pierced one of his lungs, which was now filling with blood, drowning him from the inside.

Girdner was on the floor, too, doubled over, clutching his stomach. An impressive amount of blood had already pooled underneath him. Krantz watched him get up on his knees and slowly make his way to his wife while crying in agony. He didn't get far before he fell to his side.

As he watched the ceiling, Krantz felt the irrefutable grip of fear that came right before death. As the pain became unbearable, he started to cough; foamy red saliva dribbled down his chin. Slowly, his surroundings dimmed into a black fog.

"Fuck," he wheezed through blood-soaked lips as his life slipped away. "Fuck."

CHAPTER THIRTY-SEVEN

Cape Town, South Africa

Clayton White paid the cab driver, including a generous tip, and stepped out of the vehicle, grateful for the fresh air. He collected his suitcase and started toward the main doors of the hotel. He'd taken a nonstop eleven-hour flight from Paris to Cape Town that arrived thirty minutes after the scheduled arrival time. Business class or not, the flight had been long.

The doorman gave White a huge smile and opened the door for him. White thanked him with a nod and walked into the lobby. It was a massive and inspiring modern atrium with majestic views of the sea. The sun, as red as White had ever seen it, had just lost its lower edge as it began its descent into the ocean. There was still a little bit of natural light shining through the lobby's glass dome eighty feet above. In the center of the space stood three glass-fronted elevators. Luxurious sofas, love seats, and armchairs were grouped together in various locations. A brightly lit and busy lobby bar occupied the wall to White's right. At least two dozen patrons were seated on barstools or standing around high tables, talking loudly with their favorite drinks in hand.

White didn't slow down as he walked across the marble floor, heading directly to the reception desk.

"You have a reservation, sir?" asked the receptionist, a tall, handsome auburn-haired woman in her forties.

White was about to give his name but changed his mind at the last moment. "No, it's a last-minute thing. Do you have any rooms available?" he asked, knowing from his online research that the hotel was booked to capacity.

"One moment. Let me check for you." Her long and perfectly manicured fingernails tapped on the keyboard in front of her.

White used the large mirror behind the reception desk to survey the lobby. The space was busy, but not too crowded. There was a constant flow of smartly dressed men and women, none of whom gave White a second glance. A security guard wearing black pants and a white shirt exited the men's room.

"I do have a two-bedroom suite on the concierge floor," the receptionist said, smiling at him. "It has an unbroken view of the ocean. A last-minute cancellation."

White winced. "It sounds lovely, but it's out of my budget," he said, his eyes still scanning the lobby behind him. There was a feeling he'd had since he arrived at the airport. "Do you have anything else?"

She hit a few keys and looked at her computer screen. "Not for the next two days," she replied, shaking her head. "We're booked solid."

Behind him, White noticed a single man sitting on a chair close to the elevators. He looked to be in his midthirties, had dark hair, and was wearing jeans and a pale, open-necked shirt with sleeves rolled up to his elbows. He had a folded newspaper on his lap, but he wasn't reading it. The man seemed uncommonly interested in who walked in and out of the hotel and was in the perfect position to monitor the elevators. White was too far away to see, but he wondered if the man had a coiled earpiece and was in communication with someone else.

"Are you sure you won't take the room, sir?" the receptionist asked. "It truly is our last one."

"I'll pass," White said. "Next time, maybe."

"No problem. Have a great evening," she said, already signaling the next guest to come over.

White wasn't sure why he'd decided not to stay at the hotel he had booked online, but he was listening to his gut. Something bothered him. He just couldn't pinpoint exactly what it was. As he walked toward the exit, he noticed a solitary man leaning against the railing of the second-floor balcony, looking down into the atrium. White had missed him when he'd first come in, as he had walked in the opposite direction. The man was solidly built and had short brown hair turning gray at the temples. He was dressed in black trousers and a loose-fitting black short-sleeved shirt.

Hammond's plan for his first couple of days in South Africa was for White to simply act as one of the thousands of tourists who flocked to the area to explore the wonders of Cape Town. Once White was sure he wasn't being tailed, he was to purchase basic surveillance equipment at different electronics stores across town and contact Hammond's man to let him know he was in the country. He would then wait for Hammond's contact to give him the green light in order to set up the surveillance equipment around Oxley's neighborhood, allowing White to monitor everything from the comfort of his hotel room.

This was something White had done on more than one occasion when assigned to the Protective Intelligence Division. Establishing patterns of life for people known to be hostile to POTUS was part of the job. He'd done similar missions in Iraq when he was with the 24th Special Tactics Squadron. The only differences, and they were pretty big, were that he was alone, without backup, and in a country he didn't know.

White wasn't active on social media, and his name had been kept away from the press, at least for now. No one without privileged access to the Pentagon's database would learn anything about him. He'd googled himself a few times, and the only things to come up were the citations for his military medals. There were no pictures of him nor any other personal information. Still, he couldn't shake the feeling that he was being watched. White was a trained investigator, an excellent close-protection officer, and an even better soldier, but he wasn't a spy. Operating solo wasn't his forte.

Solo or not, White knew something was afoot. And he'd been in Cape Town for less than two hours. He couldn't be certain the two men he had spotted were on to him or that they were even working together, but he would feel much more comfortable if he could establish his base of operations somewhere else.

He exited the hotel and asked the doorman for a cab. For a fleeting moment, the doorman looked at him with a stunned expression. "Yes. Right away," he said a beat later.

The doorman raised his hand, and before he could put it down, a taxi pulled up to the curb. White decided to ignore it and instead walked to the sixth taxi in line. A few of the drivers who had gathered together to chat gave him a funny look, but no one said anything. White knocked on the passenger-side window of the taxi he had selected, waking up its driver.

"You're looking for a fare?" White asked.

The driver, a stocky man with a very high forehead, rubbed his eyes and looked over at White. He leaned across the passenger seat and rolled down the window. He looked annoyed.

"You need to take the first taxi," he said, pointing toward the front of the line. "That's how it works, okay?"

White pulled out his wallet and gave the driver two twenty-dollar bills. The driver snatched the money from White's hand and unlocked the doors.

"Come in," he said.

White didn't bother putting his suitcase in the trunk. He got in the back seat and closed the door. He glanced out the window. The doorman was looking in his direction, holding a phone to his ear.

"Where to?" the cab driver asked.

Behind him, White heard a big engine roar to life and then the squeal of tires. He turned in time to see a black Range Rover speeding toward them.

"Just drive," White urged him, knowing it was already too late.

CHAPTER THIRTY-EIGHT

Naval Air Station Fort Worth, Texas

Veronica stared in shock at the screen of her phone, paralyzed by the conversation she'd just had with Noah and two other SkyCU team members. She felt as though she had been run over by an eighteen-wheeler. In the stillness of the moment, her phone slipped from her hands and her body swayed slightly, forcing her to steady herself with one hand against the wall.

Confused and angry, she wanted to scream at the top of her lungs or lash out at someone, but she was alone. There was no point. What they had feared for the last two days had now been confirmed by the engineers. Everything they'd worked so hard to accomplish . . . all of it was gone. It would take them months to rebuild the app from scratch.

Her throat tightened; tears stung her eyes. She clenched her teeth and squeezed her fists in anger.

For the hundredth time, she wondered who would feel so threatened by her or by Drain to justify coming at her in such a destructive way. A rival corporation? That was crazy. There were other ways to acquire the technology. None of these giant and publicly traded tech companies would risk losing their reputation, and their market capitalization, for sabotage and murder.

No. To be willing to go to such lengths and to risk so much just to kill the Drain mobile app and the brain behind it, somebody somewhere had to fear for their life. There was no other explanation. But again, who?

Frustrated, she kicked the wall with her bare foot, at once wishing she hadn't.

"Fuck!" she yelled out in pain.

She leaned her back against the wall, letting herself slide slowly to the floor as she gave vent to her emotions. But she was too angry to cry. Besides, she had to think. She had to stay focused.

Clay had assured her that her father had had nothing to do with the wiping of the servers. He'd told her, almost reflexively, that the CID men must have been there to protect the place. But that was just speculation, wasn't it? One of Clay's greatest qualities was that he was loyal. It was why he'd agonized about keeping their relationship secret from the Secret Service and her father. But what if his loyalty now was causing him to trust her father when he shouldn't?

The expression on her father's face, his disapproval of Drain, came back to her. SkyCU's servers had been well protected, according to Noah. It had taken someone with high-level resources to do what had been done.

Maybe the resources of the US military.

Somebody somewhere had to fear for their life.

But why would her father fear for his life?

She sat with that a moment. Then she laughed and shook her head. Clay was right. She was being paranoid. The attack at the hotel, coupled with the loss of her passion project, had her emotions stretched way too thin.

Speaking of Clay, she had promised herself she wouldn't contact him unless it was an emergency, and as much as this whole thing upset her, it wasn't an emergency. Still, she'd hoped he would have at least sent her a quick text to let her know how he was doing, and to check in.

Her anger flared again. She was pretty sure that whatever her father had tasked Clay with was related to what had happened in San

Francisco and Palo Alto. But why was it up to Clay when there were undoubtedly plenty of others her father could have assigned to the task? And didn't she deserve to know where her fiancé was and what he was risking his life for?

She glanced at her watch. Her father was scheduled to return to Fort Worth in less than an hour. Impulsively, she sent him a quick text asking him to stop by the house. Then her thoughts switched again to Clay, and her mood darkened. For reasons she couldn't explain, she suddenly grew very worried.

CHAPTER THIRTY-NINE

Cape Town, South Africa

The taxi driver reacted to White's voice and accelerated too quickly. He pulled out from the curb in front of the hotel without looking or signaling and almost nicked the rear bumper of the car parked in front of him. The taxi had barely left its parking spot when the Range Rover slammed into its driver's side panel with the solid crash bar mounted on its front, trapping the cab between the Range Rover and another parked taxi. White heard metal creak as the impact threw him off his seat, his head cracking hard against the window. Slightly dazed, he tried to open the door, but it banged against the parked taxi. Having no idea this wasn't accidental, the cab driver had gotten angry and was yelling obscenities at the Range Rover's driver.

White was trapped. On his left was the Range Rover, and on his right was the parked taxi.

Damn it!

Behind the Range Rover, another SUV screeched to a halt. Men jumped out of the vehicle just as White realized the taxi had a sunroof. Thankful for the warm weather and the fact that the driver had left it open, White exited the vehicle through the sunroof amid the loud objections of the driver. He jumped from the roof of the taxi to its front hood, followed by a quick step onto the parked taxi's bumper. White jumped off the parked car and landed on the sidewalk, not wasting any time looking behind him to see how many men were after him.

A small group of tourists had gathered at the base of the steps leading to the hotel and were blocking White's direct escape path. White sprinted through them, accidentally shoving two young men aside, their unfolded tourist map flapping in the air as one of them fell backward.

He didn't see the hotel doorman until it was too late. Homing in on him like a torpedo, the burly man tackled him. The doorman's shoulders smashed into White's exposed rib cage, knocking him off his feet and sending both of them rolling into the street. The doorman was the first to stop his momentum and scrambled to his feet. He came at White and telegraphed a right hook. White dodged to the side and buried his fist almost to the wrist into the doorman's stomach. The man doubled over and fell face first into the street, gasping for air like a fish out of water.

White dashed across the street and ran between two passing cars. Vehicles honked and swerved as their drivers performed last-second maneuvers to avoid running him over.

He had no time to think. No time to assess what had just happened. He ran. But in the back of his mind, there was a little voice that refused to go quiet.

Someone betrayed you, the voice said as White's feet continued to pound the pavement. Shouts coming from behind told him the men chasing him were also being slowed by the pedestrians.

White took the fact that he hadn't been shot in the back as good news. Clearly, someone wanted him alive. Glancing behind him, he saw five men running. Two of them made a hard left into a side street, probably in an attempt to cut him off farther down. There was nothing for White to do but run like hell. He had to slip away, but this wasn't a city he knew. He'd studied the area around his hotel prior to his arrival, but it remained unfamiliar to him, especially now that darkness had fallen.

The humidity was stifling. White could feel his sweat soaking through his shirt and trousers. His lungs were burning, but he kept pushing. He was now four or five blocks away from his hotel, and the sidewalks were filled with cheap street vendors, tourists crowded in front of them looking for a bargain. Both sides of the street were lined with shops: a men's clothing store, take-out restaurants, and coffee shops. White crossed the street again, aiming for an alleyway he'd spotted on his left next to a pizza place. He sprinted between speeding bicycles and vehicles, narrowly dodging them as he moved.

From his open car window, a taxi driver yelled something at White that he didn't understand. The man was looking straight at him, waving his fist menacingly in the air as he accelerated to block White's path—until the driver had to press the brake hard, almost running his vehicle into the rear bumper of the black Mercedes sedan in front of him. White cut across a last string of cars and hit the sidewalk on the opposite side at full speed. He entered the alleyway sprinting and almost fell on his ass, his right foot losing its grip on a shiny oil puddle. Off balance, his body slammed into the wall of one of the buildings, costing him all his forward momentum.

The alleyway was narrow, dirty, and barely large enough to accommodate the width of a MINI Cooper. White had hoped there would be back doors to the retail shops and restaurants on both sides that he could access, but this wasn't the case. There was nothing but two plain brick walls and a couple of windows far too high to be reachable.

"Damn it," he said out loud as he started to run again. The last thing he wanted was to get surrounded in the alleyway.

An instant later, White stopped dead in his tracks. The two men who had peeled from the main group two street blocks away emerged at the end of the alley.

Behind him, the three other men, all dressed in dark clothes, blocked his escape route.

Out of breath, his chest heaving, White had a decision to make. Either his pursuers had been given the order to kill him, or they hadn't. One way or the other, he wasn't going to let himself get taken without a fight.

The smaller group of two men was quickly closing the distance. Both were approximately the same height as White, but he had at least twenty pounds on them. That was the good news. The not-so-good news was that compared to the three men behind him who were panting hard from the chase, these two looked as cool as cucumbers. As they got closer, White got a better look at them. They were identical twins. Both were slim but muscular and had their hair cut tight. Their eyes were set in a cold, hard stare as they closed on White. Instead of stopping, like most people would when confronted by five men, White summoned up his strength and sprinted toward the twins.

The twins' eyes widened in surprise as White plowed through them at full speed like an out-of-control truck. With his right elbow, he shoved one of the twins hard to the side, the man's head meeting the brick wall behind him with a loud thud. The other twin, his initial surprise dissipated, lunged at White. He almost missed, but one of his hands caught White's left ankle. White fell forward. He thrust his hands out, hoping to save his head from connecting too hard with the pavement, and rolled forward. Something sharp bit into his left palm.

Broken glass, he thought as he landed on his feet. At that moment, he heard the squeal of tires as a white panel van came to a stop at the end of the alleyway. When the side door rolled open and four solidly built men jumped out, White knew he was in trouble. He pulled out the cell phone Hammond had given him. He pressed the preloaded number. The four men stood in front of him twenty feet away, confident and serious, quietly staring at him.

"What is this about?" White asked the new arrivals, forcing a smile to his lips as his right hand slid into his pants pocket, dropping the phone inside.

The largest man, who must have been three or four inches taller than White, pulled out an extendable baton and snapped it all the way open with a flick of his forearm. The man was dressed in a pair of dark jeans, with a long-sleeve gray T-shirt that did nothing to hide the hard muscles beneath. If White had any lingering doubts before, he was now convinced his pursuers didn't want him dead. Which didn't mean they weren't going to hurt him. His initial five pursuers had caught up and were right behind him. He had no way out.

"Roy Oxley wants to speak with you," the man holding the baton said.

"Roy who?" White asked, his senses on alert.

The twin White had knocked over first made his move. The man dove at White's back, trying to tackle him to the ground. White, having heard the man's feet scrape against the pavement, sidestepped to his left and grabbed the twin's extended left arm. Using the man's momentum, White spun him hard in a semicircular motion that once again sent the twin's head smack against the brick wall. This time he didn't get up. The second twin, growling with anger, wrapped his arms around White and pushed him against the wall. White swung his head back as hard as he could and felt it connect with the man's nose. The twin yelled in pain and let go, bringing his hands to his face to cup his shattered nose. White lost no time and gyrated to his right 180 degrees, striking the twin directly on the temple with his elbow. The man collapsed in a heap a few feet away from his brother.

The large man with the baton came at White, who stepped into the attack and caught the man's wrist as it was descending. Had White stayed where he'd been an instant before, the telescopic baton would have snapped his right clavicle in half. White brought his left knee up into the man's groin just as he heard the crack of a second telescoping baton firing out to its full length. The large man's legs weakened, and White stripped him of his baton by twisting hard to the left and up as the man fell to his knees. White used his newly acquired two-foot-long blunt instrument to block the strike of the second attacker, who had swung his baton toward White's opposite arm.

White kicked him in the chest, pushing the man away and creating enough distance to in turn deliver a strike with his baton. He missed the man's wrist, instead landing a mighty blow to his hand. White followed immediately with an even more powerful second strike to the man's leg. A loud snap echoed in the alleyway as the man fell the ground, clutching his broken leg with his injured fingers.

The large man who'd fallen to his knees had already righted himself. He sprang at White from the pavement. White lurched forward and met him halfway, jabbing the butt of his baton into the man's mouth, knocking out a few teeth in the process. The man fell to his side, howling in pain.

Before White could make another move, three of his initial pursuers all rushed him at the same time. White had just enough time to twist sideways when they rammed him. He fell onto his back, feeling the NSA cell phone slip from his pocket. White, pinned down by the combined weight of the three men, couldn't move. One of them swung at his face and nailed White just above the left eye. Another drove his knee squarely into his groin. White let out a strangled gasp as the three men continued to pound him.

"Syop," a frail voice said, just loud enough for White to hear. "Yoy wants him alive."

White opened his eyes. It was the large man. His face was a mess. Blood poured from his mouth through the smashed lips and broken teeth. That was why his speech was so distorted. He didn't look happy. With his left arm, the tall man wiped the blood from his chin and squatted next to White.

"Once Yoy's none we you, you mine. You'll pay fo' that," the man slurred. Then he spat a crimson shower into White's face. "Lif' him up," the tall man ordered his men.

Someone punched White in the gut, driving all the oxygen out of his lungs. The three men lifted White to his feet and zip-tied his hands behind his back. The large man started walking toward the panel van but suddenly turned around, as if he had forgotten something. He stepped forward and delivered a sharp kick to White's balls. Pain racked his entire body. Had the three men not supported him, White would have fallen to his knees.

Someone jabbed something sharp into White's neck. For a moment, he thought he'd been stabbed. But when the pain went away and his vision started to dim, he knew he'd been drugged.

His last sensation was of being thrown into the back of the panel van. Then everything went black.

CHAPTER FORTY

Naval Air Station Fort Worth, Texas

Veronica had just finished eating a ham sandwich when she saw her dad's three-car motorcade stop in front of the house. She washed her hands, placed the dirty dishes in the sink and the mayonnaise back in the fridge, and walked to the small foyer. She opened the door as her father stepped onto the porch.

"Hey," she said, letting him in. She closed the door behind him.

He gave her a quick hug and squeezed her arm lightly. "How are you, Vonnie?"

"Better," she said. And it was true. Her neck wasn't getting worse and had actually regained some of its natural color. With a bit of makeup, she thought she looked pretty good for a girl who'd almost been choked to death three days ago.

Her two-hour talk with the base psychologist the day before had helped too. She hadn't thought she needed to talk about her experience until she actually did, but she'd be lying to herself if she didn't admit the psychologist had given her some kind of emotional and psychological relief. They had penned in another appointment for tomorrow, and Veronica intended to follow through since her father insisted she stay on base for at least another two or three days.

"You want something to drink?" she asked.

He shook his head. An unfamiliar look of concern creased his face. She couldn't even begin to imagine what kind of pressure he must be under. The attempt on her life had certainly added to his stress level. Inauguration day was only weeks away. And then the real work would begin for him. As far as she could remember, her father had always been a champion at compartmentalizing his professional duties from his family life, but what happened in San Francisco had certainly blurred the lines.

It had for her too. That's why she wanted to clear the air between them.

They sat in the small living room, each taking a seat on a pale yellow sofa. She grabbed the TV remote and turned off the television, which had been set on a cable news channel.

"I'm glad you're feeling better," her dad said. "Did you talk to the FBI?"

"I did. They came twice. They were very nice. I spoke with the base shrink too."

Her dad nodded. She heard his phone vibrate in his suit pocket. "Sorry," he said, pulling it out. He scrolled down an unbelievable number of unread messages.

"How many of those do you get per day?" she asked, glad she wasn't the one who needed to read them all.

"On bad days, hundreds," he said. Then he looked at her. "But that's not important. What was it you wanted to talk about?"

"Where's Clay?"

Her father's face changed, and a look of regret flickered in his eyes. It only lasted a fleeting moment, but it was enough to make her anxiety level spike to new heights.

"Dad? What's going on?" She was surprised at how shaky and urgent her voice sounded.

It wouldn't be apparent to anyone else, but it was to her. Her father was fighting an internal battle. She could see it being played out on his tightly composed features.

"Hey!" she shouted. "Look at me."

He met her gaze. "Clayton's in South Africa," he said. "That's all I can tell you, Veronica. I'm—"

"The hell it is!" she roared, leaping to her feet, and surprising even herself with the level of aggression in her voice. "What's my fiancé doing in South Africa?"

Her father raised his hands, trying unsuccessfully to calm her down. "Please, Vonnie. Have a seat."

"I'm not gonna sit until you tell me what Clay's doing in goddamn South Africa, Dad," she said matter-of-factly.

Her father stood up and started to walk toward the door.

"If you walk out of here without telling me what the hell's going on, I'm gonna make your life so miserable you'll wish I'd never been born," she said, her voice fierce and true.

Her father stopped but didn't turn around. Never before in her life had she raised her voice to her father like that. Never before had she spoken to him with such venom. But she meant every word.

His shoulders sagged ever so slightly, and she could swear that she saw his fighting spirit drain out of him. He slowly turned toward her. His face was as pale as she'd ever seen it. Veronica sensed the impact of her words on her father. They had hit home.

"There are things that I keep from you not because I don't trust you or don't value your opinion. That couldn't be further from the truth. I keep them away to protect you—"

"I'm no child anymore, Alexander," Veronica said, cutting him off. She had him in a corner now, and she was going to press her advantage. She continued, her eyes never wavering from his. "I don't need one of your bullshit explanations. I want to know what my fiancé's doing in South Africa."

"You don't give up, do you? Just like your old man."

Veronica couldn't be sure, and she wasn't going to ask, but she thought she detected a note of pride in his voice.

———

Alexander Hammond took a seat at the dining table and gestured to his daughter to do the same, which she did. In retrospect, he shouldn't have come to the house. He should have simply called her and explained that he was too busy to stop by. She deserved the truth, but even when he was ready to share with her, she'd only ever get a version of the truth he'd told White, depending on whether White made it back alive.

Veronica was staring at him, her eyes boring holes into his forehead. She waited for him to start talking.

"I sent Clayton to South Africa to investigate a lead we had," he said, reaching for her hand. She gave it to him.

"Keep talking, Dad," she said.

"What else do you want to know?"

Her face turned red, and she pulled her hand back. "Am I gonna have to ask all the questions? I don't want to fight you over every bit of information."

Hammond almost chuckled. "Glad to hear you don't want to fight," he said, putting his phone on the table.

"Why did you send Clay? I'm sure there are hundreds of FBI or Secret Service agents who could have investigated that lead."

Hammond knew that to be true, and this was where he had to tread carefully. The good relationship he had spent decades building with his daughter was on the line.

"The investigation needed to be run outside official channels," he explained.

His daughter's eyes narrowed. "Okay. Why?"

His cell phone, which was sitting on the dining table, began to vibrate. He was going to ignore it, not wanting to anger his daughter, but knew he couldn't when he recognized the number.

Before he could grab it, his daughter did. "You take it here," she warned him.

"This isn't a game, Veronica," Hammond hissed back. "I'm the future vice president of this country. You can't ask me to—"

"You take the goddamn call here. Understood?"

Hammond couldn't afford to miss that call. It was from his contact in Cape Town. He nodded at his daughter.

"Yes," Hammond said into the phone, looking at his daughter angrily.

"Your man's been taken," Pierre Sarazin said.

Hammond tried to keep a straight face but failed. Veronica must have sensed something had gone terribly wrong because her demeanor changed from angry to fearful in the span of a second. Hammond's head started to pound.

"When? How?"

"They were waiting for him at his hotel."

How was this even possible? Only he, Girdner, and the CIA station chief in Pretoria knew about White's trip to Cape Town. And even then, Hammond hadn't given them any specifics, just the overall picture. He hadn't intended to leak White's location for another three days. He would then have used White's capture as an excuse to launch a covert operation against Oxley.

Now the timeline had changed, and they weren't ready. Hell, he wasn't even sure if it was Oxley who had him. What in hell had gone wrong?

"Are you absolutely sure?" Hammond asked. "Think before you answer."

"I'm sure. I heard it happen."

"You heard it happen? What does that even mean?" Hammond asked, his headache getting worse.

"He called me," Pierre explained. "But he didn't talk. It was as if he knew he was going to get caught and wanted to let someone know."

Hammond supposed this could be true. Pierre's number was one of the two numbers he had preprogrammed into the phone. This was certainly not the way he had envisioned the operation going, but maybe there was a way to salvage it.

Hammond put the call on speaker and logged into the special account the NSA had developed for him. From this account, he was able to monitor the whereabouts of all the cell phones attached to it. It worked like a regular Find My Phone application, but more secure. White's phone pinged back from a small alleyway six blocks away from his hotel.

"Do you know where he's been taken? I see his phone is in an alley—"

Pierre cut him off. "Whoever took him left his phone behind. Or maybe your man left it there deliberately. I don't know."

"Shit," Hammond said, turning off the speaker mode.

"What do you want me to do?"

Although he had sent White to Cape Town under false pretenses, the pattern of life White was supposed to establish on Roy Oxley was crucial for the CIA paramilitary team tasked with White's rescue. Without it, the team would be going in blind. Heck, they didn't even know *where* to go. With so many members of Oxley International Security in and around Cape Town and Kommetjie, the CIA chief of station would never green-light a covert rescue operation. It didn't matter that the station chief owed Hammond his career; he wouldn't sacrifice his men on such a shitshow operation. Not until they had something concrete to go on.

Damn it. Hammond was doing his best to control his anger. He didn't want to show Veronica how desperate he was. He glanced at her. She hadn't moved a muscle since the beginning of his call. He wasn't even sure she was still breathing.

Hammond closed his eyes. He couldn't believe that Pierre Sarazin, a French double agent, was his only chance.

"Find him, and once you do, report back to me," Hammond said. "And, Pierre?"

"Yes?"

"After this operation, you're done for good. You'll be off the hook. And I'll quadruple the amount that was deposited in your Cayman Islands account. Just get this done."

CHAPTER FORTY-ONE

Kommetjie, South Africa

White kept his eyes shut as he tried to block the pain that dominated all his senses. He felt as if his head was going to explode. He tried to open one eye, just to figure out where he was, but the effort was too much. His eyelid had never felt so heavy. He tried to stay conscious, but despite his best efforts, he smoothly slipped into a lethargic inertia again.

The drugs, he thought, remembering the stabbing pain in his neck. *It's the damn drugs.*

He didn't know how much time had passed, but when he came to a second time, the searing pain in his head had lessened to a distant throb. His neck was bent forward, straining his muscles. His chin was touching his chest. A thick drool of saliva oozed from the right corner of his mouth. He couldn't move his legs, nor his arms. He opened one eye. Then the other. A weak light filled his vision, and it took a few seconds for his eyes to adjust and focus.

He cast his gaze around. He was tied to a chair in the center of what seemed to be a wine-tasting room. There was a high vaulted ceiling with dark wooden beams. The walls were lined with oak barrels and huge canvases showcasing the South African landscape. One whole wall was made with floor-to-ceiling windows that looked down on the vineyards. Although night had fallen, powerful lights illuminated the hills outside.

Seated around a high table at the opposite end of the tasting room, White recognized four of the men he'd fought in the alleyway. At least two were armed, their shoulder holsters visible.

"What do you think, Mr. White?" a man asked from behind, a slight, almost nonexistent British accent in his voice. "Do you enjoy wine?"

White tried to reply, but his tongue was swollen and his mouth was dry. He tried to move his legs, but they were bound together with heavy tape around the ankles. He was belted to the chair with a leather strap, and his arms were fastened to the armrests with the same black tape.

White heard the man's confident footsteps behind him. They were neither quick nor slow. It was as if the man had all the time in the world, utterly unafraid of the legal consequences of having a man tied to a chair in his warehouse.

"You did quite a number on my men," he said, entering White's field of vision from the right. "One of them is still at the hospital, and another one has an appointment to see my dentist tomorrow. I have a feeling his dental bill will be hefty."

White recognized the man from the photos Hammond had shown him. *Roy Oxley.*

Oxley was of medium height, with muscular arms and shoulders, and short dark hair peppered with gray around the temples. He looked exactly like what he was: an ex-soldier. He was wearing a pair of jeans and an untucked white dress shirt with his sleeves rolled up. And brown cowboy boots. A bulge was visible on the right side of his shirt at belt level.

"You don't talk much, do you, Clayton?" Oxley looked straight at him and smiled. Then he walked to a small table where dozens of tasting glasses were set up. He grabbed a glass and walked to one of the barrels. He tilted the glass, opened the spigot, and poured a small quantity of wine into the glass. Oxley made a gesture to White that he wouldn't be long. White watched him swirl the wine for a few seconds. Oxley tasted it and seemed disappointed.

"It's not perfect just yet, but at least it's not water, right?" Oxley said, walking back toward White.

Oxley placed the glass on White's parched lips and slowly poured the wine into White's mouth. The wine stung his gums and burned his lips, but he swallowed.

"More?" Oxley asked.

White had a feeling he had to say yes, so he nodded. Oxley looked pleased and repeated the process. Once the tasting glass was empty, Oxley returned it to the table and picked up a wooden chair on his way back. He sat in front of White and stared at him.

"I have to admit that this doesn't happen often, but I'm perplexed, Clayton," Oxley said. "I really am."

White was confused, too, but he didn't think it was the right time to mention it.

"I'm trying to decide if I should trust you or not," Oxley said.

White kept his mouth shut. What the hell was he talking about?

"Are you a man of honor, Clayton?"

"I like to think so," White replied.

Oxley nodded. "Fair enough," he said. "Can I assume you were briefed about my military career?"

White's instinct was to lie and deny, and to try to slow things down as much as possible to buy Hammond some time to mount a rescue operation. He wondered if Hammond's asset in Cape Town had received White's message. He remembered putting the NSA cell phone back in his pocket while the call was still dialing. Hopefully there had been some traffic cameras that had caught the action. With a bit of luck, the NSA could locate the phone and hack the video feeds to see who had taken him and which direction they'd driven.

White shook his head. *Who am I kidding?* Hammond had warned him this was an off-the-book operation. He had no support. He hadn't even told Veronica where he was going, for God's sake. In his haste to avenge his father's death and the attempt on Veronica's life, he had gone against not only his training but also his common sense.

And here I am, he thought, *tied to a fucking chair.*

Oxley clicked his fingers repeatedly in front of White's face. "Are you listening to me?"

"Yeah," White said. "I heard you. I know."

"Tell me what they said about me," Oxley said. "And be honest."

"SAS turned MI6 agent," White said, not seeing the point in lying.

"What else, Clayton? Tell me what else they told you."

"That's it," White said. "That's all I know."

Oxley's eyes darkened, and then he abruptly clapped his hands together, creating a surprisingly powerful bang that reverberated inside the tasting room and would have made White jump two feet high if he hadn't been fastened to his chair. Even the four men seated at the high table and out of earshot turned toward them.

"Fuck you, Clayton White. Fuck you," Oxley said, rage tightening the skin of his face. "I was just starting to trust you."

Oxley got up from his chair and started to pace back and forth in front of White. White's heartbeat picked up, and a fine sheen of perspiration broke out on his brow. He was utterly powerless. He was in control of absolutely nothing.

A real damn shame, he thought, his throat drying up again. His thoughts returned to Veronica, regretting having waited so long to propose.

Enough with the regrets! Veronica yelled at him. *Get a grip, Clay! Come back to me.*

White gave his head a good shake. He wasn't powerless. The game wasn't over yet. The man in front of him had killed his father and had wanted to murder his fiancée. This wasn't something White could let go. If he gave up now, what assurance did he have that Oxley wouldn't give it another shot?

As suddenly as he had started, Oxley stopped pacing and turned to face White, his hand moving toward his holster. It was time for White to take a leap of faith.

"CONQUEST," White said, just loud enough for Oxley to hear him. "They briefed me about it, told me about your role."

Oxley folded his arms across his chest. White was glad to see Oxley's hands moving away from his holster.

"Good," Oxley said. "Did it come from Alexander Hammond?"

White nodded.

"In your own words, then, tell me what you know about CONQUEST."

"It was a special unit, led by my father, General Maxwell White, that was tasked with investigating corruption within the upper echelons of the coalition forces," White said.

Oxley was shaking his head, a huge smile on his face. "Are you being serious?" he asked.

"You were fired," White continued. "But you somehow managed to turn the tables on my father and convinced the judge he had fabricated the evidence against you."

Oxley stared at White for a few moments.

Then he began to laugh.

The sound infuriated White. It was as if Oxley was pissing on his father's grave.

When Oxley finally stopped laughing, his eyes were filled with pity, which was the last thing White expected.

"You're a pawn, and you don't even know it." Then he added, as if he was talking only to himself. "The man has no shame. None whatsoever."

"Why did you try to kill Veronica Hammond?" White asked, trying to regain some sort of control of the conversation.

Oxley pushed the wooden chair closer to White and turned it around. He sat in the chair with his forearms resting on its back.

"In retrospect," he said, "it was a miscalculation."

A miscalculation? White felt his face turn bright red. "Your miscalculation cost the lives of five Secret Service special agents under my command."

Oxley nodded. "As I said, a slipup."

White's blood was beginning to boil. He was close to his breaking point with this asshole. He wished he could free himself from his restraints, but whoever had tied him up had done a hell of a job.

"What am I doing here?" White asked.

"I knew Hammond was going to retaliate. He's not the kind of guy who can't let something like this go unpunished. I get that. So, I asked around. And here you are."

White's gut hadn't lied to him. He'd been betrayed. He was sure of it now. Hammond had lied to him when he said only two people knew about this operation.

What else had he lied about?

Oxley gave White an encouraging smile. "I see your wheels are turning," he said. "I'll tell you what I think. Hammond sent you here knowing I'd catch you. Make no mistake about it, Clayton. He thinks he'll use your capture to lobby for a covert hostage rescue operation whose primary goal wouldn't be your rescue, my friend. No, its primary objective would be to kill me."

A chill ran through White's body. It couldn't be. Hammond wouldn't throw him to the wolves like that. Never.

"You're lying. Again," White said. "I don't know what you're trying to accomplish with your bullshit stories, but I don't believe you. You murdered my father."

Oxley sighed, his disappointment apparent. "I guess this was to be expected."

His hand moved to his hip, and for a moment, White thought he was about to get shot. But instead of a weapon, Oxley pulled out his cell phone.

"Let me tell you something about Alexander Hammond," Oxley said. "It's gonna blow your mind."

CHAPTER FORTY-TWO

Naval Air Station Fort Worth, Texas

When her father's call ended, Veronica remained immobile, shell shocked at the bits and pieces of the conversation she had overheard.

"Clay's missing, isn't he?" she asked. "And don't you dare lie to my face."

Her dad propped his elbows on the table and rubbed his temples with the tips of his fingers. "Yes," he said. "Clay's missing."

"What the hell have you done to him?" she asked, suddenly feeling short of breath.

"I'm gonna fix this. I'll bring him home," he said. "Trust me."

Veronica chuckled despite the gravity of the situation. "Trust you? You have to be kidding me."

He stared at her. "What's wrong with you? You think I wanted this to happen?"

"I don't know, Dad. You tell me. You're the one who sent him to South Africa by himself."

Her father didn't reply. He kept his mouth shut. Which scared her even more. Tears were threatening to fall, burning her eyes, but she refused to let her father see them.

"You wanted this to happen? Help me understand," she whispered, feeling feverish.

"Not like this, no," he said, reaching for her hand.

She looked at her father's outstretched hand in disgust and slapped it away forcefully. He retreated deep into his chair.

"I don't understand. I just don't."

Her father sighed. "The person responsible for the murder of your protective detail, and the cyberattack on SkyCU, for that matter, is a man named Roy Oxley. I sent Clayton after him."

Did her father just admit he knew who had orchestrated the attacks? Veronica was dumbfounded. She had so many questions, but she decided to keep quiet. For now. She wanted her father to keep talking.

"Oxley is a former MI6 agent and a man I've done business with in the past," he explained. "Going through all the proper channels was never an option."

"So you sent Clay? Why him?"

"Clayton is one of the most capable men I know, Veronica. When he realized that Roy Oxley was a suspect, he decided to take the job. To avenge you."

"Don't you pin this on me," she warned him, pointing her fingers squarely at her father.

"I'm not," her father replied. "Oxley is also the man who ordered Maxwell's death."

She heard her own sharp intake of breath. "My God. I thought his chopper was shot down by the Taliban. Are you sure about this?"

"One hundred percent."

"And you told Clay about this?" she asked.

"He knows the whole story. I didn't keep anything from him."

She felt terrible for Clay. Of course he'd go after Oxley. Clay had always blamed his father's death for his mother's passing. Carolyn had stopped living when her husband died.

"What now?" she asked.

"One of my assets is looking for Clay. As soon as we find him, we'll launch a rescue operation."

Veronica watched her father carefully. She'd been grateful to grow up with a father who was quite different from Clay's. Yes, there were times when whatever crisis was going on in the world kept her father away for extended periods. But when he was there, he was fully there. He kept up with everything going on in her life and expressed his pride in her often.

Maybe it was because she considered them so close and she knew him so well, but there was something about the way he had said this last sentence that made her believe that the rescue operation wasn't her father's top priority. Getting that Roy Oxley guy was.

"If you have to pick between arresting Roy Oxley and saving Clay, what will you choose?" she asked.

Her father didn't hesitate. "I'll choose Clay over anything else. Always."

She knew her father had just lied to her face. And in her book, that was the ultimate betrayal.

CHAPTER FORTY-THREE

Cape Town, South Africa

Pierre Sarazin hurried back to the side street where he had parked his Volkswagen Polo. He opened the door and sat behind the wheel. His heart was thumping like an out-of-control bongo drum. In all his years with the DGSE, he'd never felt more alive than now, which, when considered carefully, didn't make much sense, since he'd never been in so much danger either. He didn't think the two could be compatible.

One of the first things he'd done after Oxley Vineyards had hired him was to install new security cameras. Nothing too fancy, but he wanted a nonintrusive system that would allow him to keep an eye on the facilities and the winery's grounds. Pierre's research had taught him that the fierce rivalry between the different winegrowers in the coastal district of Cape Town often led to the sabotage of costly wine-making equipment and, in two separate cases, arson. It was a sensible measure to protect the livelihood of the winery's twenty-five full-time employees. Over the last few months, Pierre had come to appreciate the dedicated men and women who showed up day after day to do the backbreaking work needed to create God's nectar. He had seen them get sticky, dirty, and sore from running all day long, up and down the vineyard hills with heavy buckets full of grapes. Pierre had developed an immense respect for them. Ensuring their safety was the least he could do.

And now he was about to benefit from it too. He unlocked his phone and tapped on the mobile application that gave him access to the twenty-five different feeds coming from the surveillance cameras installed around the property. The application took a moment to load, but when it did, twenty-five small thumbnails appeared on his screen. Pierre scrolled down the list. The cameras had night vision capability, which allowed him to confirm that the fields surrounding the wine-making buildings were deserted.

At least in the area covered by the cameras, Pierre reminded himself. There was a lot of ground the cameras couldn't see, but he didn't worry about that now. He had to work with the information he had. The last six feeds came from the cameras inside the wine-making facilities. The lights were turned on in all the buildings, but he only saw movement in one of them. The newly renovated tasting room. He tapped on the thumbnail, enlarging it to full screen, conscious there were no events planned at the vineyard that evening.

Pierre's eyes widened. He had found Clayton White.

He took a series of screenshots. The quality of the video wasn't optimal, but it would do.

He composed a text to Hammond and attached the screenshots. He pressed send.

Pierre had no idea what Hammond was going to ask from him next. Maybe that was it for him. Hammond had tasked him with finding White, and he had.

Could it really be the end of the road? He certainly hoped so. He was done with this spy shit.

CHAPTER FORTY-FOUR

Fort Worth, Texas

Upset and distraught about his meeting with Veronica, Alexander Hammond felt his mood take a turn for the worse. He didn't know what to think. She'd threatened to wreck his vice presidency before it had even started if he didn't bring White home. Hammond closed his bloodshot eyes and rested his head against the headrest of the Suburban's back seat.

"Everything okay, sir?" asked the Secret Service special agent seated to his left.

Hammond waved him off dismissively. They had a thirty-minute drive to Dallas for his meeting with an influential donor, and he wasn't inclined to spend it discussing his personal life with one of his bodyguards.

He thought of how Veronica had looked at him just before he left the house. His own daughter had stared at him with an expression of revulsion, and she hadn't even tried to hide it. It had been a crushing experience, one that broke his heart. Hammond hadn't realized until now how deep Veronica's love for White ran. He was her rock; she'd made that crystal clear.

He'd promised her that he'd choose White over Oxley, but he'd known when he said it that it was a promise he might not be able to keep. If she knew the truth about CONQUEST, about Maxwell White, about the attack on SkyCU—and God willing, she never would—she'd know that what he was doing wasn't just to protect himself but to protect her too.

No matter what it took, Roy Oxley had to die.

The ding of an incoming text message brought Hammond back to the here and now. His heart rate spiked. He read Pierre's message and looked at the screenshot the Frenchman had attached. Hammond's mind raced for a solution. Then it dawned on him. Maybe, just maybe, there was still a chance for him to come out of this unscathed on all fronts.

He ordered the driver to pull over to the side of the road as soon as it was safe to do so.

"Yessir," was the driver's reply.

To Hammond's left, the Secret Service agent spoke into the small microphone in his sleeve to advise that the motorcade was about to stop. Hammond told him he didn't want anyone else outside the vehicles. The Secret Service agent made a face but nodded. As soon as the Suburban came to a complete stop, Hammond climbed out of the vehicle and walked away from the motorcade. He didn't want the Secret Service agents to hear the conversation he was about to have with the CIA station chief in Pretoria. Not that he didn't trust them, because he did, but since the odds that this whole thing would turn to shit were high, he didn't want them on the hook.

"It's Alex," he said once his old combat buddy picked up. "Is this a good time?"

"For you? Always." The man's voice was rough and tight, just above a whisper. It had been like that since his friend had been shot in the throat during a CIA covert operation in Central America a decade ago.

"Is the team you put together ready to go?" Hammond asked, knowing this was way outside the original time schedule.

"Like, now?"

"Yes. Now."

"The team leader checked in with my 2IC at the consulate in Cape Town earlier today. They're on standby. Why has the timetable changed?"

"New intel," Hammond said, tightening his grip around the cell phone.

"Is this a sanctioned op?" his friend inquired.

"Does it matter?" Hammond asked. "Because if it does, I need to know now."

"I see," the CIA station chief replied.

Hammond held his breath, aware his friend was pondering his options.

"Is the intel solid, Alex? No bullshit."

"Intel is rock solid," Hammond replied. "I wouldn't have called if it wasn't."

There was another long pause. "You'll need to sign off on this," the man said. "That's gonna stay between you and me, my friend, and I'll shred it the minute the team's back, but I need you to cover my ass on this one in case it goes berserk."

Hammond nodded. "You got it. I'll forward you the updated details and everything I've got in a couple of minutes."

"You owe me big, Alex," his friend said. "And don't think for a minute that I won't be cashing in that chip in due time."

Back in the Suburban, Hammond typed a new set of instructions to Pierre. The DGSE agent wasn't going to be happy, but with what Hammond was promising him, Pierre wouldn't be able to resist doing one last thing for him.

CHAPTER FORTY-FIVE

Kommetjie, South Africa

White's energy was depleted. He was psychologically and emotionally exhausted, his head spinning nonstop with incomprehension. At first, he hadn't trusted the validity of the audio recordings Oxley had played to him. Audio recordings were easily altered. But the more he listened to Oxley's explanations, the less his faith in Hammond endured.

Oxley showed him correspondence—approvals and other emails— that proved CONQUEST wasn't at all what Hammond had described to him just a couple of days ago. Still, despite everything, White's brain couldn't reconcile what he knew of Hammond with what Oxley had so clearly and unequivocally exposed.

But upon hearing the recorded conversation between Hammond and a man named Abelard Krantz, in which Hammond shared the itinerary of Maxwell's helicopter flight, White felt as though he'd been stabbed through the heart. *Devastated* wasn't a word strong enough to describe how he felt.

Hammond had been as culpable as Oxley and Krantz in his father's murder. Hammond had sent his friend to his death, then turned around to comfort his friend's son, to pretend to be a surrogate father, to lie to him.

And what about Veronica? Or Heather, Hammond's wife—the future second lady of the United States? Did they know?

No. Veronica doesn't know. I'm sure of it, White thought. *And she can never learn the truth. It is not for her to bear the weight and the shame of her father's crimes.*

Humble, trustworthy, but ruthless when he needed to be, Hammond portrayed the image of the perfect gentleman-warrior. People across both sides of the political aisle trusted him. Everyone knew that the president-elect had won the election so easily because Hammond's name was on the ticket. Vice president for four years, and then who knew? The highest office was well within his reach.

This is pure madness, White thought. *Alexander Hammond is a fraud.*

In front of him, Oxley was on his second glass of white wine, seated with his legs crossed in front of him. The man had said his piece. He was simply waiting for White to come to terms with what he'd learned.

"You know what, Clayton," Oxley said, "this wine actually tastes much better on the second glass."

White wasn't in the mood for small talk. Wine was the last thing on his mind. He felt sick to his stomach.

"Did you do it? Did you kill the prisoners?" White asked, thinking about the real CONQUEST.

Oxley shrugged. "What was I supposed to do with them? Nobody wanted to be associated with these men. They were terrorists, Clayton," Oxley explained. "You were there, too, weren't you? I see it in your eyes. You served. You fought. You and I—we're the same."

White disagreed, but he wasn't about to contradict Oxley while being tied to a chair. He was stunned by Oxley's honesty. He'd at least expected some kind of denial. On the contrary, Oxley was taking full accountability for his actions, although White doubted Oxley would be as forthcoming in a court of law.

"People like Hammond entrusted me with the responsibility of dealing with these human feces," Oxley said. "Once it was clear that neither your country nor mine was going to take them in, I made the necessary arrangements. As per their request."

"Why did you tell me all this?" he asked.

"I want you to understand who Alexander Hammond really is," Oxley said, holding his phone in his left hand. "He isn't a man to be trusted."

"And you are?" White asked.

"Well, I guess it depends who you talk to." Oxley chuckled. Then his voice turned serious, almost admonishing. "But I've held up my end of the bargain and never asked for anything in return. Why? Because it's my duty to do so. Everything I've done, everything I've built, all of it, I did for my country and my family. And I swear to God that I'll spend the next decade building a better South Africa."

What scared White the most about Oxley was that the man was convinced he had done absolutely nothing wrong. To men like Oxley, killing Veronica and Maxwell were simply things he needed to do in order to *keep his end of the bargain*. Oxley, just like Hammond, had lost his bearings along the way and had never realized it. In White's mind, operations like CONQUEST were the kind that brought down empires and turned good men into monsters.

"You still haven't told me what I'm doing tied to this chair," White said. For the last hour, while Oxley talked, White had discreetly and methodically tried to rotate his wrists back and forth in an effort to loosen the heavy-duty tape. But despite his best efforts, there was still no slack. None whatsoever. That meant that for now, if he wanted to keep the slimmest hope of seeing Veronica again, he had to go along with whatever Oxley had in store for him.

"I want you to go back to Washington and tell Hammond to leave me, my family, and my businesses alone," Oxley said, standing up. "I want him to forget the incident in San Francisco and to move the fuck on. Can you do that, Clayton? Can you do that for me?"

The incident in San Francisco. The way Oxley said it made White's stomach churn. But he was in no position to say no, so he nodded.

"And you tell him that if I even feel a whiff of danger coming from him, all bets are off," Oxley continued. Then a devious smile appeared on his lips, and he said, "But if you feel the need to kill him in his sleep for what he's done to you, I won't hold it against you."

White's eyes moved to the end of the tasting room, from where one of Oxley's men was walking rapidly toward them.

"Sir?" the man said when he was still twenty or so feet away.

Oxley turned to face him. "What is it?"

White tried to hear what they were saying, but Oxley had his back to him, and his man was speaking too low.

Oxley twisted his head and cast a long and suspicious look at White, as if White had something to do with whatever his man had just told him. Oxley tapped his man on the shoulder and signaled the rest of his men to join him.

White had no idea what was going on, but there was definitely some kind of last-minute emergency. Whatever the situation was, he wanted to be ready. Unfortunately there wasn't much he could do in his current condition. Oxley left one man behind and exited the room with the three others in tow. To White's dismay, the remaining man was one of the twins from the alleyway.

The man slowly walked toward White, a cruel smile on his lips.

"My brother's in the hospital because of you," he said. "He asked me to pass along a message."

The man removed his light jacket and let it fall to the floor, next to the cell phone and documents Oxley had left behind. The twin took his time stretching his arms, his legs, and even his core muscles.

A tight, anxious feeling crept into White's chest. The man was going to beat him to a pulp.

The first punch caught White right on the chin, and it came so fast that the pain didn't register before the second one hit. The man smiled and took a few steps back, dancing and sending jabs through the air. White's ears were ringing from the punches.

"I've been working on my one-two combo for a while now," the man said. "What do you think?"

"Why don't you cut me loose, big guy—then we'll see what you can do against someone who can hit back," White said, spitting blood onto the floor.

"What would be the fun in that?" the man said, unashamed.

The man had taken a step forward when one of the doors of the tasting room opened, and in walked a small blond man dressed in a perfectly cut dark suit with a silk tie. The sound of the heavy door closing behind the new arrival drew the twin's attention.

"Hey!" the twin shouted. "Get the fuck out of here!"

The man walked in their direction and waved at the twin, a big smile on his face, totally oblivious to what was going on.

"Didn't you hear what I said? Get out of here!" the twin repeated.

"I'm sorry, but what are you doing here?" the small man said with a heavy French accent.

"No, the question is, what are *you* doing here?" the twin asked, taking a few steps toward the small man.

But the small Frenchman wasn't intimidated and, to White's surprise, didn't back down one bit. "I'm Pierre Sarazin, and I run this establishment," he said.

"I know who you are, little man," the twin hissed. "Get out!"

"No, *you* get out, mister," Pierre replied, thrusting a tiny finger into the man's torso. "Because whatever you're doing, whatever this is, you'll have to continue elsewhere. We have guests coming in half an hour for a tasting."

The twin remained silent for a moment. He looked at his watch in disbelief. White fully expected him to punch the small Frenchman in the face, but he didn't. Instead he turned toward White, a deep sense of frustration evident on his face.

Then there was a gunshot. And another. The frustration in the twin's face evaporated and was replaced by a look of complete disbelief.

He sank to his knees, looking at White as if asking for help. He stayed there for a second or two, then fell forward onto his face. Dead.

Behind the fallen man, Pierre was holding a black pistol. He moved to the back of White's chair and cut the leather strap with a sharp knife. White caught a whiff of Pierre's cologne.

Only the French would wear perfume to a gunfight, he thought, smirking. Pierre moved to the side and started working on the tape that kept White's left arm immobile. The moment White's left arm was free, Pierre handed him the knife.

"Do the rest. I'll cover you," he said.

"Who sent you?" White asked, cutting through the black tape.

"Alexander Hammond," Pierre replied.

White momentarily stopped what he was doing. *What?*

"Hurry up. Oxley and his men are surely on their way back," Pierre urged him. "I called his head of security and told him the chief of police was at Oxley's front door and wanted to speak with him in regard to an incident in Cape Town."

"Is that true?" White asked, working frantically to free his right leg.

"Of course not," Pierre replied. "It only bought us a couple of minutes."

"There's no way they didn't hear the gunshots," White said, standing up from the chair.

"Yeah, that too."

White knelt next to the dead man and patted him down. White relieved him of a semiautomatic pistol holstered at the small of his back. He also pocketed a small combat knife he found in the man's rear pocket. He heard engines approaching.

ATVs, White thought, recognizing the sound.

"They're coming. C'mon, hurry up," Pierre pleaded, already jogging toward the door through which he had entered.

"Go. I'm right behind you," White said, gathering together the documents Oxley had shown him earlier. He also took Oxley's cell phone, on which were the recordings he had listened to earlier, and put it in one of his pockets. White sprinted after the Frenchman, who was now waiting for him at the door.

"Where's your car?" White asked, taking a moment to ensure the pistol he'd taken from the dead twin had a round in the chamber.

"Oh, we're not leaving by car," Pierre replied, his eyes on the screen of his phone. He tapped a button, and the exterior spotlights switched off. "There's a helipad a quarter mile from here. They'll pick us up in twelve minutes."

"Who's they?"

Pierre shook his head. "I'm sorry, I don't know. But we need to go."

White was speechless. What kind of half-cooked plan was that? But it wasn't as if he had other options.

"Just follow me, okay?" Pierre said. "Ready?"

White nodded. "Ready."

CHAPTER FORTY-SIX

Kommetjie, South Africa

Roy Oxley was steering his four-wheeler down the path toward the tasting room when all the exterior lights across the vineyard suddenly switched off.

That fucking Frenchman was going to regret this. Oxley was going to skin that frog alive, and he would do it slowly while making sure that Pierre Sarazin, or whatever his real name was, didn't die before Oxley allowed him to.

Oxley swore under his breath as he ducked under the small windshield of the ATV to avoid the dust being churned up by the wheels of the four-wheelers in front of him.

With half his regular protective detail in London with his wife and kids, plus the two others that White had incapacitated, Oxley had only six men on the premises. He prayed that the two gunshots he'd heard coming from the tasting room hadn't killed Pierre Sarazin. There would be hell to pay if the small man was dead.

Although he had authorized one of the twins to rough up White a little, Oxley hoped he hadn't made a costly mistake by leaving the man alone with White. Keeping White alive was a priority. Oxley had seen the transformation in the American's eyes as he had divulged a deluge of damning evidence against Alexander Hammond. White might not have realized it yet, but he'd become Oxley's most powerful weapon against

Hammond. That's why Oxley was going to ensure White left here alive. He didn't think White had it in him to kill Hammond, but who knew what the future held? Oxley had seen stranger things happen.

He'd let White go, but the Frenchman . . . whether Pierre was working for Hammond or someone else didn't matter. As long as Oxley could curl his fingers around the Frenchman's throat.

Oxley came to a sliding stop next to the tasting room. He turned off the ATV's engine and signaled his men to do the same. He grabbed a suppressed M4 off the back rack of the ATV and turned toward his men.

"Fire only if you're fired upon," Oxley said, taking the time to look each man in the eyes. "I want that French cockroach alive."

Oxley sent two men to cover the rear of the building before joining his two remaining men, who were already lined up against the wall on the right side of the door.

"Three, two, one, execute," Oxley said, as the first man entered the tasting room.

The man in front of Oxley, seeing the first man going left, turned right. Oxley automatically went left, scanning for threats. Three seconds after the first man had stepped inside, Oxley's team had taken control of the tasting room. But none of it changed the fact that Oxley was now down to five shooters.

"They can't be far," Oxley said out loud. He walked toward the center of the space, looking at the dead twin. He'd been shot twice in the back.

Damn you, Pierre, Oxley thought. Then he froze, his heart skipping a beat. Where was his phone? His file folders?

"Fuuuck!" he shouted, mad at himself for being so careless. "Fuuuck!"

His men were looking at him eagerly. Oxley knew what they sought from him. They wanted his permission to kill White and Pierre. As tempting as it was, Oxley had to stay the course.

"The rules of engagement haven't changed, gentlemen. Find them!"

CHAPTER FORTY-SEVEN

Kommetjie, South Africa

White heard the four-wheelers the instant Pierre opened the door. They sprinted across the small dirt path and jumped over a short stone wall that bordered it. The moon was high in the sky and provided just enough light for them to see in front of them. They had covered less than fifty meters when the ATVs' engines stopped.

In front of him, Pierre got down to one knee. White did the same.

Alert, White remained silent, listening. In the distance, the waves were breaking onto the rocky shore. Closer to him, a gentle breeze caused the vines to whisper in a soft and quiet sway. Then he heard something else. White closed his eyes so he could concentrate. There it was again, the faint crunch of someone cautiously walking on a dirt road. White estimated the distance at twenty, maybe twenty-five meters.

"Let's go," Pierre said, in the process of standing up.

White grabbed his arm and pulled him close. White placed his index finger on his lips, signaling Pierre to stay quiet. The Frenchman nodded. Despite what he'd done inside the tasting room, the man looked frightened and completely out of his natural environment. A thin layer of perspiration on his forehead gleamed in the moonlight. White wondered who Pierre was working for. DGSE? Swiss Intelligence? Not that it truly mattered. The man had saved his life, and White would do what he could to protect him.

He allowed himself to take two long but silent breaths, hoping Pierre would do the same. White closed his eyes again, trying to pinpoint exactly where the steps were coming from. After a few seconds, he concluded that whoever had been walking on the dirt path had stopped. Had Pierre's silhouette been spotted? That sent a chill down White's spine. He was about to change position when the steps resumed. He froze, holding his breath. The steps were much closer than they were a minute ago. And, worse, the faint crunching was now coming from two different directions and getting closer.

White gently squeezed Pierre's arm to get his attention. Pierre snapped his head in White's direction, looking at him with wide eyes, his upper lip quivering.

"Stay here," White mouthed to him. "Don't move."

Pierre shook his head and pointed farther down the vineyard. White squeezed Pierre's arm harder.

"Stay here," he mouthed again. This time, Pierre nodded. White glanced at Pierre's hands to make sure his finger was off the trigger. The last thing they needed right now was an accidental discharge that would give away their position. He was glad to see that Pierre's finger was on the frame. White moved rapidly and silently, making sure to stay on the grass and away from the dirt path. He used the thick vines as concealment and covered approximately thirty feet before he stopped to listen. White stayed immobile for what felt like ten minutes but was in fact less than thirty seconds.

What betrayed Oxley's man was his odor. The man was a smoker. A deadly sin. White assessed the distance separating him from the man at less than ten feet. An easy shot in any circumstances. But the second man worried White. Where was he? Was he covering his partner? Had he left?

White didn't want to commit before he had the answer, but the man forced him to when he stepped over the small stone wall and through the row of vines White was using as concealment. The man emerged nine feet in front of White, holding a rifle in his hands and looking in the opposite direction. He was tall and bald, with a thick neck. Not an easy man to take down silently, so White didn't even try. He raised his pistol and sent two rounds into the back of the man's head.

White was moving before the man had even hit the ground, aware that his muzzle flash had given away his exact position to anyone close by. It was the right move, as someone opened up with multiple three-round bursts. Bullets streamed through the vines, shredding the loose foliage where White had been seconds ago.

Resisting the urge to fire blindly, White stayed low and waited, hoping the man would cross over to confirm his kill. The man called out something, but White's ears were ringing. He couldn't be sure if the man was requesting backup or calling his dead friend. One thing was for sure, though: the man was almost on him. This was confirmed when a small, thin man wearing glasses emerged from the vegetation less than five feet from White.

Unlike the man White had just killed, this one was looking right at him. Before the man could get off a shot, White fired twice, hitting him center mass. He sent an additional bullet under the man's chin and up into his brain. He grabbed the man's rifle, an M4, and inserted a fresh magazine before heading back toward where he had left Pierre.

With his ears ringing from the gunfight, White had to trust that Pierre wouldn't shoot him by mistake. He shouldn't have worried, because the Frenchman hadn't moved at all. In fact, he was curled up in a ball, his pistol on the ground next to him. Whatever adrenaline had pushed Pierre through shooting the twin and the rest of these events that were clearly out of the ordinary for the reserved spy had clearly deserted him.

"We need to move, Pierre," White said. "Come on, buddy. Get up."

But Pierre refused to move. He didn't even look at White.

White cursed. They had less than five minutes to get their asses to the helipad. They weren't going to make it.

CHAPTER FORTY-EIGHT

Kommetjie, South Africa

Oxley was startled by the two pistol shots, but by the time his man returned fire with three-round bursts, Oxley was already sprinting to the door at the opposite end of the tasting room. He stepped outside just in time to see the silhouette of a man jump over the stone wall. The moment the silhouette disappeared into the vines, two more shots were fired, followed by a third one a second later.

Oxley clenched his jaw and took cover behind a row of empty oak barrels. He signaled his two men to do the same. He resisted the urge to race after Pierre and White. He couldn't afford to move too quickly now. If two of his men had fallen, that meant that White and the Frenchman were now armed with rifles. Oxley asked the man on his right to call back the shooter he had sent to cover the main exit. He needed more manpower.

"Who's at the gate?" Oxley asked.

"It's Ricardo, sir," his man replied.

"Tell Ricardo to grab some NVGs from the armory," Oxley said. "Tell him to hurry his ass up."

Oxley realized how unprepared he'd been for this. He had let himself get soft and complacent. It had been way too long since he'd last gotten into a good fight. He had let Krantz run the day-to-day operations of Oxley International Security and had instead focused his time and energy on growing the shipping company and his social engagement initiatives. His sky-high heart rate confirmed the fact that for the last few years, he had spent way too much time in boardroom meetings and not enough at the firing range or at the gym.

In his mind's eye, Oxley visualized the map of his winery. Were Pierre and White heading toward the ocean? Was there a boat waiting for them close by? That couldn't be. Oxley had only learned from Krantz three or four hours ago that White was on his way to Cape Town. There was no way someone could have mounted a rescue operation so damn fast. Oxley knew from experience how treacherous the rocky shores at the edge of the vineyard were. Simply stated, maneuvering a boat close enough to shore—especially in the dark—to allow two men to board was risky business. And a deadly one if attempted by anyone not familiar with the waters around Kommetjie.

What else was there? What would *he* do if he was the one who needed to escape?

The helipad, Oxley thought. Were they going for his helicopter? The thought sent a cold spike of anxiety through him. No, it was impossible. His chopper was at the Port Elizabeth International Airport for regular scheduled maintenance, and he wouldn't get it back to Kommetjie for another week or so. He was about to dismiss the idea completely when the man on his right caught his attention.

"Sir! Listen."

Oxley strained his ears for the sound of anyone approaching. He stood still for several seconds. Then he heard it too. It wasn't someone's footsteps; it was the distinctive thump of spinning rotor blades clattering into the dark sky. It was coming from the ocean. Oxley scanned the horizon, searching for the chopper's position lights, but he couldn't spot them.

"Get on your ATVs and take position fifty meters on the north and west side of the helipad," Oxley ordered the two men squatting next to him. "Questions?"

There were none. "Make sure you don't turn on your lights," he reminded his men. "You don't want to lose your night vision."

"Understood," one man replied.

"I'll wait for Ricardo and the NVGs right here," Oxley said. "Then we'll regroup around the helipad."

Both men nodded. Oxley rested his M4 on top of an oak barrel and scanned for threats. "Go!" he ordered.

He heard his men's boots pounding against the dirt path behind him as they raced toward the front of the building, where they had left their four-wheelers. Oxley once again cursed his lack of readiness. If he'd had a pair of NVGs with him, it would have given him the technical advantage he needed to swiftly end this little escapade. At least Adaliya and the kids were off the property. That had been a good call.

The helicopter was getting closer. Oxley had no difficulty hearing the whine of the chopper's turbine engine. The fact that Oxley couldn't see its navigation lights told him everything he needed to know. This was indeed a rescue operation. But for whom? Pierre or White?

The sound of the helicopter approaching was soon drowned out by revving engines of the two ATVs that sped past Oxley. Oxley watched as his men navigated the dirt path with one hand on the ATV handlebars and the other holding their rifles. The ATVs' brake lights came on as his men slowed down to take a sharp bend in the path.

And that's when Oxley saw the muzzle flashes followed by the silhouette of one of his men being thrown off his four-wheeler.

CHAPTER FORTY-NINE

Kommetjie, South Africa

White shook Pierre gently by the collar. "C'mon, snap out of it, Pierre. We need to move."

Though he'd gotten most of his hearing back, White's ears were still ringing, and he wasn't sure how loud he was speaking.

Pierre didn't respond. He was in a fetal position, rocking back and forth. It wasn't a pretty sight. White slapped him across the face. Pierre looked at him, confused.

"Hey," White said. "I need your help, buddy. Can you help me?"

Gradually, Pierre stopped shuddering, and his short legs unfolded. He got up to one knee and gazed at his surroundings, his eyes blank and unseeing.

The roar of incoming ATVs gave White an idea. It was risky, but it was an opportunity he couldn't afford to miss. Not if they wanted to make it to the helipad in time for their pickup.

"I'll be back," White said to Pierre. Grabbing his M4, White started running parallel to the dirt path, staying close to the grapevines in an effort to stay concealed for as long as he could. In case a shooter was waiting for him on the other side of the vines, White didn't want to show up too close to where he had last been seen.

In front of him, the vines took a sharp turn to the right, signaling a similar bend in the dirt path. White anticipated the ATVs would slow down right before the curve, unless the drivers wanted to flip their machines onto their sides.

They were getting closer. Almost on his heels. It was now or never.

White hopped on top of the small stone wall and raised his M4. The ATVs were a bit farther away than he had expected, but it wasn't all bad. It gave him an extra second to adjust his aim. The ATVs were running without their front lights, but the moon provided enough illumination for White to align the front sight of his rifle with the torso of the man driving the lead ATV, now only a hundred feet away.

White exhaled and pressed the trigger five times in quick succession, his rounds slamming into the man's chest, knocking him off his ATV. The ATV, having lost its driver, hit a bump on the dirt path and changed direction, heading straight toward White at thirty miles an hour.

White dove to his left and onto the dirt path just as the ATV struck the wall with an ear-splitting crash, sending bits of metal and stones into the air. The ATV caught fire but didn't explode. White, who had landed on his stomach, raised his head just in time to see the second ATV coming straight at him.

He rolled hard to his left, leaving his rifle where it lay. The right front wheel of the SUV missed him by less than an inch but rolled over his M4. White watched in disbelief as the driver locked the wheel and tried to turn the ATV away from the upcoming wall.

The ATV almost tipped over and sent the driver flying off his seat. The driver bounced against the dirt path and rolled a few times, finally coming to a stop against the stone wall. To White's surprise, the man instantly jumped back to his feet, like nothing had happened. He looked to his left and right, no doubt searching for his rifle. White didn't know where the man's weapon was, either, and since he wasn't convinced his own rifle wouldn't blow up in his face after being run over by the ATV, they stood facing each other in silence.

With lightning speed, the man pulled a knife from his rear pocket and opened the blade with a flick of his wrist. White did the same with the knife he'd seized from the man's dead colleague.

The man attacked with speed and agility. Like White, this wasn't his first knife fight. White blocked the man's initial strike and backed off, trying to create some distance, despite knowing that he had to attack. In a knife fight, the person playing defense usually ended up dead. That advice had come from a gifted knife fighter: Maxwell White. The words of his father, during one of the rare times they'd bonded over military training, still echoed in his mind.

You will get cut. You will get hurt. Don't be afraid of the pain. What you need to concern yourself about is the protection of your vital organs. Be the aggressor, Clay. Always be the aggressor.

White feinted a looping thrust to the man's head. The tactic worked, and the man was suckered into a defensive cross slash. White easily avoided the blow and stepped into the opening he had created with a counterthrust to his attacker's neck, his blade sinking into the man's throat. By the time his opponent's knife had slipped from his dying hands, White had already pulled his blade from the man's neck and driven it into his heart. The man fell backward, twitched twice, then went still.

White ran to the dead man's ATV, which had come to a stop against the stone wall. The ATV's engine was still running, and it looked like it hadn't sustained any critical damage. Wedged between the front of the ATV and the stone wall was the man's rifle.

White reached for it, but as he did, he heard a voice behind him say, "You going somewhere, Clayton?"

White, startled and still slightly out of breath from the fight, raised his hands in the air and slowly turned toward the voice. Fifty feet away, Roy Oxley, now equipped with a pair of NVGs on his forehead, was pointing a rifle right at him.

CHAPTER FIFTY

Kommetjie, South Africa

Pierre Sarazin snapped his eyes open and looked around. His body jerked up at the sound of a loud crash not too far away from him. For a moment, he wondered where he was. Then he remembered. The last thing he recalled clearly was that he couldn't breathe, that he'd had to sit down. Then White had left him. Where was the American? Had he abandoned him?

In front of him was his black pistol. Pierre took it in his hand, vividly remembering the two shots he'd fired with it into the back of one of Oxley's men.

Merde! What happened to me? Never in his life had his body shut down on him like this. He glanced at his watch. It was almost eleven o'clock. The helicopter. Had he told White about the chopper? He couldn't remember. Hammond had been very specific about this. The chopper was going to land on Oxley's helipad at precisely eleven o'clock, and it wouldn't stay longer than sixty seconds.

The helipad was a quarter of a mile away. There was no way Pierre could cover the distance on foot in so little time. He suddenly jolted his head toward the cloudless night sky, certain he had heard the sound of a helicopter, but his eyes couldn't find it. If the helicopter was close by, he had no time to lose. Maybe White was already waiting for him at the helipad?

Pierre stood up, holding his pistol with both hands. He remembered hearing the sound of ATVs, which gave him an idea. He carefully stepped through the vines and banged his knee against a meter-high stone wall that bordered the dirt path. Not far to his right was the tasting room. But it was what was unfolding fifty meters to his left that took his breath away—a scene he could see clearly thanks to the burning ATV.

Clayton White was in the middle of the dirt path, fighting with someone and completely oblivious to the two men approaching him from behind. Pierre's body became rigid when he watched White stab the man he was fighting with in the neck and again in the heart a second later. Pierre wanted to scream at him, to let him know that two armed men were almost on him. But what purpose would that serve? Pierre would lose the only advantage he had left. Surprise.

The thing was, he wasn't even sure he could fire the pistol again. Just thinking about shooting someone else gave him the creeps.

Shit. He had no choice. There was only one way out of this. Mustering up all the courage he had left, Pierre headed toward danger.

CHAPTER FIFTY-ONE

Kommetjie, South Africa

White didn't know if Oxley had spotted the M4 trapped between the stone wall and the four-wheeler. His NVGs were up on his forehead, unneeded due to the ATV on fire. It was possible he hadn't seen it. But White had another problem. He had no idea if the rifle had a round chambered or not. And even if it had a round in the chamber, and even if he could reach it, how was he supposed to take down two men before being himself mowed down by bullets?

"Who's picking you up?" Oxley asked, taking steps toward him. "I heard a chopper hovering over for the last few minutes. Friends of yours?"

White kept his hands up but held himself ready to pounce if given the opportunity.

"You know what, Roy? I have no freaking idea," he replied.

Oxley sneered. "So this is Pierre's master plan? Speaking of him, where is our favorite Frenchman?" He scanned to his left and right with his rifle. "Is he with you?"

The man walking next to Oxley looked behind him and probed the darkness with the help of his NVGs. He suddenly stopped moving and brought his rifle to bear, aiming toward the vines.

"Sir! Movement to—"

The man was interrupted by three muzzle flashes coming from the right side of the dirt path. The man's head snapped back, and he collapsed before he could return fire. The instant Oxley started to pivot toward the gunfire, White sprang into action and rolled to his left, snatching the rifle. Then he heard two quick shots, his brain acknowledging that the shots hadn't come from a pistol like the three previous ones.

White locked the butt of the rifle into his shoulder just as Oxley gyrated back toward him, his M4 up. White squeezed the trigger. Oxley spun and fell to the ground. White, keeping a watchful eye on Oxley, scanned the area for other dangers. Behind him, a helicopter was making its final approach toward the small hill where the landing pad was.

"Pierre?" White shouted. "Pierre?"

Damn it.

White jumped on top of the stone wall and vaulted through the vines. To his left, Pierre was sprawled on the ground, motionless. White hurried to him.

Less than a quarter of an inch apart, two neat bullet holes had hit Pierre below his right shoulder. White's throat tightened as he bent over to take Pierre's pulse. The little Frenchman had saved his life twice today. It should have been White lying inert in the grass, not him.

Pierre's pulse was weak and irregular, but he was alive.

White let go of his M4 and placed Pierre's pistol at the small of his own back. He then whisked Pierre onto his shoulders in a fireman's carry and jogged along the vines until he reached the sharp bend. He had just stepped off the stone wall when Oxley called out.

"Is that your chopper on my property?"

White turned to face the man. This time Oxley was armed with a pistol, and White noticed he was holding it in his left hand. The right side of Oxley's shirt was soaked red, his right arm dripping blood and coloring the dirt path with dark red blotches.

"I already told you," White said. "I don't know who they are."

"How long have you known Pierre?" Oxley asked, taking a few steps toward White.

White shook his head. "Less than an hour," he replied.

Oxley's lips curled into a half smile, but it evaporated as fast as it had appeared. White noticed something in Oxley's eyes he hadn't seen before. Was it nostalgia? A sense of understanding? Truth was, White didn't care what the man might or might not be thinking. Roy Oxley had tried to kill Veronica, and for that reason alone, White wouldn't hesitate to finish the job he'd started if given the chance. The only thing that mattered to him in that moment was to bring Pierre to a hospital.

"You're free to go, Clayton," Oxley said. "Just remember what we talked about, yes?"

White nodded and took a step toward the ATV.

"I said *you* were free to go, Clayton. I didn't say anything about the Frenchman."

"He's dying," White said. "I'm not leaving him behind."

"Then we have a problem, don't we?" Oxley said, aiming his pistol at White's head. "And there's also the matter of my phone. I'd like to have it back."

White didn't care about the phone. But there was no way he was going to leave Pierre behind.

"You know what, Clayton?" Oxley said, his eyes turning dark. "I'm done being nice. You have three seconds to drop that sack of shit to the ground or—"

Oxley never finished his sentence. The top of his head exploded in a pink mist.

White looked over toward the chopper. The helicopter was painted with a matte black that made it almost impossible to spot at night. White knew that whoever had shot Oxley now had *his* head in his optics.

White nodded and started to jog toward the ATV. He had a flight to catch.

CHAPTER FIFTY-TWO

Kommetjie, South Africa

White had finally managed to stop the bleeding, and Pierre's pulse had stabilized. He wasn't out of the woods yet, but at least White had given him a fighting chance. The chopper had two well-equipped medical emergency bags, and despite flying so low that the wash from the rotor was kicking up spray from the surf, the pilots were doing an amazing job of keeping the aircraft stable.

"You've done that before, haven't you?" one of the four CIA paramilitary men asked, speaking into his helmet microphone. The man had a long black unkempt beard and piercing green eyes. Like the others, he was dressed in nondescript tactical clothing bearing no insignia.

"I was a combat rescue officer in my past life," White replied.

"And now?" another one asked. White thought the man looked like his fallen friend Marcus Thompson. The man's shoulders were too large to fit into a single seat back.

White shrugged. "I honestly don't know. Up until a few days ago I was with the Secret Service. Name's Clayton White, by the way," he said, introducing himself.

"No fucking way," the skinniest of the men said. "*The* Clayton White?"

White stared at him with a puzzled look on his face.

"Vice President-Elect Hammond held a press conference and talked about what happened in San Francisco. He spent half of it thanking you for saving his daughter's life," the man explained.

White cursed under his breath. Hammond was taking control of the narrative.

"That's true," confirmed another operator. "And congratulations are in order, right?"

"What did Alexander Hammond say?" White asked, feeling sick just pronouncing the man's name.

"About the engagement? To his daughter, Veronica?" the man replied, his tone indicating he wasn't sure if he should continue with the subject or not.

"Anyhow, the VP-elect said you're a fucking hero," jumped in the operator who looked like Marcus. "That's good enough for us."

White forced a smile. "I appreciate the help, guys," he said before taking a long pull from the energy drink one of them had thrown at him. "Thanks for showing up on time."

Then, one after the other, they introduced themselves to White and gave him a fist bump. All of them were former military, and they all had a story to share about the great Alexander Hammond. As he listened to the men sing the praises of the vice president-elect, White realized that no matter what Oxley had told him about Hammond, he was going to have a hard time convincing anyone that Hammond was anything other than an American hero.

EPILOGUE

INAUGURATION DAY
US Capitol
Washington, DC

White was almost standing to attention as he watched the newly elected president of the United States take his oath of office less than twenty feet away. It was a still, cool day, and the sun hung high above the Capitol, which was much more pleasant for the large crowd that had gathered to witness the swearing-in ceremony than the storm that had raged with unabated fury for the last two days.

Veronica squeezed his hand three times in rapid succession. That was their own private *I love you*. Since his return from South Africa, they'd spent every single day together, and White had enjoyed each second he'd been with her.

Pressured by the news media and White's newfound minicelebrity status, the Secret Service had closed the investigation into his actions in San Francisco and had swiftly concluded that he hadn't broken any rules or regulations. They'd gone as far as to offer him a position at their training academy, which he'd flatly refused. Instead, he'd submitted his resignation. Within days, virtually all the government agencies he had ever heard of had contacted him with an offer of employment, even NASA. When White learned that the position NASA was offering him wasn't as an astronaut, he had said no to them too.

At some point White had wondered if all these calls were due to his qualifications or to the implicit access to the vice president that hiring him would give them. Of course, none of these agencies knew White and Hammond had barely spoken since his return from South Africa.

Pierre, who White had learned did in fact work for the DGSE, was still at Walter Reed. He was getting better by the day, which pleased White very much. He'd become good friends with the small Frenchman, and so had Veronica. They spoke almost every day, mostly about wine. Never about South Africa.

A week after his return from Cape Town, White had rented a safety-deposit box at a local bank. Since he didn't know who he could trust, or what to do with Oxley's cell phone, he'd left it there, making sure to remove the SIM card. He was going to think long and hard about how to deal with Hammond's betrayal. For now, Hammond had no idea how much White knew about CONQUEST, or that White had learned the truth about Hammond's involvement in his father's murder.

And the fact remained: the underwater graveyard was still there. And it continued to be a threat to Hammond.

White had the feeling that his fiancée was aware of the unspoken problems between White and her father because her attitude toward her dad had changed drastically. When White had tossed out the idea of moving to Washington State three weeks ago, she had jumped on it. She'd even applied for a teaching position at the University of Washington.

They were leaving tonight.

White couldn't wait to start this new chapter with her. He didn't know what the future held for them, but he wasn't going to take Veronica for granted. He was going to be present for her, and responsive to her needs.

And I'll keep you safe. Even from your dad. I promise.

After the swearing-in ceremony, a couple of young political staffers came to White to ask permission to take a selfie with him. The way he sent them scurrying away earned him an elbow strike in the ribs from Veronica. At the joint congressional inaugural committee luncheon that followed, he couldn't stop staring at Vice President Hammond, his disgust for the man evident. By betraying Maxwell's trust, Hammond had committed an unpardonable sin, one White wasn't about to forgive. Or forget.

In the deepest part of his heart, White had always held out the hope that one day he and his dad would grow closer, that they would somehow find a way to make things right between them.

Which would have pleased Mom very much, he thought.

But Hammond had crushed any hope of that ever happening. A succession of painful memories suddenly flooded in as images of White's mother's lifeless body surfaced in his mind. He ground his teeth in anger as he cast his eyes back to Hammond, incapable of wrapping his head around the fact that the man was now the vice president.

It wasn't right.

"Are you okay, Clay?" Veronica asked him, her concern obvious. "You're shaking, baby."

"I'm sorry, Vonnie," White said, standing up from the round table. In front of him, the small garden salad and the chicken fettuccini remained untouched. "I just need a bit of air. I'll be right back."

He kissed Veronica on the head, squeezed her shoulders three times, and walked outside the ballroom.

"Hey, Clayton," one of the Secret Service agents said.

White nodded at him but kept walking. His phone vibrated in his suit pocket. No caller ID. He took the call anyway. Maybe NASA had changed their mind about the astronaut program?

"This is Clayton," he said into the phone.

"Look behind you." White recognized the voice instantly. It was Alexander Hammond.

White did look behind him, but he continued walking. Hammond was fifty steps behind him, followed by a lone Secret Service agent.

"Can we talk?" Hammond asked.

White ended the call and sat on one of the wooden benches set against the wall. Hammond gestured to the Secret Service agent that he needed privacy and that he shouldn't get any closer. Hammond took a seat next to White.

The two men remained silent for what seemed like an eternity. White didn't mind. He wasn't the one who was going to start the conversation.

"All right, Clayton," Hammond finally said. "How do you want to proceed?"

"About what?"

Hammond sighed. "What the fuck's wrong with you? You're still pissed about South Africa?" he asked. "I moved heaven and earth to get you into that chopper. I called in every favor the CIA owed me."

"You did it because Veronica threatened to destroy you on social media if you didn't get me back," White said, not one bit intimidated by Hammond. "You used me."

"You're lucky to have her at your side," Hammond said, his eyes hard and his voice nettled.

White wanted to ask him what would happen if Veronica wasn't his fiancée. Would Hammond murder him too? Like Maxwell?

He held Hammond's gaze. "You're the vice president now. The eyes of the public are going to be on you—a lot more than when you ran JSOC. And those eyes are going to be watching for any misstep you make. And you can bet your ass that my eyes will be among them. And so will your daughter's."

White saw Hammond's body stiffen, his jaw muscles tensing. "What's your point?"

"My point?" White said, resisting the urge to bang Hammond's head against the solid marble wall behind him. "Drain is going to be back up and running soon, and Veronica will be traveling and promoting it all over the world. You're going to support her—no matter where it takes her. Even to the Arabian Peninsula. And you're going to ensure that she's protected by the best Secret Service agents. I might not be one of them anymore, but I know that they're uncorruptible, that they'll follow their oath to protect her—no matter what instructions the VP gives them. Are we clear on this?"

Hammond's stony expression didn't waver, but White's eyes caught a flicker of something that might have been fear.

"But yes, you were right, Alex," White said. "I'm a lucky man. And by the way, Vonnie and I are leaving tonight."

This time, Hammond's eyes opened wide in surprise. "Where?" he asked, as if he had just swallowed broken glass.

"As far from you as we can," White said, getting up and walking away.

ACKNOWLEDGMENTS

The first thank-you goes to my readers. Thank you for your attention and your time. There aren't enough words to properly express how grateful I am. It's always such a pleasure to interact with you online. Thank you for your messages. Keep them coming—because they keep me going!

This book would not exist if it wasn't for my marvelous team at Thomas & Mercer. I'm extremely proud to be associated with such a talented lineup of publishing professionals. I am forever indebted to my acquiring editor, Liz Pearsons. Thank you for your support and spot-on editing. You're truly a joy to work with. Thanks, too, to Grace Doyle, Sarah Shaw, Laura Barrett, and Lindsey Bragg. Thank you to Caitlin Alexander, who with Liz made countless suggestions, large and small, on how to improve the book. You're a literary genius!

A special thanks to my good friend and literary agent Eric Myers at Myers Literary Management. Thanks for everything you do for me. I know I can count on you. Thanks to my writer friends Marc Cameron, Mark Greaney, Joshua Hood, Jack Carr, James Hankins, Don Bentley, Brad Taylor, KJ Howe, Rip Rawlings, Brian Andrews, Jeff Wilson, and Kyle Mills for their support and kind words.

A big thank-you to the guys over at the Crew Reviews: Sean Cameron, Mike Houtz, and C. E. Albanese, all of them terrific writers in their own rights. Thanks to the Real Book Spy, Ryan Steck. You've become a trailblazer, my friend!

Finally, I wish to thank my children, Florence and Gabriel, who are a constant source of inspiration and laughter. You brighten my life. And to my fabulous wife, Lisane: every single day with you is a gift. I'm so lucky to have such a wonderful life partner. Your love means everything to me. Thanks for believing.

ABOUT THE AUTHOR

Photo © 2013 Esther Campeau

Simon Gervais was born in Montréal, Québec. He joined the Canadian military as an infantry officer and was commissioned as a second lieutenant in 1997. In 2001, he was recruited by the Royal Canadian Mounted Police and became a federal agent. His first posting was in Toronto, where he served as a drug investigator. During this time, he worked on many international drug-related cases in close collaboration with his American colleagues from the Drug Enforcement Administration. His career switched gears in 2004, and he was placed with a federal antiterrorism unit based in the Ottawa region. During the following years, he was deployed in several European and Middle Eastern countries. In 2009, he became a close protection specialist tasked with guarding foreign heads of state visiting Canada. He served on the protection details of Queen Elizabeth II, US president Barack Obama, and Chinese president Hu Jintao, among others. Gervais lives in Ottawa with his wife and two children.